NO
COMING
BACK

ALSO BY KEITH HOUGHTON

GABE QUINN THRILLERS

NO COMING BACK

KEITH HOUGHTON

MYS
Houghton

Text copyright © 2015 Keith Houghton

Published by Thomas & Mercer, Seattle

www.apub.com

Amazon, the Amazon logo, and Thomas & Mercer are trademarks of Amazon.com, Inc., or its affiliates.

ISBN-13: 9781503947481
ISBN-10: 1503947483

Cover design by bürosüd° Munich, www.buerosued.de

Printed in the United States of America

For Jason

My son—who sadly passed away during the writing of this novel.

A beautiful comet,
That blazed brightly but briefly in our lives,
Before returning to the heavens,
To shine among the stars,
Evermore.

'Some secrets are better left buried.'

Prologue

Life rarely turns out how we expect it to.

As far back as I remember I wanted to be something I wasn't. It didn't matter what, providing it got me noticed, mentioned in the press, or at the very least put me on a level pegging with my brother.

Aaron was everything to me.

Although he was shorter by a head, I looked up to him. The golden child—excelling without effort—three years my senior, with three times my stature. He was able to elicit praise from my father without breaking a sweat.

In many ways, I loved him. In many ways, I envied him.

My father ran a tight ship. He was ex-navy and as hard-headed as an icebreaker. He grew land legs after meeting my mother, and together they dropped anchor in Harper, my father's hometown, living in the house built by my grandfather before buckshot blew out his brains. My mother was a photographer by day and my father's keeper by night. She was the gentle to his rough, the salve to his salt. By the time my beautiful brother came along, my parents were respected members of the community, integrated, happy. For a while they led a picture-postcard lifestyle, the three of them, in their cookie-cutter home, in their little bubble of bliss.

Then one day it popped, and nothing was ever the same again.

I was a mistake, unplanned, unequal, and, as such, unloved by my father. My big brother's little brother, physically longer, taller, maybe even smarter, but never measuring up in my father's eyes. My mother did her best. My father did his worst. Together they canceled each other out.

From day one I was plagued with illness. An unhealthy child, God's reject, weak and gawky. A freak. I grew up quickly and sickly, all of it in my brother's shadow—in that cool slipstream where the sun never shines—and the pride in my father's eyes soured whenever they fell on me. I was the second son of second-generation immigrants. Raised on tough love and scraps. Sunday sermons delivered with absolute gusto and manners metered out with the back of a hand. Ours was a hammer-and-nails home, built on hard work and 'be-grateful-for-small-mercies' footings. From the moment I could suckle, I had hand-me-downs and issues.

Darkness became my only shelter.

As we grew older, Aaron taught me to pick a cause and to believe in it. Carry it to the ends of the Earth if need be. Embrace it. See it through to its conclusion.

Aaron was everything to me.

In my eyes, he could do no wrong. He was the living embodiment of perfection. Saintly. Worshipped by our father and adored by all. I didn't just want to be like him, I wanted to be him.

Sometimes we don't get to choose.

Sometimes life has other plans.

Chapter One

Would you be so quick to dig your own grave and then to lie down in it?" a well-meaning counselor asked, eighteen years ago, when I was trapped in that awkward metamorphosis between child and man.

I was midway through a private therapy session at the time, with nobody eavesdropping at the door, and no one videoing for posterity or being overly judgmental. The counselor was a good-hearted man, keen to fix me. It wasn't our first rewiring session and it wouldn't be our last. We were both invested, focused. New medication and a month of intensive psychiatry had me itching to talk, to offload. I wanted to share, needed to.

For as long as I could remember there had been something dark and bottomless inside me. An abyss, swirling with black smoke and thorny sparks. His sessions had brought me to the brink, and all I wanted to do was to let go.

But he held me back, hand raised, halting my imminent confession. "Save it for your priest," he said. "I don't need to feel the weight of your burden to know it's pulling you down into hell. Some secrets are better left buried."

I never fully appreciated what he meant, until now.

Keith Houghton

It's after three in the morning and blacker than tar in northeast Minnesota. Cold enough to bite off skin. I am at my family home on the outskirts of Harper, scooping away shovelfuls of snow from the frozen backyard, digging for the hatch that leads to my grand-father's defunct bomb shelter. Even in the dead of night and after an absence that stretches through all my adulthood I have every right being here, but I shouldn't be. A backhanded invitation never makes for a warm welcome. The insides of Satan's snow globe, that's what this place is to me. Hell frozen over.

The shovel strikes metal, sending shockwaves up my arms.

The truth is, I needn't have come. I have no unpaid debt to clear. No compelling obligation, either moral or emotional. What I do have is every reason to keep my distance, to stay in the Twin Cities, where I am relatively safe and hidden from the ghosts of my past.

Yet, here I am.

I get my first glimpse of the hatch, just as my cell phone starts to sing. I stab the blade into the snow and fumble the phone out of my pocket before the noise wakes the dead and every dog for miles around.

I don't recognize the number. "If this isn't the state lottery, I'm hanging up."

A male voice snickers at my words, rolling down the connection like distant thunder. "Trust me, son, that kind of money is both baggage and a burden. Brings nothing but bad luck and sob stories. And I should know; I wrote most of them myself."

Even though I haven't heard it in years, I know this voice. It's unmistakable—like a funeral dirge:

Lars Grossinger.

Whenever I watch a Lee Marvin movie I can't help but think of the man who practically owns Harper. They could be siblings, Lars and he. But the real clincher is his gravelly voice. They are one and the same.

"This is a burner phone," I say. "How'd you get the number?"

"Son, one thing you should know about me is I can get where water can't. Where there's a will and a weakness, there's generally a way."

I haven't spoken with Harper's homegrown marvel since I was seventeen, and I'm not sure I want to speak to him now. I let the impatience show in my tone. "What do you want, Lars? And don't say to welcome me home. I don't believe for one second you're calling to chat about the good old days. Not at three o'clock in the morning, and especially seeing as how there never were any good old days."

He laughs. It sounds like a bulldozer tearing down a church. "That's my boy. I see age hasn't blunted that gilded edge of yours. You were always a razor, Jake. It's one thing I admired. Cut straight through all the bullshit. Despite what you might think, I am glad you're back. Got to be a blessing, whichever way you slice it. Just a damn pity it's not under better circumstances." He clears his throat. "Sentimentality aside, you're right: this isn't just a courtesy call, it's a job offer."

At this point I should hang up, turn off the phone, and go back to shoveling snow. Better yet, bury the cell along with my childhood memories, here in the backyard of my family home, and walk away, never to return.

But I can't. Not yet.

My thumb hesitates a fraction too long over the *end call* button and Lars takes advantage of it:

"What's this? The idea of working for the *Harper Horn* not very appealing anymore? I seem to remember a time you begged me to give you a break. You were all hung up on becoming the next big Pulitzer Prize–winning journalist. Said you'd do just about anything to get it, too. Sell your soul if you had one."

"I was a kid."

"We've all been kids, son. Not all of us were as driven as you were at that age. Who knows where you'd be right now if things had turned out differently?"

For a moment I picture a past. One of those color-grained Super 8 recordings of family barbeques and kids learning to ride bikes: images of my wonderful children at milestones from birth to graduation; of my lovely wife, Jenna, with her homemaker smile and our big house in upstate New York; of a glittering career of accolades and achievements; of a life bursting with love and hope and happiness, with more glorious years ahead than behind. But it is not my past. It's not even my life. And I have no right picturing it.

"Don't renege on me now, son," Lars says into my silence. "Remember, you owe Lars Grossinger."

Me, and every damned soul in town.

"Besides, we both know this is not too bad of a deal," he continues. "So quit with the stalling. I've sent someone to come pick you up. Should be with you any minute now. Do us both a favor and take the damn job. Trust me, son, you won't live to regret it."

———

I am still mopping crystallizing sweat from my brow and mulling over Lars's closing comment when I see the beam from a flashlight scope out the side of the house. A woman's voice isn't far behind it:

"Hello? Jake? Jake Olson? You hiding away back here?"

The house is in total darkness, deadened by a canopy of snow, but the backyard is lit by a kerosene lamp. She must have seen the weak glow and come to investigate. The flashlight sweeps across the snowy backyard, searching over dimpled mounds and icicled outdoor furniture before finding my face. I squint between gloved fingers, unable to see through the intense glare and my own condensing breath.

"I expect you've already spoken with Lars," she says as she approaches, boots crunching snow. "In which case you should already know why I'm here."

There's still time to back out, to tell her to take a hike and to stick Lars's job offer where the sun never shines. But there's something about her voice that roots me to the spot.

She emerges into the kerosene glow and the flashlight falls from my eyes. She's about my age, with short blonde hair and a face cut like a diamond. Eyes that look older than the rest of her. She wears a curious expression and a big padded parka with a Stars-and-Stripes stitched on the sleeve.

Breath smokes from her lips. "Hello, Jake. It's been a while, hasn't it? Cold enough for you?" She comes over and punches me playfully on the arm. "What's this? Cat got your tongue? Why the puzzled expression? Don't you recognize me? We were inseparable, once." She pouts at the crease formed on my forehead. "For the love of Pete, it's me: Kim. Okay, so I had long mousey hair and Coke-bottle glasses, and maybe that's why you're gawking?"

"Partly," I admit with a stiff nod, "but mostly because you're a cop."

The pout plumps into a pucker. "Jeez, you got me there. The uniform gave it away, did it?" She opens her arms, wide. "So how about a big hug for old time's sake? Come on, don't be shy. Or would you rather not be seen fraternizing with the enemy?"

⁓

The black-and-white Ford Interceptor driven by Sergeant Kimberly Krauss of the Harper Police Department smells of mango and leather. I am not a fan of car fresheners; they asphyxiate.

"I hope you won't hold it against me," she says as she rolls the steering wheel against the ice-rutted back road. "Being a cop, that is. I'm not completely insensitive; I can imagine how you feel about the whole police thing. If it's any consolation I didn't plan on being an officer of the law. It kind of just happened."

Kimberly Krauss.

I haven't spoken with her in private since my world imploded. Neither of us were much more than children back then. Restless saplings pulling up roots instead of laying them down, oblivious to what would become of us.

"You never made it out?"

"From Harper? Not through lack of trying. I did escape, for a while. I got as far as college and *this* close to saying goodbye forever. Believe me, after what happened, I had every intention of never coming back."

"But you did."

"Sure. But not through choice. My mom was diagnosed with cancer and everything kind of went on the back burner after that."

"Sorry, Kim; I didn't know."

She smirks it off. "How could you? Anyway, during the chemo she needed constant round-the-clock care and I was happy to do my bit. So I came home from college. I'm not complaining; things worked out okay for me, all things considered."

"You became a cop."

She glances my way and smiles. "You got me. I suppose, given the family history, it was inevitable. Walking in my father's footsteps."

The Interceptor bounces over a pothole, jolting us in our seats.

Everything is frosted on the tree-lined lane, like a scene from a chiller movie. Shadows scurrying from the bright headlights. A month of snowfall has blanched the northern states and turned the side roads into deathtraps. It doesn't stop Krauss from driving dangerously fast. In a blur, I catch sight of boot prints running along the edge of the roadway, left there no more than an hour before by my own heavy feet.

"Speaking of which, how is your dad? Is he still the police chief round here?"

Another glance. This time there's a sparkle in her eyes, as though she's expecting the question and has an answer already lined up. "You'll be glad to hear not for a long time now. It's been eighteen years, remember? A lot's changed. As a matter of fact my dad retired the same year you left. We've worked our way through two more chiefs since then. These days, Shane Meeks is the big boss. You remember Meeks?"

Another name I haven't heard in years, or forgotten. Shane Meeks was never a fan of mine and I don't need to confirm it out loud; Krauss remembers, too, and sees it in my face.

"He's a good chief," she says. "He's changed."

But wolves rarely make great domesticated dogs.

"I thought he was in it to the death, your dad?"

Her eyes move back to the road. "He was. Then something weird happened. It was his fiftieth birthday, a month or so after you left for St. Paul. We were all there, all the usual suspects, including your aunt and uncle, your dad, everybody having a good time and celebrating, enjoying the party. Then, from out of the blue, he stood up and announced he was quitting the badge. Just like that. It took us all by surprise."

"Did he say why?"

"Not in so many words." Krauss chuckles to herself, as if savoring a private joke.

It's clear she loves her dad. No reason why she shouldn't. As far as I remember they were as thick as thieves. He did everything in his power to protect his little girl, and probably still does.

"Jake, I'm pretty sure he was having a midlife crisis. In the weeks leading up to his birthday he was in a permanent bad mood, complaining all the time and picking fights with my mom."

"She survived the cancer?"

7

"This was the year before her diagnosis. But, yes, she did. If you remember anything about my mom, it should be she's a fighter. She beat the cancer hands down. But it took both her breasts and her marriage. Sometimes my dad is as shallow as a creek in a drought."

Krauss is no longer smiling, gaze fixed ahead. I can see it hasn't been easy on her, and I wish I'd been here to lend my support. Sometimes it's harder when you're an only child.

"Soon as he retired, things really started to deteriorate at home. Eventually, my mom threw him out, and that's when I came back from college to do my bit."

"What happened with your dad?"

"He moved into our cabin up at the lake. We all thought he'd turn into a crazy hermit, but he picked himself up after a while and converted the place into a sports outfitters. Now he runs kayaking schools in the summertime for the tourists."

Before I can catch it, a drowned memory rises to the surface, as real as the moment it was created:

It's late afternoon in early summer, and mayflies swarm the shallows. The sky is vermilion, and the tree-bristled hillsides stand silhouetted against the calm water. I am standing in a vacuum, on the muddy shoreline, with my fists bloodied and sweat stinging my eyes. Clothes torn, dirtied, spattered with blood—not all of it mine. The memory is scary, uncomfortable. I push it back under, into the swirling darkness, holding it there until the weight of it drags it back to the deep.

"Of course, I've tried talking him out of it time and again," Krauss continues, bringing me back to the present, "but he's determined to stick it out. Says he likes the solitude. Gives him time to reflect. I worry about him, you know? He'll be seventy in a couple of years. He's all alone up there, which isn't sensible this time of year."

We hit the highway with a thud. Slush splashes the windshield. Automatically, the wipers skim it off. The Interceptor fishtails on the level roadway, leaving overlapping arcs in the thin layer of fresh snow. Krauss floors the accelerator as the vehicle straightens out. The headlights pick out a set of tire tracks disappearing into the dark, and we head northeast at a pace, climbing through woods entombed in winter.

I watch Krauss through the corner of my eye.

It feels strange being in her company again after being apart for so long. Unreal, like I've been transported into the future, with no memory of what lies between. Not just unreal . . . weird. The Kimberly I know, the Kimberly still living in my mind, is a seventeen-year-old girl. A bookworm with a boyish figure and a twisted sense of humor. One of my closest friends from day one of kindergarten. We did everything first together: conquered creeks; climbed cliff faces; crossed the lines and laughed about it afterward. Dumb kids, thinking we knew better than our forebears, thinking the world was ours for the taking. This version of her is more woman than I've seen in eighteen years. It will take some getting used to.

She catches me spying. "I know, it's bizarre, isn't it? I can't believe it myself, that you're actually here. Truth be known, Jake, I never thought you'd come back. Of course, I kept my fingers crossed. Your uncle told me you were making a new life for yourself in the Cities. For a while I was tempted to reach out, to get in touch."

"Kim, you should have."

"I didn't want to push it, you know?"

Krauss has questions for me. It's to be expected. Questions not just about my past, but about me as a person, all bottled up for nearly two decades. Despite our history I am an unknown quantity, and she's law enforcement. She must be wondering how the intervening years have changed me, altered my perspectives, shaped my thinking and maybe even my preferences. Krauss was always the inquisitive one—a trait no doubt honed by her profession. She would always pry, dig, cajole, always wanting to know what I was

9

thinking or feeling, but then choose to be annoyingly evasive if I ever turned the tables. It was one of the few things about her that used to get under my skin. I know she will bide her time and pick her moment to peel back my layers. I'm worried she might not like what she finds.

We pass an abandoned car. It's off-road and leaning into a ditch, the rear wheels off the ground. Recent snowfall has already begun smudging its features. Somebody has drawn an unhappy face in the snow on the tailgate window.

"Kim, where exactly are we going?"

"Lars didn't mention it?"

"We both know Lars: he keeps one hand close to his chest while the other is picking your pockets."

She laughs. On the surface Krauss has changed dramatically, but her sudden laughter is the same hyena whoop that I remember with fondness. The sound of it brings back bittersweet memories of the busy weeks immediately prior to my uprooting; of short evenings studying in her bedroom, with a pile of textbooks and unspoken words between us; of long nights on the phone, philosophizing and playacting, planning futures and vocalizing dreams.

None of it would come to pass, for either of us.

We really screwed up.

"You're right," she admits with a nod. "Lars does play a mean hand of poker. And he does make everyone who owes him pay their dues. But you'll be relieved to hear he's not quite the same self-serving megalomaniac he was when we were young. I've gotten to know him better in his old age, and I can solemnly vouch that he does have a human side. The world's moved on since Lars ran the show with an iron fist, and he's accepted he's no spring chicken anymore. Of course, he still has his thumbs in everyone's pies, but these days he's mostly a recluse. When he's not at home with the drapes drawn he's locked away at the printing press."

"The roar of the wild waits for no man."

Krauss smirks at my vocalization of the slogan joyfully emblazoned on the top of every edition of the *Harper Horn*. "It's a truckload of bullshit, isn't it? But, God bless Lars, he believes every last word of it."

"That's because he writes it."

We share a laugh. It feels natural, comfortable.

"So what's the story here, Kim?"

"I'm not completely sure. I got a heads-up from a friend at the Sheriff's Office. She said some hunters were making their way down from the lake before nightfall when they came across something unusual. They called it in as soon as they picked up a signal."

"Did they say what?'

She shrugs. "If they did, she didn't know it. But you can bet your life it's something big; they don't dispatch deputies out here and at this hour for the fun of it."

Up ahead, the tire tracks swerve off the highway and follow a fire road as it curves its way uphill though the woods. Krauss slows the Interceptor and makes the right. Then we are being jiggled around in our seats like kids on a Coney Island roller coaster. We pass beneath overhanging trees weighted with snow. I know where this trail leads. We've been out here many times before tonight, in our youth, just the two of us. Kids exploring the world, their emotions, and each other. We both knew our way around back then, and I'm sure things haven't changed a whole lot since. But there's a cool unease uncurling in my belly, something I can't put a finger on or ignore.

Lights twinkle through the dark. Rotating red-and-blues splashing vivid color across an otherwise monochrome scene. The lights belong to a Tahoe sporting Sheriff's Office decals. No one inside or standing around. Krauss brings the Interceptor to a controlled stop and we climb out.

Beyond the glow of the turret lights everything exists in tomb-like blackness. Everything still, as though the snow is deadening every sound.

Krauss hands me a flashlight and lights her own. The beams burrow deep into the woods. She points toward multiple elongated footprints snaking away into the trees. "Looks like they went that way. You coming with?"

Off-road, the snow is easily two feet deep. We wade, leaving runnels. The going is all uphill and hard on the knees.

The foreboding in my belly is gathering momentum. It's hard not to think about what lies through these trees, farther upslope. The memory is clamoring for attention. But I keep it at arm's length.

"So what were you doing back there," Krauss asks as we climb, "in your backyard, with the shovel, at three in the morning, like a weirdo?"

"Are you asking as a friend or as a cop?"

She glances at me through fogging breath. Her gaze is filled with interest, but it's underpinned with suspicion. "I'm asking because I'm curious, okay?"

I look away. Those eyes were always able to see through me, but not without seeing everything on the inside first.

"I was checking if something was still inside the old bomb shelter."

"In the dead of night? What have you got stashed back there, Jake—the family silver?"

I point through the trees. "They're up that way."

Distantly, two separate flashlights are visible off to one side, much higher upslope, lancing though the dark. Faint voices permeating the funereal hush. The terrain rises steeply directly ahead, forming a thick folded blanket of meringue-like snow, broken only by black-boned trees. I know this area well. So does Krauss. Without hesitating, she veers left and picks up the tracks again. Skeletal branches rise up and claw at our passing. Thirty yards later we emerge onto a flatter ridge of snow-covered rock.

"Watch your step there," she warns.

We are on the brink of a steep drop-away. A ravine known locally as The Gallows, running in a jagged line all the way up to Hangman Falls. This was our hangout on hot summer days, our retreat on warm summer nights. We were explorers here. Stargazers and settlers. We climbed its height and swam its length.

I remember it fondly. But now there is something creepy about the place that my innocent childhood senses missed.

Our flashlights reach out across empty space to strike the opposite wall. White disks revealing snowy rock and shrugging trees. A frozen ribbon of water, twenty feet down, littered with broken twigs and dislodged boulders. A few overlapping animal tracks. Deathly quiet.

It's hazardous for anyone not paying attention.

Krauss points. "Looks like they're up at The Falls."

In my belly, the misgiving uncurls a little more. Decades have passed like stick drawings in a flip book, but my memory of this place is perfect, defined and drawn in blood. I push it back down, into the darkness, until it disappears completely.

One of the sheriff's men spots our approach and comes lumbering down the snowy incline to meet us halfway.

"Hey. You there," he calls, "stay back. This is sheriff's business." He's a young guy, mid-twenties, with a long face split by a thick moustache. He runs an interrogating flashlight over our faces. "Officer Krauss? What're you doing out here?"

"I guess I could ask you the same question, Deputy Milner."

"This isn't a Harper PD matter."

"I know. But we came all this way, and in the dark. It would be impolite to turn us back now. Can we at least take a look, while we're here? It's a long ride home with our tails between our legs."

Indecision twists his face. His eyes roll my way, properly, for the first time. I am not the smallest of guys. Not these days. As a teenager I was gangly, stringy, one of those cadaverous kids who shies from sunlight and never gets picked for the football team. Now I look like a guy who can look after himself. It's a look that puts people on their guard. I can see by his expression he's wondering who the hell I am and why Krauss has brought me out here, uninvited. My beanie skull cap and two-day stubble only add to the thuggish look.

I give Deputy Milner a perfunctory smile.

Krauss reaches up and punches him playfully on the arm. "Will you relax, Deputy Milner? We're all friends here. All working toward the same goal. No one's going to drag you over hot coals for breaking protocols. My lips are sealed."

His stance softens. "Just don't either of you touch anything."

"We promise. Don't we, Jake?"

"Cross my heart."

We follow Milner to his waiting partner, who he introduces as Deputy Hanks.

Hanks is twice Milner's age and twice his girth. His face screws itself into a ball the moment he lays eyes on me. He takes a provocative step forward and dazzles me with his flashlight. "Hey, wait a minute. You're that Olson kid, right? It is you, isn't it? You've got a lot of nerve coming back here after what you did." His hand moves to his firearm.

Swiftly, Krauss steps between us. "Whoa. Slow down there, Hanks. Keep your speed in check. Jake here's my guest, which means if you pick a fight with him you're as good as picking one with me, too. Plus, he works for Grossinger. Is that a road you really want to go down?"

Hanks is staring me out with cold distrust in his eyes, his hand hovering dangerously close to his firearm. But Krauss's words

14

eventually penetrate. No one in their right mind wants to make an enemy of the man who draws rent on half the properties in Harper.

"Stand down," Deputy Milner warns him. "We're all good here."

Reluctantly, Hanks backs off, looking pissed, but keeps his scowl aimed at me.

"Anyhow," Milner breathes, "back to business."

He shines his flashlight at a patch of roughed-up ground lying between the tree line and the rocky precipice. It's a circular disturbance of black soil and broken roots, four yards across and over a yard deep in the center. Circling it are rings of overlapping boot prints, compacting the snow.

"There used to be a tree here," he says.

Krauss nods. "Sure. Hangman's Tree."

The focus of many of our childhood exploits. An old tree with one exceptionally large limb overhanging the ravine, rubbed smooth by kids happy to drop from it into the cool plunge pool below.

"So where is it now?"

He redirects the flashlight over the edge of the precipice, into the darkened depths. "Down there."

Cautiously, we approach the drop-away. It's dicey and deadly. I keep Krauss between me and Hanks.

Flashlights probe an open grave.

To our immediate right, a towering cliff of corrugated ice rises into the night sky. A month of arctic temperatures has transformed the waterfall into a ribbed wall of dirty ice. We're about a third of the way down, on a level with a fringe of icicles, each thicker and longer than my arms. The Gallows is deeper here, at least fifty feet and eerily quiet. Our beams drop to the uprooted tree standing upside-down at the foot of the falls. The trunk is a thick column of mossy wood, propped up against the ice cliff. Its upturned root system is a tangled mass, gnarled with frozen soil and snow. Farther down, the snow-thickened crown has smashed into the ice covering the plunge pool and partly broken its way through, pushing up big jagged ice slabs before refreezing.

But the toppled tree isn't the focus of our attention.

Something is caught up within the bare roots. Something that the eye recognizes as foreign. It isn't immediately noticeable—it's the same general gray color as its surroundings and blurred by snow—but the more I look, the more it takes shape.

And the more defined it becomes, the more I realize exactly what it is I am staring at.

I hear Krauss mutter *"that's different"* as I get out my cell phone and snap a photo before Hanks can say otherwise.

Chapter Two

Well harbor secrets. Some are so dark even light doesn't intrude. Living, breathing, walking saints are rare on the ground. People lie, cheat, steal, kill. Most of the time their indiscretions go undetected or overlooked. Sometimes the past catches up and demands a hearing.

"This is a bad idea," Krauss insists as she pulls the Interceptor against the curb. "I'm telling you, Jake, we should wait on all the facts to come in before jumping to conclusions. Let me take you home instead. Sleep on it. Things always look different in the daylight and with a clear head."

She means well, but I'm too energized to consider resting.

Krauss and I are back in sleepy Harper, outside a smallish house at the end of a quiet lane. We haven't shared more than a handful of words on our way back to town. She knows I was never big on fruitless conversation, and has left me to stew in my silence. Quite rightly, she senses my unease and I sense it's making her uneasy, too.

"Please, Jake. Reconsider."

A salted front walk connects the street to the house. Shoveled snow piled high on either side. It's the same scene repeated outside every home in Harper.

This is Ned and Nancy Luckman's place: a two-floor, brick-and-wood construction that backs onto the Harper golf course. Like the rest of its neighbors, the house is deep in darkness, and doesn't look like it's changed much since my leaving. But the stark reality is, everything changes. Sometimes it's slow, gradual, evolving or decaying over years and decades, so slow that we barely notice. Sometimes it's abrupt and things are never the same again.

The last time I sat here like this was with another girl, Jenna Luckman. Making promises that would never be fulfilled. I owe it to her to keep this one.

I open the door and climb out. "Thanks for the ride, Kim."

Krauss leans across the seat. "At least let me tag along. For emotional support."

She wants to, desperately. But the hard line of my mouth is answer enough. Krauss is protective, always was, but this is my responsibility.

"I'll call you," she shouts as I close the door.

I give her a wave and she drives away. Then I draw a deep breath and roll the tension from my shoulders.

I must look a mess. Sleep-deprived, unshaven, clothes that went out of fashion years ago. I have no idea what kind of reception I am about to receive, if any at all. People are quick to say that time heals all wounds, but it's a lie. Anyone who has lived through trauma or tragedy will attest that time is no solace. Time is a sentence on the soul, stretching out the pain.

I stamp slush from my boots, straighten my hat. There's a thrumming in my ribcage, like a frightened bird is trapped inside and trying to peck its way to freedom. I've been here before, lingering at this very threshold, feeling equally nervous, equally useless. But this time I won't be taking a girl to the movies and hoping for a kiss.

I pull off a glove and press the doorbell, let it ring for long seconds.

For a moment I am seventeen again, conscious of my gawky appearance and anxious about introducing myself to *the parents* for the first time. My mouth is bone dry and my feet won't keep still. I am not the most popular kid at school. I don't stand out in any particular class. I don't play quarterback for the football team. I won't be picked as valedictorian. I don't shine like my brother. I am your average Joe—Mr. Unexceptional—destined to do well but never to excel. I'm not sure her parents have plans on settling for second or even third best.

Maybe it's a good thing they never had to.

A light comes on inside the house. I lift my finger from the buzzer. Heavy feet sound on creaking wood, a man's voice cussing as he fumbles with the locks. The door swings inward and I come face to face with a ghost.

The Ned Luckman of my memory is in his forties, with a chunky physique sandblasted from years of hard outside labor. A broad smile in a happy face. A husband, a father. Someone with everything to live for. But the man standing before me now is a weathered husk. A leathery face with a frosting of white stubble on a loose jawline. Sunken eyes under a heavy brow. He must be in his sixties but he looks ten years older than that. He wears a quilted robe over thick pajamas, and a slightly irritated expression.

The last time I saw Ned we were still on speaking terms, but I have no way of knowing how time, my absence, or the influence of others might have altered his feelings toward me. I remember he was good friends with Lars, and I know Lars is a master manipulator.

"Hello Ned," I say before he can place my face. "It's me: Jake."

"Jake?" The word leaks from his mouth like his last dying breath. There is a scent of stale alcohol on it that hasn't come from mouthwash.

"I know it's the middle of the night and this is a complete surprise, and I'm sorry for turning up uninvited like this. I was planning on visiting you and Nancy tomorrow, but something came up tonight and it couldn't wait. I have some urgent news. I think you need to hear it. Can I come in?"

"Jake Olson?" His mind fumbles around in the dark for a few seconds before realization dawns. Then his rheumy eyes widen, as though he's witnessed a miracle. "By the love of sweet Jesus, is this really you standing here?"

I pull off my hat. "In the flesh."

My worry is unfounded; Ned steps out onto the porch, his bare feet on the freezing timbers, and throws his arms around me, hugs me tight. Hugs me like a father should hug his son. Not that I'd know. The embrace is unexpected, but I reciprocate. I have not hugged another man in eighteen years, though many have tried. Ned feels like a bag of sticks, frailer than any man should feel—as brittle as someone who has visited hell and can speak of it.

"Thank God," he breathes stale booze against my neck. "We never thought we'd see you again." He squeezes me some more, all of it weakly. I go with it. If he feels my cool tension it doesn't dilute the warmth of his greeting.

When we disengage I see tears in the corners of his eyes.

"Jake, I can't believe it's actually you. It's a miracle. When did you get back?"

"Just tonight."

"Tonight? And you came straight over here?" His face is an odd picture of joy. I'm not sure I want to be responsible for it; after all, I am the bearer of bad tidings.

"Bless you, Jake." He steps back inside the house and flaps a hand. "Don't just stand there. Come in, come in. I'll fix us both a drink and you can tell me everything. Hurry; it's cold enough to freeze piss out here."

No matter how many prayers we perform or deals with the devil we make, our past is woven into the fabric of time and cannot be undone.

"I can't believe it's you," Ned murmurs again as I follow him into a cozy living room. He turns on lights and asks for my coat. He switches on one of those halogen heaters and points it in my direction. The orange glow burns into my retinas. "It's a pity Nancy won't be able to join us, though. She'd be thrilled to see you."

"She isn't here?"

"She's upstairs, sleeping like a baby. It's virtually impossible to wake her once she's had that pill of hers. Gives you an excuse to come again tomorrow, like you say. Now make yourself comfortable there, Jake, while I get those drinks."

I settle on the edge of the couch as he pads over to a liquor cabinet in the corner. He rattles out a pair of tumblers and a whisky bottle.

"I'm sorry it's so late," I say again.

"Ah, don't worry about it." He comes over and hands me a whisky. The glass is half full and enough to put me out like a light. "I'm at that point in my life where I sleep better during the daylight hours anyway. Cheers." He chinks his glass against mine, tips his head back and downs a mouthful. "Jeez, that hits the spot, don't it?" He drops into the couch next to me. "So, Jake, you're back."

"I am."

"Of course, I want to hear everything, in your own time, when you're ready. I know it's been tough and I don't want to rush you any. Maybe you can come over for dinner once you're settled back in?"

"I'd like that."

"Great. Nancy will be over the moon. It'll give her something to focus on. A bit of hope, you know? In the meantime, what's this urgent news of yours?"

My throat tightens even before I start to speak, as though there's a noose being drawn around it. Quietly, measuredly, I tell him about my ride up to The Falls with Kimberly Krauss. As he listens, his head nods slightly, eyes growing larger as my account reaches its climax. Finally, I get out my phone and show him the picture. He puts on his reading glasses and takes the phone in his bony hands.

The image of tangled tree roots burns away its pixels. The camera quality isn't great and there's no pinch-zoom on the burner. But there's no mistaking the human skull and rack of bones poking out of the snow and soil. It looks like a child's marionette, carved from bleached wood, broken and left outside in the wintertime. Pale roots protrude through every gap and every crack, stitching it all together. No signs of any clothing or flesh. Maybe some hair. It's hard to say for sure.

It's definitely a human skeleton.

"It's Jenna," I say over a dry tongue.

A wave of guilt washes suddenly over me. All at once I'm thinking maybe Krauss is right, that this is an impulsive move and I shouldn't be here, doing this to these people at this unholy hour. On our way back to town, while I was beating myself up, convinced that I was seeing Jenna's skeleton in those roots, she'd told me to wait on the official ID, that until it came back I had no rock-solid proof that the remains were even Jenna's, and that to inform the Luckmans they were, without the forensic confirmation, was arrogant at best and downright insensitive at worst.

But something inside me feels a connection. I can't ignore it.

Ned is unmoving, hypnotized by the image and petrified by my words.

Things could have played out very differently.

I imagine sitting here under changed circumstances. Sharing anecdotes over whisky with my jolly father-in-law. Showing interest in his carpentry projects while we set the world to right. It's how we bond. The lighthearted conversation between Nancy and my wife wanders through from the kitchen, riding on the back of delicious cooking smells. They could be sisters, happy hens clucking over their brood. Farther still, the joyous squeals of mischievous children can be heard in the yard as they chase the dog with a hose, slipping and sliding on the soft summer grass. Then Jenna appears in the doorway, radiant as ever, and my heart quakes. This is what happiness feels like. And I have no right feeling it.

"Are they sure it's her, Jake?"

The killer question. I feel my cheeks flush. "My understanding is they'll need to run tests. Confirm the ID, for sure."

"But they do think it's her, right?"

"They didn't say outright. But I'm convinced."

"Sweet Jesus," he breathes.

I avoid mentioning anything about DNA sampling, cross-checks, the Luckmans being exposed to difficult questions, maybe from the media, definitely the opening up of old wounds, another agonizing funeral, the whole cartwheeling circus coming back to town.

He hands back the phone, as though it's contaminated with something deadly. "Her disappearance hit us hard. But we were hopeful, in the early days, you know? The lack of a body kept it from being real. Stopped it from being final. We thought she'd turn up someday alive, out of the blue. But she never did. I guess deep down we always knew this day might come. But it doesn't make it any less shocking when it does." He lets out a long, tremulous sigh and rubs shaky hands over his grizzled chin.

There are a lot of unspoken words in that breath. A mouthful of *should-haves* and *didn't-dos*. I've had plenty of my own, swallowed them down or spat them out against unsympathetic walls.

23

I reach out and touch his arm. "Ned, I'm sorry."

"Ah, forget about it, Jake; it's not your fault. Sure, things have been difficult. No parent should lose their child, you know? But you get used to the loss after a while. Of course, you never really move on. You just learn to live with it. God knows there are people suffering far worse in the world than us." He closes his eyes and drains the rest of the whisky.

Ned Luckman is a good man and I feel for him. I'm unsure if he's drowning his sorrows or celebrating their conclusion. His whole outlook on life changed with the disappearance of his daughter. He's spent years in limbo, holding a candle. My news has poured ice water on that flame. It doesn't bring closure, I realize; it removes his purpose.

He reaches for a framed photograph on a side table and brings it into his lap, nursing it.

I catch a glimpse of a blonde-haired girl wearing a Harper Bobcats jersey. In her hands are blue-and-white cheerleader pompoms, with the half-filled bleachers of Harper High ascending in the background behind her. Players practicing. There's a big grin lighting up her face. She is full of life and the focus of every male eye in the stadium. No idea of her fate and what was to come less than a month later.

Ned sees me looking and hands me the picture. "Go ahead."

I hesitate before taking it fully. He pushes it into my grasp. This is the first time I have held Jenna in half a lifetime.

Jenna!

She looks younger than I remember. A fragile blossom of youth, soon to be crushed underfoot. The image I have of her—the image branded onto my mind's eye—is all woman, mentally aged over time to keep up with my own passing years. But I am thirty-five now, a grown man, and I realize with a start that this is the picture of a girl. It never felt that way at the time. To us we were mature, fully grown. But the reality is, Jenna has remained forever seventeen, and always will.

The clawing unease is back in my gut.

"Belle of the ball," Ned says with the glimmer of a proud smile. "You caught her at her best there, Jake. It's one of my favorites."

I nod, gripping the frame as the photo comes to life in my memory:

"Tell me you got it?" Jenna calls on the day it was taken, as if it's happening right here and now. She shakes the pompoms fiercely, while her fellow cheerleaders sing out the Bobcat's praises.

"You're spoiling the routine," I call back.

"No way! I promised my dad a really cool picture of me cheerleading. So did you get it?"

I shrug and glance at the camera, as though by doing so I can see if the positive light from Jenna's beaming smile has worked its magic on the negative inside, like it does with me. "I guess I think so. Want me to take another, just in case?"

"That's why I bought the film, dum-dum! Take the whole lot!"

And so I do. I snap away, the bristling boyfriend, while Jenna skips and bounces, performing neat choreographed kicks and jumps, flashing her dazzling smiles and exuding infectious energy.

If anyone wonders what a snapshot of heaven looks like, here it is. A perfect moment in time, captured and preserved.

It rips me up on the inside.

Now it's my turn to feel a consoling hand on my arm.

The Luckmans have strategically positioned other photographs of their daughter around the room, so that she is always in the frame. They all show her at the same age—the age she was lost. Most of them taken by me on that glorious spring day. The last photos of her ever taken. There are none of Gavin, her older brother. It's as though he has been relegated to other parts of the house or forgotten entirely. Only dead Jenna dominates the living room.

Science teaches us that matter cannot be destroyed, only altered into something else. I kidded myself for years, thinking she'd come back to me from the grave, as a resurrected spirit, but she never did.

I swallow over a thick throat. "Ned, you do know, if I could go back and undo what was done, I would."

He smiles. It's the smile of a man who has been to hell and back. "Life's all about lessons, Jake. What good would it be if we never made mistakes?" He takes the photo from my lap and positions it back on the side table. "Speaking of which, I heard about your old man, and I'm sorry. You got my sympathies there. It's not going to be easy for you dealing with everything that's to come." He notices me pull back slightly from the comment. "You want to talk about it, Jake?"

"Maybe some other time." I get to my feet, suddenly itching to get out into the cold. "I really ought to be going. It's been a long night on the back of a long day. Rightly or wrongly, I just thought you should be the first to hear the news. I'll check in with you again tomorrow, see Nancy while I'm at it, if that's okay?"

"Sure." He accompanies me to the front door, feet shuffling on the boards. "One more thing," he says as I step outside. "He's still out there: her killer. Walked free all these years. You're here now. You can do something. Make amends. She deserved a life. We all did. So what are you going to do about it, Jake?"

Chapter Three

O ne day, when I was seven, my mother walked out the front door and never came back. At the time, I was too young to understand the complex nature of adult relationships, but I was old enough to understand that crossing my father came at a price, and normally any dues owed him were paid in blood.

I think about my mother on the walk back home from the Luckmans'. The sad truth is I have few intact memories of her. Those that do survive are grainy images. Flashes of feelings, evoked by emotion. I am sure that more exist, but they lie shrouded in darkness, deep down, where I don't dare go.

The house is mortuary cold.

I dump my snow-heavy boots on a rubber mat and power up the furnace. The house hasn't been heated in a week, or more. Frost on the inside of the window panes and ghosts in the shadows.

Four unanswered messages lie in wait on the answering machine in the kitchen. I press the *Play* button and listen to the recordings as I drink week-old milk from the fridge.

Deep in the bowels of the house, the ancient furnace stirs to life. Knocking pipes tapping out the tune from *The Exorcist*.

If Ned has his way he'll have me chasing down his daughter's killer, to do unto him that which he did unto her. An eye for an eye. Old Testament retribution brought bang up to date. But Ned hasn't done it himself. It's one thing to follow your heart instead of your head, but when it comes to the crunch, killing another human isn't like swatting a fly. It takes a completely different mindset to deliberately take a life. And once it's done, there's no coming back. Their ghost will haunt you for the rest of your life.

The milk is on the verge of turning, but I gulp it down without complaint; I've drunk far worse in my time. By the looks of things, there's not much of anything worth eating in the fridge: some amorphous foodstuffs that have grown fur coats for the winter. Cupboards offer little more in the way of sustenance. I dig a fist into a box of opened cereal and munch on a handful of stale cornflakes as the first answering machine message comes to life:

"Olson, this is Chief Meeks. Long time no see. I heard you were on your way back to town. Call me the minute you get in, and I mean the minute. I've got paperwork you need to sign and forms you need to fill out. Plus, I need to lay down some ground rules. Call me. I mean it, Olson. Don't piss me off and make me come looking for you."

This is the first time I have stood in this kitchen as an adult. It feels smaller, cramped, but otherwise the same. Olive green walls and stained countertops. Everything still in desperate need of updating, fixing. As with the rest of the house, it remains as it was the day my mother walked out, the day my father dived into the bottle and never resurfaced.

The second message is mostly static but contains a background noise that sounds like a TV with the volume turned low. No one speaks into the phone itself. The recording lasts about thirty seconds before it disconnects.

I wash the cereal down as the third message clicks on. A woman's voice, saying:

> *"This is a message for Jake Olson. Hello, Mr. Olson. My name's Dr. Beth Townsend. I'm calling about your father. I believe you are the next of kin and you've been apprised of the situation. It's my understanding you're on your way home. Please return my call on this number as a matter of urgency, or at your earliest convenience. I'm working the night shift at the hospital this weekend, so if you'd like to speak face to face, I'll be here. Thank you."*

In my pocket, my cell phone vibrates. It's a text message from the same number Lars called me on earlier.

One word: *Well?*

With clumsy thumbs I type back *Meet me at Merrill's at 7.*

On the answering machine, the fourth and final recording clicks in. It comes with the same indistinct TV noise as the previous anonymous message, but this time a male voice growls through the static:

> *"You knew the rules, duckweed. Come back and you die. I thought I'd made it perfectly clear. Your funeral. Now you're a dead man walking."*

Chapter Four

These days, Tolstoy was feeling every one of his seventy-three years. Decades of living to excess had finally caught up with him. There were only so many knocks and scrapes a body could take before it was wrecked. But what man thought about becoming dust when he was shining like a diamond?

It was early; not yet dawn. And, typically of late, Tolstoy was sitting astride a toilet, sweating, trying to pee what felt like bits of broken glass through an inflamed urethra.

His wife had reminded him he was no spring chicken. She'd urged him to slow down, to take things a little easier. After all, it wasn't as though they couldn't afford the hired help; they were comfortable, with bank balances in the black. Shouldn't he be sitting back and enjoying the ride instead of driving down the fast lane with his foot stomped on the gas?

A year ago, she'd warned him to listen to his complaining body or pay the price if he didn't.

Ten months later, the debt had been called in.

With watering eyes, Tolstoy caught sight of his ghostly reflection in the bathroom mirror and let out a labored breath. The aging black man glaring back at him was still a hulk by all comparisons, still the stuff of children's nightmares, but he could see where his affliction had melted muscle, turning hard slabs into sandbags. He wasn't stupid; he knew it was only a matter of time before he faded away altogether, and the thought made him all the more determined to make his final days count.

An acidic trickle drilled its way through and he gasped with pain.

Cussing under his breath, he finished up and then made his way to the back of the house, stooping through doorways as he went. This wasn't his home and he didn't know his way in the dark. A man called Blake lived here. Tolstoy didn't know Blake and Blake didn't know him, but between them they did know a mutual acquaintance, and that was the reason for the visit. Politely, Tolstoy had introduced himself, by profession and connection rather than by name, and Blake had been accommodating, to a point.

"Man, I am so sorry about that," he said to Blake as he entered the dimly lit kitchen. "I got this thing going on, you know? Damn nuisance. And no amount of medication hits the spot." He ran himself a cool glass of water and glugged it down in one. Maybe it would force his bladder to play ball? Probably not.

Blake was standing at the breakfast bar. He was a thin-faced guy with salt-and-pepper hair and shifty eyes. There was no blood on his lips, no blackened eyes or broken teeth, no facial evidence to show he'd been roughed-up, but he had been. Verbally. There was real fear carved into his panicked expression, the kind of fear that causes a grown man to wet himself all over the kitchen floor.

Unexpectedly, Tolstoy was jealous.

"Please," Blake implored him quietly, "I'm begging you. Don't wake my wife. She'll be up anytime soon as it is. You need to be long gone from here before then."

Tolstoy stuck out a ledge of a lip. "That a fact? So what worries you the most, Mr. B—your lovely lady finding out you spent the rent money on cocaine, or the fact you've pissed yourself all over her clean kitchen floor?"

His words came out a shaky whisper: "You don't need to do this; I said I'll give you the money."

"Sure you did. And that's mightily generous of you. Seeing the error of your ways and wanting to make amends is commendable. Good for you, Mr. B. But it's my job to make sure you understand the danger you've put your wife in. That way, it'll never happen again." Tolstoy moved closer and Blake visibly cowered. At eight foot tall, and even in his seventies, Tolstoy had the menacing presence of a standing bear. "See, I could have just as easily slipped in here, nice and quiet, and slit her throat while you both slept. But I didn't. This is your one and only warning. You with me, Mr. B?"

Blake let loose a snotty whimper, nodded tightly.

Both of his hands were palm-down on the beech countertop, both pinned in place by steak knives stabbed through the soft webbing between the thumbs and the index fingers. Not enough to completely tear the skin into flaps, but sufficient to prevent him from pulling free and calling the cops. Trickles of blood had pooled on the wood.

"Please." There was a distinct tremor in his voice. "I'll give you all the money. Every last penny. Just don't hurt my wife."

Tolstoy slid Blake's checkbook across the counter and slapped a pen down next to it. "So write the check and we can both go back to bed." He reached over and pulled the steak knife out of the Blake's right hand.

A minute later, Tolstoy was on his way back to his pickup when his cell phone vibrated in his pocket. He took it out, squinting at the small screen. It was a text message from an old friend:

"Jake Olson is back in town. You know what needs to be done."

Chapter Five

H arper isn't what you might call a pulsating metropolis. At best, the population teeters around the two thousand mark. At worst, that number swells in the summertime into the six figures. The reason? Harper is what's known as a gateway community. A frontier town, clinging to the edge of the great outdoors. Last call for every East Coast city slicker with a permit and a canoe.

In any other town, Merrill's Diner would be a trendy coffee shop or a fast-food outlet. One of those big-brand clones that have elbowed their way onto every intersection and kicked out the competition. The one thing small towns have in their favor is charm, and it protects them from the big-boy franchises. Merrill's has stood on the corner of Charlotte and Main for what seems like forever, or at least since jukeboxes ruled the roost, and that in itself is a lifetime ago.

I used to come here all the time with Jenna.

It's impossible not to fill my thoughts with her as I sit here waiting, staring through the window at the street lights holding back the dark. Jenna was my first love. It meant something, still does. Recently, I think about her more than I have in years—still spellbound by her bright blue eyes and the way the rest of the world dimmed in the brilliance of her smile. Pathetic, I know. A counselor once told me I have a fixation with my feelings for Jenna and an idealistic way of remembering her, both of which act as an overcompensation for her absence. Maybe so. But it doesn't make me feel or think any differently.

Ned and Nancy aren't the only ones who have held a torch for her all these years, I realize. Discovering her remains doesn't just bring closure, it brings finality and has left me on a knife's edge.

I press achy shoulders against the back of the booth and draw a slow breath. A tall mug of coffee is warming my hands. I think about the messages on the answering machine, especially the anonymous recordings. Unsurprisingly, I have enemies in town. People who'd rather I never came back or, better yet, that I'd died in the Twin Cities and spared everyone the heartache. Any lesser person would run a mile. But I'm not easily scared these days, or deterred.

On the wall, a TV is showing a 24-hour news channel. The scene depicts a Middle East warzone: shelled buildings, speckled with bullet holes; dazed survivors scurrying for cover under the thunder of incoming artillery; dusty babies crying in mothers' arms; broken bodies mangled in the rubble. It's the kind of foreign shore where my brother would have defended his country. The clip could be current or ten years old; same scene every day of the week, year in and year out. Far enough from Minnesota to make it somebody else's problem.

With a sucking noise, the diner's door opens, allowing a gust of freezing air to blow in and ruffle the napkins. On the back of it comes an old man in a padded parka. One of those Russian-style ushanka fur hats is curled up on his head like a sleeping mink. He walks with the aid of a cane but his gait remains awkward. He is thinner than I remember, as knotty as driftwood. He spots me and pulls off the ushanka to reveal a cap of snowy hair atop a head that seems out of proportion with the rest of his withering frame. He looks every bit the harmless retiree, half the man of my memories. But I know looks can be deceptive. You don't need weight to have gravitas.

"Thanks for your consideration, son," Lars Grossinger complains as he slides into the booth seat and fixes me with a slanted smile. "Have you any idea how deadly it is out there for a guy with a stick?"

I spread my hands. "Neutral territory."

His gaze scans the deserted diner. "Haven't been in here in a while. Sure looks like no man's land. Still, I don't bite, you know? Not with these teeth."

"They serve better coffee here."

"That's what I'm counting on."

As if on cue, a young waitress floats over. She's all of sixteen, pretty in an uncluttered kind of way. She fills the mug in front of Lars and tops mine to the brim. I wonder if she has any inkling about the identity or even the history of the man she's now serving. Lars nods his gratitude, then picks up the sugar dispenser and proceeds to load the drink. With a rumble, he orders pancakes with blueberries, syrup, and extra butter.

"How old are you, Lars?"

He pulls off gloves. "Eighty-something. To tell you the truth, by the time you reach my age, it's a bit of a blur. If it's my blood sugar you're worried about, don't be; I'm not. They have medication for everything these days. Besides, we all got to die sometime, right? The way I figure it, we might as well enjoy ourselves on the run-up." He nods toward the departing waitress. "You want some breakfast, son? It's on me."

I shake my head. I don't want to owe Lars any more than I already do.

"Okay, so let's just cut to the chase." He removes his fur hat and sets it on the seat next to him. "One thing I do remember about you is meandering conversation was never your style. So let's talk business. What's my story?"

"There isn't one."

He gives me *the look*. I know it's the look Lars makes whenever he feels deceived. Ordinarily, it causes most people to quake in their shoes. Not me, not now.

He leans forward. "Son, let's you and I get something straight here: there's always a story. It may not be immediately visible. It may take some digging, some inventive thinking. But there's always a story. Kim called me after she dropped you at the Luckmans. She told me exactly what you found up there by The Falls and what you believe it means. If that ain't newsworthy, you better tell me what is."

This is my chance to tell Lars to keep his job, to prove to him I'm not the malleable kid he remembers. I've been away from Harper and my father long enough to grow an iron backbone and a steel skin. Unlike most townsfolk I was never completely in Lars's pocket. Had I stayed in Harper things might have been different. As it is, I owe him for supporting me in my hour of need, but that doesn't mean I owe him my life.

Lars blows at his coffee and cautiously takes a sip. "Look, son, I know going up there this morning has probably opened up old wounds and got you on the defensive. It's understandable. I'm no ogre here. I empathize. But a deal's a deal, right? You agreed to go out there and get me a story."

"Even if the truth is it's yesterday's news?"

"The truth is what we make it." He breathes the words, as though by saying them any louder he'll invoke the devil himself. "Son, are you and I operating on the same frequency here? If your hunch pays off and you're right about it being Jenna up there, then it's not just newsworthy, it's serendipitous. Trust me, son, we need to get this story landed before the sharks get a sniff of it."

When I was a boy I would never have looked Lars directly in the eye, but I do now. "Kim assured me you'd mellowed with age, but I can see you're still just as fixated as you always were."

"That's because it's in the blood, son. I'm obsessed with the truth. It's all we have. It defines us, shapes us. It's the only thing we take with us beyond the grave. Never mind your chivalry and your patriotism, it's the truth that keeps men like you and me up at night. Someone needs to be its voice. And that's our job."

I've heard his little speech before, and I'm still unimpressed.

I lean back in the booth and drop my shoulders. "Lars, it's been eighteen years. The people had their conviction. No one's interested."

"And that's where I beg to differ. There's no statute of limitations on murder, Jake. Not in Minnesota. The people need to know what really happened to Jenna, where it happened, and by whose hand. Do you want the world to go on thinking it was you who killed her?"

Another killer question. The worst one.

With heat rising in my belly, I glance toward the kitchen, fearing that the waitress has overheard Lars's declaration. Thankfully, she is nowhere to be seen, and my speeding heartrate slows a little. My reaction is automatic, and one that has been repeated a hundred times over the preceding six months.

"Most of the town believe I killed her," I say, keeping my voice low, even though I have nothing to be ashamed of. "It's the way it's been since I was seventeen and I can't see it changing just because her remains have been found."

"It will if you find her real killer. That's the reason you're here, isn't it?"

"Partly."

"So this is your chance to set the record straight. Give the people what they want: the truth. Find her real killer. Expose him. I don't buy for one second you don't have intentions to do exactly that." He sees the darkness in my eyes and adds, "Be its voice, Jake. Work with me. We're on the same side here. Like it or not. We're up to our necks in the truth business and there ain't a damn thing we can do about it."

He neglects to say *his version of the truth* business.

A smirk tries to force its way onto my lips, but I hold it back. Provoking a cobra is never a good idea. Thanks to his ownership of the local press, Lars has written what he calls the truth in Harper for over fifty years. That's a long time to warp perspectives without succumbing to your own hype. Listening to him, I'm not sure he can tell the difference between the truth and a donkey in a dress.

Lars sits back and lets out a long breath. "Okay, so I know what you're thinking: the truth is whatever people choose to believe. I accept I've played my part in that outcome over the years. God knows there are times I haven't been completely forthcoming with the unabridged version of it. See, my hands are up. I'm a sinner. We all are. When I was younger I had axes to grind and soapboxes to climb. Stupidly, I believed I could make a difference and that the *Horn* was my way of fixing things. After all, the pen is mightier than the sword, isn't it? When we peel back the layers of lies, the only thing left behind is the truth."

He spreads his hand. "Look, Jake, let me be perfectly honest with you. I'm too old to fight anymore. My time here on Earth is limited; I'm not getting any younger and God knows I've had a good run at things. I need to make peace with my maker while I still can. I've made some bad choices over the years. We all do. None of us are angels. Before my time expires, I need to set the record straight—just like you. I know you're not in my fan club. I respect you for it. A man should have his principles and be willing to stand by them, no matter what. I just want you to know I've always done my best by you, son. And that's the God's honest truth. This job offer of mine, it's an olive branch. A new start. I'd like it to be long term. I'm not going to be around forever; I need someone to run the *Horn* after I'm gone. I need someone I can depend on. Someone with sharp eyes and a nose for a good story. Someone out for—"

"Revenge?"

A smile makes a brief appearance. "I was going to say for the good of the people. But if that works, who am I to say otherwise? The truth is, in the short term, I need a dependable reporter and you need a regular paycheck. Whichever way you slice it, this is one heck of a deal for us both, right?" He takes something out of his pocket and slides it across the tabletop. It's a plain white envelope, thickened by its contents. "Go ahead, count it. There's a thousand dollars in there. Consider it an advance on your first month's wage."

I shake my head. "Keep your charity."

He leaves the envelope where it is. "Loosen up, son. I know you got your education in prison. Top marks with flying colors. Got that journalism degree, too, I hear. So quit playing hardball and put all that learning to good use. Think about it. Everyone believes you're a convicted murderer. Who else is going to give you a job round here?" He pushes the envelope to my side of the table. "We'll get you started on a basic two thousand dollars a month. Plus commission."

It's probably double the salary of his last reporter, and I tell him so. Harper isn't exactly a hubbub of news stories. No high demand for investigative journalism hereabouts.

He dismisses my hesitance with a wave of his liver-spotted hand. "Want to know something? Your mother was the best photo-journalist I ever worked with. She was the best. I owe it to her to make good with you. Besides, I'm cash-heavy these days, and I can't take any of it with me."

I take a mouthful of cooling coffee, one eye on the envelope.

The waitress brings his pancakes. Lars tucks an oversized napkin in the neck of his sweater and dives in.

Up until a couple of days ago, I cleaned tables in a mall in St. Paul and bedded down in a hostel. The job wasn't riveting and the accommodation wasn't The Ritz. Lars's job offer is a good one. Generous. Better than the roll of ones dwindling in my pocket. It will provide security and a means to stay in Harper—if that's what I want.

We all have a price. But do I want to owe Lars my soul?

One thing I am sure of is that being on Lars's payroll comes with expectations, obligations. Lars never does anything without good reason. Once you're indebted to him, your life is his to do with as he pleases. Sure, I need the money, but it's all about the lesser of two evils and what I'm prepared to live with, or not.

It's hard not to get burned when you're fascinated by fire.

Lars swallows down a mouthful of pancake. "Must have come as a shock, that scene this morning. Don't pretend you don't give a damn, Jake, because I know you better than that."

"You know nothing about me, Lars."

"I know enough. I've kept track of you over the years. I know you have principles, that you're loyal, that you're a survivor. I know you wanted the Luckmans to hear it from your own lips, rather than read about it in the paper. That takes some balls. You got a conscience and that's golden in my line of work." He wipes whipped cream from his lips. "That discovery this morning, some might say it's more than coincidence that this hits the fan the minute you walk back into town. If I were a God-fearing man I'd say it's divinely ordained. So I'll ask again: what's my story?"

Acquiescing, I bring up the photo on my phone and slide it across the tabletop, past the untouched envelope. One of his wiry eyebrows tilts at the picture glowing on the screen, then the ruddy color drains from his skin as his eyes focus properly on the image.

I've never seen Lars look even remotely shocked before. It's the most emotion I've seen from him that isn't fueled by anger.

"She was buried under the tree," I say. "The bedrock is close to the surface up there. It looks like the snow weight got too much for it and brought the whole thing down."

"Is this Hangman's Tree?"

"Yeah."

He picks up his coffee and slurps, loudly.

There's a tremor in his hand. Coffee-stain liver spots jiggling on loose skin. "Are they positive it's her: Jenna?"

"How many other women do you know who have gone missing in Harper?"

He shrugs. "Hard to say for sure, son. A lot of holidaymakers, explorers, and general outdoorsy people come through here. No one keeps tabs on anyone. Who's to say it isn't some lone hunter on the wrong side of a bear?"

"Stuffed under a tree?"

"I'm just saying. It's not impossible. Wolves take their prey back to their dens all the time. What we're looking at here could just be the result of some unlucky hillwalker failing to measure up to the great outdoors."

Lars's points make sense, but something about his quick-to-dismiss reaction feels off somehow and I can't quite put my finger on it.

I watch him take another long look at the picture, as if memorizing every detail, every brittle bone fragment. He's definitely shaken, and I'm surprised by it. Lars has seen his fair share of skeletons over the years, most of which he's skinned himself, but this one has him itching to run a mile.

"You take any more photos like this, any high-definition close-ups?"

"You're lucky I got this."

41

He nods. "I'll get you fixed up with a real camera. So what did the sheriff's men say?"

"That they're treating it as a recovery operation. Once they ship the remains back to Duluth, they'll run the DNA to confirm the identity. Aside from that, like I say, there's no story here, Lars. The people had their conviction for Jenna's murder a long time ago. As far as the state's concerned, the case is closed."

But Lars doesn't look convinced. "Well, like I keep saying, there's always a story, son. You just have to read between the lines." He points at the phone. "If you're right about this being Jenna, then it's the biggest story to hit Harper in recent history. People need to read it and we have a responsibility to publish it." He leans forward, over his pancakes, suddenly wearing the face of a man on death row. "Make no bones about this, Jake. There are opposing forces at play in this town. A clear divide between the truth and the lies. You've experienced it for yourself; it's robbed you of half your life. Those same people have perpetrated a cover-up for years. As purveyors of the truth, it's our duty to expose them for what they are." He pushes the envelope across the table. "So you need to decide which side you're on and where you're prepared to make your stand."

Chapter Six

A yellowish glow blanches the eastern cloud cover as I hunch into my coat and head away from the diner. The sidewalk is salted, but patches of ice lie in wait underfoot. It's quite a trek back to the house on Prescott. I haven't slept in over a day, and only intermittently before that. Caffeine is giving me a welcome burst of energy, but I know it'll be short-lived.

Lars has told me to call into the office Monday morning, to sign contracts. But I'm not sure I'll take him up on his offer. Then again, I'm not sure I'll decline it either. Certain situations have taught me the benefits of mutual backscratching. One thing is clear: if I am to go about my business in Harper unhindered, then having Lars Grossinger's weight behind me will help open doors and loosen lips. Even at a personal price, I'd be a fool to ignore that kind of leverage.

A car creeps past, taking it easy on the slushy surface.

Jenna fills my mind as I head home.

I think about her a lot—more so in the first few years following her disappearance, and recently, very recently, following my homecoming. She never fully leaves me, never has. I feel her presence when I close my eyes, smell her scent on other people, all of it provoking memories:

"Where do you see yourself ten years from now?" Jenna asks as we stare at each other over milkshakes, the day she leads me to believe we can run away together, a week before my world implodes.

"With you, of course," I answer, stupidly, before even thinking.

That's the one thing I learn after she's dead: I speak before engaging my brain. Early on, it gets me in trouble—sometimes big trouble—and I am never able to talk my way out of it. But beatings make for great teachings. They teach me restraint, diplomacy, the power of silence. But it's all too late to save me and Jenna.

"Maybe in a house by a lake," I add, again without giving it any real thought. "With kids and a dog. Yeah, that would be nice, perfect."

My outburst of visceral honesty makes her laugh. It's genuine, and without a hint of condescension. Of course, I am heavily biased. I am seventeen at the time, smitten, and Jenna can make cuss words sound sexy.

She smiles. "Okay then, how many kids?"

"I don't know. Three, four. As many as you'd like! Whatever makes you happy, Jenna. Us happy."

At this point in our relationship, Jenna and I have been seeing one another for three months. It's still fun and curious, but we both sense there's a seam of seriousness underlying our interactions. Don't get me wrong, we are happy with our slice of the pie. As happy as any dating teenagers with bright futures lighting our way should be. But we're both aware that dating is base camp and there's a long, hard climb ahead if we ever hope to reach the summit before sunset.

The views will make it all worth it, won't they?

Jenna's laugh settles into a smile, sucking blood into my cheeks.

I love that smile, that pure, brilliant, infectious smile. I can't imagine thinking anything different, or ever living without it.

Playfully, she reaches across the tabletop and caresses my hand. "Jake . . ."

My skin tingles at her touch, as it always does. The electricity that moves between us is anything but static. Her fingertips dance on the back of my hand, keeping tempo with my heartbeat. Cheesy to the point of puking, I know.

"Exactly how will we live by a lake when you're a successful *New York Times* journalist and I'm a trailblazing surgeon?" she asks.

Small town people with big player dreams.

"Well, let's see . . . for starters I'm pretty confident New York has lakes. We can live in a big house outside the city. You know how much you love the water, the woods. Maybe have an apartment in the city during the week, overlooking Central Park."

"New York." She breathes the words with awe, as though this is the first time she's pictured herself anywhere other than humdrum Harper.

Jenna isn't intimidated by the thought of uprooting and beginning again. It excites her. And, right then and there, it excites me, too.

At seventeen, we both know it's a glimpse of a possible future, from a distance, through rose-tinted lenses. We both know there are a million and one obstacles standing in our way, preventing us from ever getting there: detours, distractions, landslides. Journalism is my chosen path—just as hers is medicine. The end of high school is in sight. College is in our crosshairs. We have discussed our dreamed destinies, in depth and in every detail. We are aware of the pitfalls of studying apart, of attending different academies. The general consensus is that long-distance relationships fail. We aren't naïve. We know the odds are stacked against us. But we have to try. We *want* to try. How else can we realize our dreams if we never have them to begin with?

"Pulitzer Prize winning journo," she grins.

"Head of neurological surgery," I reply.

"Two girls."

"Two boys."

"A house by the lake."

"Don't forget the dog!"

We laugh and slurp our milkshakes like teenagers without a worry in the world, reveling in escapism and what could be.

A week later she is gone. Taken. Lost. Possibly dead. And all our imaginary flights of fancy are clipped, crashing to earth, aflame.

I never saw Jenna again. My childhood sweetheart.

Until today.

"Olson."

I look up from my feet, so distracted by my thoughts that I haven't noticed the cop car pull up to the curb ahead of me or the officer standing next to the open passenger door. It's not Krauss's Interceptor. It's a black-and-white Ford Mustang with black alloys. One of those muscle cars driven by men with inferiority complexes. The officer has a metal *Chief* pin on his collar, polished to perfection.

Shane Meeks.

He's early forties, with short white-blond hair and irises the color of glacial lakes. Imagine a grown-up version of a child from the movie *Village of the Damned*, and here he stands. The similarity is not restricted to his external appearance either. Internally, Meeks is just as disconnected from his humanity as one of those soulless Hollywood half-breeds. As a teenager, Meeks was a bully. On several occasions the only thing standing between me and his fist was my brother. More than once there was no intervention.

"Get in," he says. "I mean it, Olson. Don't mess with me. Get in. I'm not asking."

I drop inside. Meeks goes round to the driver's side and slides in behind the wheel, closes the door.

The vehicle smells of coffee and cologne. Both of them cheap.

"Congratulations on the promotion, Meeks. They say scum always floats to the top."

My comment is rewarded with a sneer: "Don't get smart with me, Olson. This isn't a good day to get smart. Close the door; you're letting the heat out."

I don't. I leave one foot on the road. "What do you want, Meeks?"

His lips curl with contempt. Meeks never hid the fact he disliked me, loathed me. He had his reasons. None of them made any sense.

"Let's you and I get something straight from the get-go," he says. It's not quite a snarl, but the sentiment's the same. "It's Chief Meeks to you now. I'm the law in this town. Round here, I'm top of the food chain. I own people like you and I don't like the smell of bullshit. One whiff of it and I'll come down heavy, like a brick shit house falling from on high. You get me? If you think Harper's a soft landing, you're mistaken. Give me an ounce of trouble and you'll pay for it by the pound."

This is our first conversation as adults and already he's acting childish. I'm not intimidated by his little *get out of Dodge* speech. Meeks is small-fry compared with some of the bullies I've had to deal with, insignificant. We both know it.

His colorless eyes frisk me over. Balls of inhuman ice rolling round in their sockets. He's smaller than I remember, just like everything else around here.

He taps a piece of chewing gum from a packet and pops it in his mouth. "Harper's not the same place it was twenty years ago. Most folks have moved on. Got themselves whole new lives. They don't need some convicted troublemaker dredging up the past and making them feel uneasy all over again."

"That's not why I'm here."

"Yeah, sure. And I guess time will prove it one way or the other. I heard what happened with your dad and I'm sympathetic to a point. He was a better man than you'll ever be and didn't deserve a runt like you, and that's the only reason I'm giving you a little latitude here. All the same, it's a big mistake on your part coming back. Jenna's murder hit this town hard. Feelings still ride high in some quarters. Everybody knows you killed her. Understandably, some folks still hold a grudge."

And I have no doubt Meeks is one of them.

Prior to my arrest, Meeks had an unhealthy interest in seeing Jenna's killer brought to a swift justice. Meeks knew Jenna through association with Gavin, her older brother, who was his best buddy in those days. They were a deadly double act, like an evil Abbott and Costello. Back then, Meeks was a patrol officer in his mid-twenties, but I knew he had his sights on Jenna, despite both the age and intellectual difference. His jealousy was palpable whenever he saw the two of us together.

"For the record," he continues, chewing the gum, "I've spoken with your PO in St. Paul. You're lucky you've got a nice guy there. He was real accommodating, illuminating. So we have this agreement in place. While you're in my jurisdiction, you'll be checking in with me on a daily basis—without fail—or you risk violating the conditions of your parole. You get me? So that means staying out of trouble, Olson. I mean it. It's my job to keep the peace; I don't need to hear anyone complaining about you upsetting them."

It sounds like Meeks learned all his lines from a B-movie. Monotone stereotype. His intention is to intimidate, but he doesn't scare me one bit, not anymore. I say nothing; words can incriminate. Meeks isn't thrilled with my homecoming, and he won't be the only one. I'm a dagger, plunged through the fabric of the community, and Harper is tight-knit. When things are that close, gossip spreads like bloodstains.

"And that includes going where you have no right going," he adds, referring to my trip to The Falls this morning. "Keep your nose out of police business."

"Sheriff's business," I correct.

His top lip pulls up, like he's just tasted something unsavory. "Don't take advantage of my charity, Olson, or I'll ship you back to Stillwater quicker than you can shit yourself. Now get out of my car."

Chapter Seven

The hunter was invisible—nothing more than a stain on the snowy terrain. The white camouflage parka and matching padded pants were bulky but necessary if he wanted to remain warm and undetected. It was freezing up here on the mountain, and maintaining any single position for any length of time wasn't recommended. But stillness was a hunter's best disguise. Anyone glancing his way would see a seamless surface of undulating snow, luminous with light and striped by shadows, with no hint of his presence. Even the white surgical tape wrapped randomly around the hunting rifle made it look more like a fallen tree branch than a deadly distance killer.

People were moving within its crosshairs: a red-headed girl taking photographs, the shriek of her camera clawing against the uneasy silence; a thickset guy raking back snow, huffing and puffing; men and women with Day-Glo orange vests pulled over their thick winter coats, serious expressions pinned on hung heads. A single word was splashed across the front and back of their bright orange vests. In a large black typeface it read: *Sheriff.*

Those who weren't scratching at their scalps were either bagging evidence or jumping to the echoing commands of a barrel-chested lieutenant standing on the rim of the ravine. The recovery operation was in full swing here at Hangman Falls. Everything businesslike and organized. But the tension was intense, clotted by people impatient to get down off the mountain. No one wanted to be on crime scene cleanup on the weekend and in freezing conditions.

A flick of his wrist brought the frozen waterfall into view.

His elevation on the opposite side of The Gallows provided an eagle-eye panorama of the activity below.

The boys and girls from the Sheriff's Office had spent the last hour trying to figure out a safe way to recover the human remains lodged firmly in the upturned tree, without causing injury or embarrassment, or damage to the evidence. But the location was proving a challenge. The exposed root system was three yards out from the edge of the ravine and about the same distance down. Everything precariously balanced against the frozen waterfall, on a knife's edge. One wrong move, one clumsy boot, and the entire tree would topple, taking the skeletal remains down with it, and maybe a couple of heavy-handed deputies, too.

Finally, after a heated discussion, a bright spark had come up with the brilliant idea of rappelling down the frozen waterfall. The lieutenant had given the plan the thumbs-up and two snowmobiles had been anchored in the frozen runoff at the brim of the falls. A pair of jaw-clenching deputies had rappelled down, armed with battery-powered saws. Now they were in the process of trying to disentangle the human skeleton from the root matrix. The body had been under the tree a long time, long enough for roots to invade every gap and entwine around bone, suffusing it. Time had welded it to the tree, and their handsaws were jumping around on the swollen wood like bugs on a hotplate.

What they needed was an experienced lumberjack, someone who would throw a harness around the root ball, lop the whole thing off and then hoist it to safety. But that would mean wasting even more time, and time was not something they had in abundance out here; white flakes had begun to fall from the sky again and this time tomorrow the root system would be crusted in a foot of hardening snow.

Distantly, somebody hollered for attention.

The hunter swept his rifle sights across the scene.

The shout had come from a female deputy standing a little way back from the drop-away, in the disturbed soil area where the tree had once stood tall. She was holding an object up in the air and gesturing at the barrel-chested lieutenant to come take a look.

The hunter adjusted the focus on the scope, bringing the object into sharper detail.

It was a woman's purse, dangling on a leather strap from the end of the deputy's metal wand. Faded brown leather, with leather tassels and what looked like a sunflower design stitched into one side. Distinctive. It was caked in soil, but otherwise better preserved than its owner.

He'd seen the purse before, he remembered with a jolt. He knew whose purse it was, knew the implications that came with its discovery. And he knew it would mean an unplanned trip into town to share the bad news.

Chapter Eight

The encounter with Meeks leaves me prickly. The one thing I value is my privacy. I cherish it. These days I make a big deal out of it.

I walk off my edginess, boots cemented with slush, legs leaden by the time I get to the house on Prescott. The exercise has me thinking about my brother when we were kids:

"Will you quit whining?" Aaron asked, a lifetime ago, as he prepared to embark on his daily five-mile jog into the National Forest and back.

It was a brilliant summer's day, the world split equally into green and blue. Aaron was sixteen at the time, with the clean-cut looks of a poster boy and the toned body of an Olympian. Shorter than me, but solid.

"Exercise is good for you, little brother." He grinned, showing healthy teeth, as if to confirm it.

"It's hard work," I argued. It was a puny reason. All I had. It fit in with my weedy physique.

Aaron continued to grin at me with the winning smile of an athlete at the top of his game. My brother walked or ran everywhere, always had. He participated in every sport played in Harper, excelling in all. His energy levels were phenomenal, enviable. Unlike me, he had the stamina of a marathoner. I tried my best, but I was not the sporty type. I didn't have the genes for it. Even at thirteen, I preferred my sports from the comfort of an armchair.

"Trust me, Jake. You'll live longer."

But not forever. That was my point. No one does. Not even my super-healthy, fitness-freak brother.

The house on Prescott is thawing out. Musty odors of drying plaster. Creaks of warming wood. I spend the next six hours sleeping restlessly, unable to find comfort or stop my mind from replaying the morning's events. It's like this now, and has been since my release from prison. It's difficult settling down without someone else's metronomic breathing to regulate my own. The irony is, in the early days of my incarceration, that very same stranger's breathing used to keep me awake.

When I do sleep I dream of death. Often it's somebody else's. Sometimes it's my own.

Eventually, I wake to find myself on the floor, tangled in damp linens and wedged between the bed and the wall. Disoriented. For a moment I think I hear the wake-up call echoing outside, boots stamping on gray cement, bolts being drawn back, but it's just the banging of pipes against loosened pins.

I relax in my nest, but only a little.

I can smell Jenna and my heart is racing.

Six months have passed since I got the stamp of approval on my parole. For me, time has stood still. The world I left behind is dead. Friends have moved on. Family has passed away. Trends have come and gone and come around again. While I've been resisting change on the inside, the outside world has changed beyond all recognition, almost as though I have emerged from a coma into an alien world.

In some ways reintegration is harder than incarceration.

"No one warns you before you get out," I'd told Denis Flannigan, my designated parole officer, as I sat in his cluttered office in St. Paul, a day into my newfound freedom.

Flannigan had cigarette-stained fingertips and a missing front tooth. He was a wiry redhead with skin so freckly he looked like an accident in a paint factory.

"So what do you think they should do, Olson," he'd said in his thick Irish accent, "provide handbooks and the like? Get real, will you? State Corrections is dollar-poor as it is. They got better things to spend their money on other than wiping your miserable backside. So get used to it, brother. You're institutionalized. It's going to take time to readjust. Who knows, maybe you never will. The sooner you accept your old life is gone and there's no going back, the sooner you can start building you a new one. Better than the old. Same as I tell all my boys. You've done the hard part. You survived prison. You did good. Congratu-fucking-lations. So now you've got to learn to survive out here, too. Stay good. You getting me?"

The truth is, psychologically speaking, I was institutionalized within weeks. Fate sealed in a concrete box with no way out.

People think imprisonment takes away choices. It doesn't. Every day I made decisions, most of which were designed to grease my life and stop the abuse from sticking, but mostly to survive. Choices I would never make on the outside, or ever even contemplate. Prison life is all about adjustment. Those that fail to adapt either die or wish they had. Daily routines help, especially as the weeks drift into months and the months fade into years. They keep you focused, grounded. They denote the passage of time. But nothing prepares the mind for release, for exposure, for the bigger bad world to confirm your insignificance. I came out of Stillwater time-shifted and forgotten, and I haven't quite caught my breath.

My phone rings on the nightstand. I extricate myself from the tangled linens and pick up, "Hello?"

"How you doing there, sleepy head?"

"Kim? How'd you get my number?"

"Lars. Obviously. I figured you'd be sleeping, so I hung back from calling too soon."

I rub grit from my eyes. "What time is it?"

"Almost two. It's the weekend and it's snowing. We should do something."

I get to my feet and pull back the drapes, squint at the gleaming world outside. Big flakes are tumbling lazily from a breezeless sky.

"What do you have in mind?"

"Skinny-dipping up at the lake?" She hears my snicker and adds, "Seriously, though, how'd things go with the Luckmans?"

"Better than I expected."

"Yeah? That's good, Jake. I'm pleased for you. They've been through a rough patch. Now they can move on. So I was wondering about grabbing something to eat. I'm thinking a late breakfast or an early dinner? My treat."

I almost say *"what's your agenda, Kim?"* but then remind myself she's just being friendly. The fact of the matter is I'm not used to people being pleasant for no reason. I'm used to ulterior motives and coercion. I have to remember she's looking out for me in the same way she always did. There's no harm in her believing a kindly face will help shoehorn me back into Harper life. I have enemies. Krauss is a police officer. Keeping her close will soften attitudes.

I stretch stiff neck muscles. "It sounds like a plan. But first, I have business I need to take care of. Can we meet at Merrill's, later, say around four?"

"Sure. Just don't keep me waiting. Okay? If you decide to back out, let me know. You've got my number now. Use it. You can call me anytime. Night or day. I mean it, Jake. I want you to know I'm here for you. Besides, we've got a lifetime of catching up to do. It's going to be great."

Jail time can change a man for the better or for the worse. More often than not he doesn't get to choose which.

I hang up and rub fingers through unkempt hair.

Whenever I feel disjointed I stick to routines.

Preprogrammed, I scoop up the mound of blankets from the floor and smooth them out on the bed, tuck everything in nice and tight. Plump the pillows even though I haven't used them. Then I go to the bathroom to urinate, wash, brush teeth. I left my razor in St. Paul. No big deal; the stubble makes me look mean, and a little meanness might not be a bad thing right now. I crank up the shower and sluice away dried sweat, soap up my hair, rinse. Then I return to the bedroom to dress in clean clothes pulled from my duffel bag, mostly donations to the hostel. Everything either a little too small or a little too big, but clean.

Downstairs, I count the thousand dollars in the envelope from Lars, for the third time. I'm not sure what to do with all this money.

I know there will be bills to settle, debts to clear. I'm not sure how far it will take me or go toward satisfying my father's creditors.

I stuff some twenties in a pocket and head to the kitchen, flush the remains of the stale cereal down my throat.

All the while I'm thinking about Jenna rotting away under that tree for all these years, visualizing the worms and the beetles pervading her soft skin, picturing her decomposing flesh swarming with maggots. Cruel roots sucking every morsel of goodness out of her. I wonder how many lovers have rolled entwined in the shade of that tree, oblivious to the carnage underway beneath; how many laughing children have climbed its leafy limbs to spy pirate ships from its crow's nest, unaware of the skull and crossbones buried at its base.

Mittened knuckles thud against the kitchen window.

I look up to see a man peering through the grubby pane, recognizing the round and ruddy face of my uncle. He sees me looking and waves. I open up the door. "Owen?"

"Hey there, big fella. What're you doing cooped up in here on a nice day like this? It's glorious outside. You should be out there, soaking it all up." He bangs snow from his boots and steps into the kitchen, brings a flurry of snow in with him. Without stopping, he pulls me close and hugs me tight. "Great to see you, Jake. You're home at last, finally, where you belong. Harper hasn't been the same with you gone." He lets go. "When did you get in?"

"Later than planned. Early hours of the morning. I just got up."

"Well, that explains why you didn't answer the first time round. I came over after sunup. I saw the heat was on and banged on the door, but you didn't answer. Catching up on your beauty sleep, was you?" He grabs me by the chin with his mittened hand. "Will you look at you? All grown up and back home! Wait till your aunt sees what a hunk you've become."

I smile away his harmless sarcasm. "How is Julia?"

"Oh, she's good, you know? No doubt looking forward to seeing her favorite nephew. Looks like it'll have to wait until after the weekend, though; she's away visiting her sister in Hibbing. She's sick with the flu—her sister, that is, not your aunt. Bad timing all round, I guess. So, you got in late, did you?"

The interstate had been at a crawl. Traffic jams trailing snowplows. Overworked police and red road flares. One or two crashes and cars overturned on the roadside.

"Owen, I'd make you a coffee, but we're fresh out."

He flaps a mittened hand. "Ah, no bother. The doctor warns me I drink too much of it as it is. I get these palpitations, you know? Arrhythmia, he calls it. He thinks it's the caffeine. I don't tell him I have a weakness for pastries."

"You should watch your cholesterol."

"Sure, like it'll make a difference. When your time's up, that's it and there's nothing you can do about it. God knows best, always does." He glances around us, at the disorganized kitchen, at the mold crawling up the window frames. It's probably the first time he's stepped foot in here since before my mother left. His nose wrinkles. "Boy, this place smells, and in a bad way. You had a rat die round here?"

I smile. "Probably."

I like my Uncle Owen, always have. He's like a big lovable teddy bear. One of those people who gets on with life without complaint. Together with my Aunt Julia he runs Harper's busiest homegrown general store, right in the heart of town. His outlook on life is sunny side up. *Fix what's fixable and make the most of what's not.* But it hasn't always been this way. Before I was born, Owen used to hit the bottle harder than my father—so much so that my aunt had threatened him with divorce. Luckily for them, he saw sense and has been on the wagon ever since.

I always sensed my father hated him for cleaning up his act.

Then again, Owen and my father have always clashed.

As boys they rarely saw eye to eye, often verbally sparring and frequently falling out to the point of throwing punches. If any brotherly love existed between them at all, it was a one-way street and all from Owen's end. My father had issues, even then. He fostered an unhealthy need to compete with his older brother. But he never could. Owen was good at everything he put his hand to and my father despised him for it.

As men they stayed out of each other's way, on opposite sides of town, only coming together for Sunday service and at family functions, and only then when forced to out of obligation. I knew my father envied Owen's popularity, the house he lived in, maybe his position of power in Harper's community. Envy ate away my father from the inside out, always did, and not just with Owen. The irony is, my uncle is the least competitive person I know.

"Well, will you take a look at this?" he says as he inspects the fridge. "It's like the theory of evolution in here, and a bad case of salmonella waiting to happen. Oh my. I hope you've not eaten any of this stuff." He sees my eyes dart to the empty milk carton on the counter, and makes a disapproving face. He closes the fridge. "I'll see about getting you some provisions sent up from the store, fix you up until you're settled in. In the meantime, you're welcome to eat at our house. Like I say, your aunt's away, but I'm sure I can rustle up a decent meal for the two of us. I remember you love my pot roast."

"I do, and thanks. I'd like that."

He flaps a hand. "Hey, it's no big deal. It's the least I can do. We're family, right? Comes with the territory. Plus, it's my seventieth birthday next week. It'll be a great opportunity to get together and celebrate your homecoming properly." He looks me over with doleful eyes, and I sense what's coming next: the reason that brought me back to Harper. He spots my automatic withdrawal, even though I try to hide it. I don't exactly run away and cower in a corner; it's more of a subtle creeping of the flesh. "I'm guessing you haven't seen your dad yet?"

"No. But I will."

"You should. It's only right. Prove you're a better man than he ever was."

"Owen," I let out a sigh, "I said I will. I just need to pick my moment to go out to the hospital. It's difficult."

"But you've got to do it."

Owen's right. I know I have to. I know I don't really have a choice. I know I am only delaying the inevitable, the unavoidable. I know I will put it off for as long as I can. I know once it's done I'll have closure. I know it's not that easy.

Owen performs a slow and measured nod. "You're right; it's a big deal. Hey, I get it; I'm no Neanderthal here. Came as a shock to us all. We thought he'd go on forever, but this brain bleed of his knocked him out cold. In spite of everything, you must be going through hell. God knows, no one would blame you if you turned your back on him. He never treated you right. Not from day one. Sure, he had his reason. But that wasn't your fault, big fella. He was wrong taking it out on you the way he did."

"Water under the bridge."

Owen misses the tension in my response. "Yeah, well, we tried telling him over the years, your aunt and me. We tried making him see sense, but he wouldn't listen. Your dad was stubborn like that. Come to think of it, he was the definition of bullheaded. No wonder he ended up lonely and alone. He never bounced back from your mom walking out."

My father isn't the only one.

I let out a shaky breath. "It hit us all hard—because he hit my mother hard. It was all his fault. Everything. He brought it on himself. She did what was best for her own survival. She left him and got as far away from him and Harper as she could."

He nods. "Hey, don't think I'm making excuses for him. I don't condone marital violence in any shape or form, or any violence at all for that matter. But the demon drink can do that to a man. Your dad's not the first and he won't be the last. His decline accelerated after your brother left, too, you know that, don't you?"

But my leaving had no impact.

"He lost his health, his mind, his faith. You do know Aaron never came back either?"

"My father wasn't easy to live with."

"That's for sure. Like rats in the attic. Still, I never thought it would end this way. Like it or lump it, Jake, you're all he has. It's down to you now. You're the man of the house. I know it's tough, but you've been through worse, right? I know you'll do the right thing." He reaches out and pats my arm. "I'm here, if you need me. I still have my seat on the council, which gives me some sway in town, if you need it."

"Thanks, Owen. I appreciate it."

"No problem."

Out of everyone, Owen is one of the few people to champion my corner without question and without reward. Although he was unable to visit me religiously every month in Stillwater, he did visit a couple of times each year, especially in the early years, and that is more than can be said for anyone else. Not once has he questioned my innocence. Not once has he bought into the lie. You can't buy that kind of loyalty. It's golden. It's familial.

"Oh, and before I forget," he says. "Your dad has papers here somewhere. Insurance stuff, you know? Maybe even a will. You need to find them, just in case the worst happens and he doesn't pull through. Last thing you need to worry about is the bank calling in a loan or something."

Chapter Nine

B y the time Owen leaves and I venture outside, the snowfall is heavier, thicker. A sheet of muslin is drawn across the sky, mummifying the snow-deadened landscape. Noisily, I crunch my way down the side of the house, shovel in hand, blowing flakes from my nose as I go. The backyard beckons, but it can wait.

The upshot of my uncle's visit was an urgency to investigate my father's affairs. As soon as he was gone, I broke the lock on the writing bureau in the living room and rolled back the lid. My father's filing system consisted of bills and bank statements, in ripped envelopes piled high, and all of it in no particular order.

A quick rummage revealed no land deeds or insurance policies, but I did find a photocopy of his Last Will & Testament in a manila wallet. It was positioned on top of the dog-eared paper clutter, as if deliberately put there for me to find. Heart thudding, I pored over its contents. The will was signed and dated the year my mother walked out. The legal jargon was of no interest, so I skipped straight through to the beneficiaries section, too realistic to be hopeful; I knew my father wouldn't leave me a crust of bread if I were starving.

One beneficiary: the holy building directly across the street from the house on Prescott. The Harper Community Church. My father's beloved obsession, and the one thing in his life aside from Aaron that he loved unconditionally.

I grew up in its shadow, and its legacy lives with me still.

A snowdrift has barricaded the garage doors shut. I get to work with the shovel, chopping at it like a mad axman. The effort of clearing the concreted ice warms me up a little. No strength for it earlier.

Images of Jenna's skeletal remains play on my mind:

This morning, as we headed down off the mountain and into town, I asked Krauss: "What happens next?"

Her expression was solemn. "Once they recover all the bits and pieces, they'll send them to the ME's office over in Duluth. Run tests to determine the exact cause of death. Don't be surprised if they come back inconclusive. Eighteen years is a long time to be under the earth."

"Blades and bullets leave marks on bone."

"They sure do. But you can't tell from a skeleton if the person was asphyxiated or even had their throat cut."

Krauss's comments should have spooked me, but they didn't. In my head, I have played through all the scenarios of that fateful night, time and again until I am left dizzy and directionless. As a species, death fascinates us. When we're young and healthy we can only conceive of death happening to somebody else. But there's no discrimination. Death has no favoritism. Sooner or later it's our turn to take a bow.

During long, lonely nights in my cell I thought about Jenna being abducted, bludgeoned unconscious, bundled into the trunk of a car, taken somewhere remote, raped and beaten, then fatally stabbed or shot before finally being buried in a shallow grave out in the woods or dropped to the bottom of the lake.

I have held her hand and walked through every step with her in meticulous detail. Every heartbeat. Every breath. Every scream.

I have changed the locations, the circumstances, the variables. I have seen her bleed, her bones break, her eyes glaze over. No matter how many times I rewind and run through it again but with different setups, the outcome is always the same:

Jenna dies every time.

The truth is, I have a preoccupation with Jenna's death and I can't escape it. It's coiled up in my DNA. It's all I've known. It's part of me.

About a year into my sentence, my psychiatrist assured me:

"Repeatedly going over events beyond our control is a perfectly normal predisposition."

It explained my craziness, or made it less alien. She went on to tell me it was healthy, restorative. Over the preceding six months she'd worked hard at unraveling my layers of complexity, digging deeper than anyone else had done previously. She'd uncovered a vein of truth. The treasure was within touching distance and she had no intention of letting it slip back into obscurity.

"The mind is a composite of realities," she continued. "Replaying traumatic events and working through alternative outcomes is its way of compartmentalizing the incomprehensible. Reflection, analysis, and conjecture are all constructive functions. It shows that the mind is trying to come to terms, to deal with sudden loss or unwanted change. Think of it as a Band-Aid for the brain."

Speculating on Jenna's death was healthy, it seemed, at least for me. Nevertheless, I spent sleepless nights worrying over the days leading up to her disappearance, wondering how I missed the signs, how I failed to notice the dark stranger watching her from afar, watching and waiting for his moment to pounce, to strike, to shatter my world into a million bloody pieces. Who was he? Where had he come from? Why did he choose Jenna? Why wasn't I there for her when she needed me the most?

"The world is full of bad people," the psychiatrist said matter-of-factly. "When they enter our lives and cause mayhem we try to rationalize their actions as best we can in our own terms. We compare their deeds to the moral framework we are comfortable with. We try and understand their motives, their mindset. But madness cannot be so easily pigeonholed and reasoned away. Sometimes people are evil. They do very bad things, despite our best efforts to the contrary."

I spent even more fruitless days hypothesizing on how Jenna met her fate, and what she was thinking in those final moments before he cruelly ended her life. Did she plead to be with her mother? Did she cry for the future she knew she'd never have? Did she think of me? Did she blame me?

Torturous thoughts were unstoppable, uncontrollable. They invaded in the dead of night, when my guard was down, in those quiet moments when I was at my most vulnerable.

The psychiatrist told me that chastising myself for being unable to foresee, prevent, and ultimately save Jenna was normal behavior, natural. When we lose someone close, that's what we do. A personal inquisition. What could we have done differently? What could we have done to force fate to switch direction? What could we have done to intervene?

An endless stream of questions. And not one single answer to stem the flow.

Back in Harper, I shake the memory from my head and stab the shovel deep into the snow.

The psychiatrist knew her stuff. But thinking of Jenna kills me every time.

The garage doors complain about rusted hinges as I drag them apart. A waft of something dead brushes past me and escapes. I discard the shovel and step inside. Things smell musty in here, bad, worse than the mildewing kitchen. A sagging workbench stands beneath a pegboard prickled with nails and rusted tools. Cartons of screws, slowly being absorbed into the moldy surface. Underneath, packing boxes gone waxy with age. The small window at the back is veiled with webs. Mouse droppings litter the floor.

My father's prehistoric Ford Bronco is fossilizing beneath a stained tarp. Dust billows as I pull it back. The vehicle looks like it hasn't been let out in years, and has been going to seed for much longer. Red paintwork masking rust. A testing kick at the tires shows they are soft but surprisingly doable.

In another time, I hear my father's voice saying:

"They don't build them like this no more."

The words came as I was soaping it down one sunny Sunday afternoon, trying to make a good impression, one of many.

"Put your back into it, boy," he commanded. "Get all the crap out from under those fenders. You don't want to give that rust any excuse to make itself a home."

I was sixteen at the time, hoping to build enough trust in him to be permitted behind the wheel. In fact, I was running around doing every chore I could find, just to stay on his good side, if there was one. Three months and twelve washes later I was allowed to run the Bronco up and down the driveway for the first time, but not under my own supervision, and not without one or two coarse corrections.

I hook gloved fingers under the door handle and give it a tug. The driver's door isn't locked, but it might as well be. Rust has welded it shut. I put my back into it and wrench it open. It obliges with a yowl, and brown flakes fall to the floor.

Then I hesitate before climbing completely inside.

The stench of my father is overwhelming. It cuffs me on the chin and claws at the walls of my stomach. Decades of sweat and Marlboro Reds, ingrained in the vinyl. Hostile.

I wish I could say the smell of him brings back happy memories, but it doesn't.

Incredibly, the engine starts after a dozen turns, sputtering and wheezing and blasting soot into the rear of the garage. I rev it, gently at first, then harder as the Bronco finds its feet. According to the dials on the dash, the tank is almost empty, needle touching red, but hopefully enough juice to get me into town.

I crank the heater to max and head out. The Bronco slews and freewheels its way along the back road, black soot booming from the exhaust.

Feels weird.

The last time I sat in this seat, Jenna sat in the other. We were happy, tunelessly singing along to "Nobody Knows" by the Tony Rich Project—our favorite song at the time—laughing and fooling around. Teenagers with hopes and dreams and no idea how easily they could be torn asunder.

"Why don't we just keep driving," she suggested, her slender hands tapping along to the tune on the radio. "God knows it's a crazy idea. But there's nothing stopping us, right? We could just leave and never come back. Start our lives together someplace else. Just the two of us." She implored me with heart-tugging eyes. To me, right in that moment, Jenna was the epitome of everything I desired. The idea of running away together was electrifying.

"What about school?"

"Screw school! Jake, you are such a Mr. Do-Right! Loosen up a little, will you? Who cares anyway? This is our life. Ours to do with as we choose. I don't know what you think, but I don't want to be one of those people who look back and wish they did things differently. Do you? We should make the most of it. Live while we're young. No regrets."

At that point in our relationship I had real feelings for Jenna, feelings that were deeper than mere friendship, the kind that screamed when we were apart and purred when we were together. I wanted nothing more than to spend the rest of my life in her presence, every waking moment and every sleeping one, too. Gagging, I know. I'd heard all the horror stories about young love turning sour with age. I knew, statistically, we were already doomed to fail. But this felt different. I *knew* it was different. I couldn't imagine a life without her in it. We were young lovers, on the verge of a great leap. Not into the unknown, but into each other.

Anything was possible if we wanted it hard enough. Right?

Jenna was still staring beseechingly at me from the passenger seat, waiting for my response, for an answer that could change both our destinies forever. I was about to take the plunge and gush out an *"all right, let's do it!"* when she stuck out her tongue and announced:

"Jake, I'm joking! Jeez, you are so adorable, but you're way too serious sometimes! Come on, let's go get milkshakes at Merrill's and fantasize some more."

Like so many times since then, I kept the crushing disappointment from darkening my face. I loved Jenna for all the wrong reasons, but I hated her for all the right ones.

Days later she was gone, missing, then presumed dead, murdered.

"She skipped school today," her father told me, the day after she went missing, the day we were all baffled by it.

Officer Meeks was there, at the Luckmans', in their living room, taking notes and already trying to pin her disappearance on me.

"I thought she was home, sick," I answered, blankly. "We all did. Ask anyone." It was midweek, midterm, and as far as I knew Jenna had never played hooky before.

Meeks eyed me suspiciously. "Did you two break up?"

"No. Like I've already told you a million times: I wasn't with Jenna yesterday, after school. I don't know where she was, or went."

"And you didn't see her at all today?"

"Not once."

Jenna's father shifted to the edge of his chair. Already he was looking like a father who was thinking something terrible had happened to his little girl. "Jake, help us out here, will you?" His tone was a mixture of anger and parental perplexity. "As you can appreciate, we're worried, scared even. Jenna didn't come home last night. Her bed wasn't slept in. We know she was in school yesterday, but she didn't come home afterwards. We need to know where she went. If you weren't with her, who was?"

"I wish I had the answer. Honestly, I do." That way, I could have put their fears to rest and told them something that would have made sense, even to me. The Luckmans had been kind to me, treated me like a son. I owed them the truth. But the truth was, I had no idea what happened to Jenna after school. Jenna and I were an item, but we weren't joined at the hip. She was free to come and go as she pleased, and strong-willed enough not to seek my consent either way.

Meeks caught my attention. "If not you, Olson, then who was she with?"

I shrugged. "Ruby?" It was a clutching-at-straws guess and sounded like it. "Have you asked her? She's her best friend, you know? They're always hanging out together when we're not."

"We've already spoken with Miss Dickinson and crossed her off the list. Ironically, she thought Jenna was with you. In fact, that's what Jenna told her." Meeks glanced at his notepad. "She says, and I quote, '*Jenna said she'd had an argument with Jake and wanted to sort things out,*' and that's all she knows."

"She said she was with me?" My words came out single-file, my cheeks heating up incriminatingly.

Behind us, Jenna's older brother paused his pacing long enough to snarl: "Yeah, you were fucking her, duckweed. Of course she was with you." Gavin was seven years older than me and Jenna, the same age as Shane Meeks, and with the same aggressive mentality.

Jenna's tight-lipped mom flapped a censuring hand in his direction.

Jenna's dad cleared his throat disapprovingly. "So level with us, Jake. You're not in any trouble here. You can tell us the truth. Was she with you? It's okay if she was. It's okay if the two of you were doing stuff you don't want us to know about. We've all been teenagers. We just want to get to the bottom of what's happened, that's all. Know she's safe. Even if she asked you not to tell us anything, we need to know."

I made a pained face. "I'm sorry, Mr. Luckman. Really, I am. I'm just as cut up about Jenna going missing as everyone else. But I'm not hiding anything here. I'm telling the truth. I didn't see her after school. I know it's no use to anybody, but I don't know what else to say except that this is wasting precious time. It's getting dark. We should be out there looking for her." I got to my feet, but Meeks pushed me back to the couch.

"Out where, exactly?"

"I don't know!" Panic strained my voice. Desperation indistinguishable from guilt. This was the longest Jenna had been incommunicado since we'd been dating. In some ways I felt responsible, but only because I was her boyfriend and I should have known *something*, anything to mitigate their anxiety. But I was as clueless as everybody else.

Meeks rose up in his seat and cornered me on the couch. "Listen to me, Olson. You're this close to me throwing you in lock-up for the night. Now spill the beans. Out where in particular? Is there something you want to share with us?"

I glanced from Meeks's accusing eyes to the frightened faces of Jenna's parents. Mr. and Mrs. Luckman were dying to gobble up any scrap of information that would help them understand what was happening. But how do you begin to get your head around the idea your child had vanished without trace?

At this point, thirty-six hours had passed since they last laid eyes on their daughter. Jenna was missing and everything was up in the air. They needed something with weight to tether it down. Unfortunately, my answers were without substance.

"Several of the faculty witnessed you arguing with Jenna yesterday, during your free period."

I rotated my wide-eyed gaze back to Meeks, who was looming over me. "That's ridiculous. We weren't arguing." My cheeks felt hot enough to glow in the dark.

The Luckmans were looking on, mesmerized like jurors hearing a killer's testimony for the first time.

"We weren't arguing," I reiterated, pulling back on my anger.

"What, then?"

"We were having a disagreement."

"Same thing."

"No, it's not. Arguments lead to break-ups. And we definitely didn't. I don't know where Ruby's got her information from, but she's mistaken. Jenna and me, we were expressing a difference of opinion, that's all." I glance at the Luckmans. "There wasn't any animosity."

"That's not what several eyewitnesses say."

I turn back to Meeks. "They're lying."

"Really? So let me get this straight. You're calling Mrs. Peterson, the head of science, a liar?"

"No."

"What, then?"

"I don't know!" I was cornered, exposed. "Okay, so maybe we were a touch louder than we should have been. It was no big deal. It was just a stupid argument."

"I thought you said it was a disagreement?"

72

I scowled at Meeks.

"What were you arguing about?"

The Luckmans were watching, lungs billowing with bated breath. It was the first they knew about our altercation. It hadn't come to blows. But they were her parents and it was their job to be protective.

Awkwardness swelled in my chest. "I can't tell you."

"Because it has something to do with her disappearance?"

"No. Because it's private, and it has nothing to do with this situation." I pull myself up on the couch, forcing Meeks to back off a little. "Now, can I please go or am I under arrest?" My heart was thumping, lungs collapsing. I needed air. All at once I needed to get outside and run.

Meeks glanced at the Luckmans, then back to me. "No, Olson, you're not under arrest. But everyone can see you're being evasive and that doesn't look good for you. Something's not right here and we need to get to the bottom of it. Like I said right at the start of this interview, it's in your own best interest to answer my questions fully and honestly. Holding back just makes you look like you're not telling us something. So work with me here. Where were you yesterday evening, after school?"

"Nowhere." It was a pathetic response. A knee-jerk reaction from a teen forced out of his comfort zone. Sweat was beading on my brow, making me look as guilty as a cat burglar caught with his hand in the safe.

"Define nowhere."

Automatically, I glanced at my hands, suddenly conscious of the slight bruising on my knuckles. There was a noticeable tremble, but no blood. I tucked them under my thighs before anyone noticed. "If you must know I was up at The Falls."

"Hangman Falls?"

"Yes."

"Why?"

"Because that's where I go when I want to get away from everything."

"You go up to The Falls?"

"It helps me think."

Momentarily, I closed my eyes, finding myself transported to the lip of the ravine, my bones jarred by the crashing water. Above me, the setting sun has turned the sky blood red. Down below, the mercury surface is infested with flies. Some of them come up to investigate the blood dripping from my fingertips. My breathing is labored. Mud on my clothes and matted in my hair. Sweat soaking my skin and muscles still quaking in the aftermath of exertion.

"What were you getting away from, Olson, up at The Falls?"

"Home," I answered, opening my eyes. "My father. My brother."

"Not what you'd done to Jenna?"

"I didn't do anything to Jenna." This time, through gritted teeth. Then I turned to the Luckmans and repeated the statement, less forcefully, hoping they'd believe my sincerity.

Meeks nudged my foot with his boot. "Hey. Look at me. So what got you running all the way up to The Falls, by yourself, on the evening Jenna went missing?"

I released a hot, weary breath. "Last week, my brother announced he was leaving home to join the military."

Jenna's dad leaned forward. "Aaron signed up?"

"Against my father's wishes. They went to war with each other over it. They were still arguing when I got home from school yesterday. I didn't want Aaron to go. I begged him not to. But his mind was already made up. I tried to reason with him, but he stormed out of the house. My father started smashing the place up. I was upset."

"So you went up to The Falls?"

I nodded. "To clear my head and to get away from it all. It's where I go. I wasn't with Jenna and I didn't see her."

A mask of dissatisfaction was hardening Meeks's face. "Anyone else vouch for your whereabouts?"

I shrugged. "I wasn't thinking about an alibi." I got to my feet. "Now, can I go? My father's expecting me home."

"Sure," Jenna's dad said. "Thanks, Jake."

"Just don't leave town," Meeks added. "You know more than you're telling us, Olson, and the truth will come out, sooner or later."

At first, and in spite of my interrogation, the police were empty-handed, with no leads, no clues, and no idea where Jenna might be, alive or dead. Nothing to go on except that she argued with her boyfriend, in school, in front of witnesses, the day she disappeared. There was no trace of Jenna running away; her purse was missing but her clothes and personal belongings were all in her room, exactly as she left them before heading off to school. There were appointments penciled in her planner and arrangements to hang out with friends the coming week. Her disappearance wasn't just unexpected, it was a mystery. What teenage girl went anywhere for any length of time without her makeup? There was no record of her purchasing either a train or bus ticket. No sightings of her hitching a ride or leaving town. No mention to any of her closest confidents that she was planning an escape.

One moment she was there, the next she was gone.

And I floundered like a landed fish.

"Jenna was not the running away kind," Ned Luckman reported on the front page of the *Harper Horn*, three days into his daughter's disappearance. *"We had a happy home life. Jenna excelled in her studies. She was popular and planned to study medicine. We're thinking somebody has taken her. There's no other explanation. We're asking anyone who knows anything to come forward. No matter how small or seemingly insignificant your information, it might help the police find her. We're praying for our daughter's safe return. Please pray with us."*

Already, he was talking about her in the past tense.

Lars Grossinger, who was good friends with Ned Luckman, ran with the story and didn't stop running with the story, or an ever-evolving version of it, until an arrest was made. Increasingly, the Harper PD was put under pressure to produce results. My uncle held meetings in the town hall, at first to share information with concerned townsfolk, and then to work out search strategies. Nearby woodlands were combed, but it proved impossible to sieve through even a fraction of them with limited manpower.

There hadn't been a single recorded abduction or kidnapping in Harper's history, and there was no blueprint to work from.

As time passed and nerves got frayed, Chief Krauss made it his personal mission to solve the riddle of the missing girl. He was fastidious, a dog with a bone. He re-interviewed everybody connected with Jenna: family, friends, acquaintances, me. He went through everything with a fine-toothed comb: who was where and when; who saw what and where; who noticed anyone acting suspiciously or any visitors in a sudden hurry to leave town. It was the cusp between spring and summer. Fishing season had begun and there were strangers underfoot.

With volunteers brought in from neighboring towns, Chief Krauss organized wider searches of the local wood- and wetlands. They even used sniffer dogs and somebody claiming to be a psychic. They found nothing. No scent of Jenna anywhere other than where they knew she'd been. The chief posted her picture at all the bus and rail services within a fifty-mile radius. But no one reported seeing Jenna Luckman.

The only recurring report was that I was seen arguing with her the day she disappeared.

Then, as the days became weeks and Jenna failed to resurface, the police began thinking of her disappearance as an abduction. When her torn sweater was found in my father's truck with her blood on it, their missing-persons case moved up a gear to homicide. From there, it was no great leap of the imagination to conclude that I had continued our argument after school, when we were alone. And it hadn't stretched the scenario too far to think that the argument had ended badly, for Jenna, and by my hands.

Inescapably, one by one, the fingers of blame pointed my way, like dominoes falling. No physical body was ever found. No signs of a struggle in her family home. No evidence to suggest foul play other than the torn and bloodied sweater found in my father's truck, which I tried to explain away, to no avail:

"We were up at the lake," I told my police inquisitor. "It was weeks ago, way before she went missing. I don't recall when exactly. I know it was raining. We ran for cover. She got her sleeve snagged on a tree and she had to tear it free. She picked up a deep scratch. We were soaked, so she left her sweater in the truck. She must have forgotten about it. I know I did. Do you think for one moment I'd leave it there if I killed her?"

The smoking gun. It was what the cops called culpability and what prosecutors called circumstantial evidence. Add that to the fact Jenna and I were seen arguing right before her disappearance, and it was enough to accuse me of her murder.

"The boyfriend did it!" became the unifying cry.

True or not, I was guilty.

"But I'm innocent," I protested as I was processed into the system, fingerprinted and photographed. I pleaded with Chief Krauss, begging him to rethink my arrest, appealing to his good nature. "This isn't right. You know me. I'm at your house all the time, with Kim, studying. You can't do this! Listen to me. I didn't kill her! You can't do this! I'm innocent!"

But no one was interested in the squeals of a pimple-faced seventeen-year-old who'd killed his girlfriend. My complaints of injustice were whispers in a whirlwind. I had no solid alibi—or at least none that I was willing to share—even though one did come from an unexpected source:

"He was with me, the whole evening," Kimberly Krauss told her dad, in my defense. "You have to let him go, Dad. Jake didn't do anything wrong."

The chief couldn't prove she was lying, but he didn't believe her either.

"We were together," she stated defiantly. "All evening. Just the two of us." She was doing her best to cover for me, literally lying through her teeth, but the chief dismissed her—especially when I failed to corroborate her story independently.

"I don't want her in any trouble," I told him from behind the bars of my cell in the basement of the Harper police station. "Kim has nothing to do with any of this. Nothing. I didn't see her at all the evening Jenna vanished. I swear to God."

Chief Krauss was happy to accept my word at face value. The last thing he wanted was his daughter implicated in a potential murder investigation and causing a conflict of interest for him.

The case against me was simple and went like this:

Jenna wanted us to break up and I couldn't stand it. We argued about it, both in school in public and afterwards in private. Things got heated and Jenna's life was ended in a crime of passion. I covered up her murder and disposed of her body, never to be found.

The headline read: *Jilted lover kills beautiful girlfriend.* Case closed.

"Just quit with all the pretense and tell us where you hid the body," Chief Krauss growled at the tail-end of a grueling three-hour interview. Kim's dad was a balding man with sweat patches staining his shirt. Breath as foul as some of his accusations. "Give me something to take to the prosecutor. Anything, before they ship you out to Duluth. Work with me here, Olson. Stop this craziness spiraling out of control while you still can. You know the Luckmans. They deserve to know the truth. Don't deny them the chance of burying their daughter. You're not that kind of monster, are you?"

But I had nothing to give. I was empty, consumed by blackness. His blunt words beat me up and left me broken. Silence can be incriminating.

Shell-shocked, I was sent to pretrial detention, where I learned my lawyer was being provided by Lars Grossinger.

"Your mother was a valued employee of the *Harper Horn*," the lawyer explained. "Mr. Grossinger thinks it only right that he should pay back her loyalty by helping you in your hour of need."

For whatever his reason, Lars didn't believe I'd killed Jenna. He put his money where his mouth was. It meant I owed him, if and when the nightmare ever ended.

At trial, my defense was defenseless. It wasn't cheap, but they crumbled under the weight of the prosecution's sustained offensive. They argued I was an angry teen with daddy issues, someone who didn't like to hear the word *no*. They brought in psychiatrists specializing in teen angst. Talked about my upbringing, my issues, my emotional withdrawal, my failure to take my medication following my mother's leaving. They made a big fuss about the fact that I was on mood-stabilizing medication in the first place. The world heard about my volatile state of mind, about how I was pinned with a label from an early age. They focused on the fact that my father had regularly beat up on my mother, about how my witnessing it had influenced me subconsciously, about how my mother had eventually left home to escape his brutality, about how her abandonment had traumatized me, and how I channeled all that pent-up rage into strangling the life out of an innocent seventeen-year-old cheerleader.

The jury heard that our argument in school was probably the catalyst and therefore probable cause. Jenna's torn and bloodied sweater was a preponderance of proof. They went on to construct whole scenarios where I disposed of Jenna's body in the woods, coated it in lime to throw the tracker dogs off the scent—lime I had access to in my uncle's general store. Or I tied rocks to her feet and dropped her in the lake. It was all circumstantial, all wrong, all believable, all bullshit. Sure, I wept like a little girl, but there was no sympathy for me. No juror buying my sobs. I was found guilty of Jenna's murder and sent to the Minnesota Correctional Facility at Stillwater to begin a twenty-five-year term.

My life was over. Just like hers.

Almost two decades passed by behind bars, time in which I grew, matured, planned. I learned how to manipulate the swirling blackness within me, using it to keep me alive. Using it to control the flow of memories. Then, from nowhere, I was granted parole and it was as though someone had breathed new life into my corpse. I left Stillwater with two goals: to find the person responsible for killing Jenna and to clear my name.

From my basic means in St. Paul, I spent weeks researching people back home, events, comings and goings on the lead-up to her disappearance. I was determined to uncover her real killer and to prove my innocence to the world. Even if I had to kill to achieve it.

Chapter Ten

E ven those who knew his real name referred to him as
Tolstoy, despite the fact he was neither of Russian descent
nor a great author. The nickname had been his for as
long as he could remember, bestowed upon him by an elementary
school teacher as a play on words against his real name of Warren
Peets. He didn't mind the moniker; it made him sound distin-
guished and came with an air of authority, which was everything
in his job.

Tolstoy had been born in a small fishing community clinging
to the Gulf Coast in Louisiana, but he'd lived out his entire adult
life here in Harper. Compared with the South, Minnesota was cold,
even in the summer, and in spite of his thick skin he'd never quite
acclimatized. Lately, the chill had taken permanent residence in the
marrow of his bones.

Tolstoy had never felt a desire to marry and to father children,
although he was and he had. When he was twenty-one he'd met a
local Harper girl who didn't mind the fact that his head scraped the
ceiling, and together they'd started a family, leading a comfortable
life in the house on the southern edge of town that had been their
home for the past fifty years.

In his heyday, Tolstoy had been a force to be reckoned with. He could proudly boast he'd never lost a fistfight or an argument, even though he avoided both if he was able. With his towering frame and his three-hundred-fifty pounds of muscle, his presence didn't just dominate, it intimidated. Protective parents pointed him out to their children as someone to be avoided from the other side of the street. To them, he was an enforcer, fearsome, never to be crossed. To their kids, he was an ogre, fascinating, and the stuff of urban legends.

But to those who mattered the most he was a gentle giant and a loyal friend. The kind who would willingly take a bullet or leap into a swollen creek to save a neighbor's cat.

He thought about the text message on his phone as he followed the red Ford truck through town.

"Jake Olson is back" the text message had read, and he knew exactly what had to be done.

Chapter Eleven

I leave the Bronco parked at the end of a steep driveway and make my way up a slippery front walk toward a dilapidated house. The property is a tired construction of buckled walls fighting a losing battle against rot and neglect. A thick cap of snow presses down on the roof. It looks like the whole structure could collapse at any moment under the weight. Silvered wood with flaky remnants of yesteryear's paint. Empty windows like blackened eyes. A moldy Christmas wreath hangs on a rusty nail on the front door. We're a month beyond the holidays and the wreath hasn't been changed in years.

"I'm not interested," a woman's voice calls as I rap my knuckles against the wood. "Whatever it is you're selling, I got plenty already."

"It's Jake Olson," I call back. "Open up."

"Who?"

"Jake Olson. I used to date Jenna when we were in high school. Jenna Luckman."

I hear footfalls approach. A lock turns and the door swings open. Immediately, I am hit by a blast of cooking smells mixed with tobacco and questionable cleanliness.

The woman standing in the doorway is as rundown as her home. Wintry skin-and-bones in a summer dress short enough to give chills. Years of erosion have worn her away. Instead of softening her features, time has sharpened them into crags and ravines. She has a bleached blonde thatch with black roots, pressing down on a face that has seen too much of hardship and decided to simply give up. There are food stains on her neckline and a map of bruises on her bare arms. I can see from the dullness in her eyes and her slight sway that narcotics play a leading role in her life.

The penitentiary introduced me to every drug imaginable. Sometimes we have no choice. I try not to sit in judgment anymore.

"Hello, Ruby. How've you been? It's Jake Olson. Do you remember me?"

Shadows lengthen in the gullies of her face. It takes a moment for her to make the connection. She probably hasn't heard my name mentioned in almost two decades, and thought about me even less. One thing I've learned is that we all share different memories of the same events, including people. Just because I remember her doesn't necessarily mean she remembers me.

"Jake Olson?" She sucks hard on a hand-rolled cigarette before blowing the sweet smoke to the side. "You're shitting me, right? The same Jake Olson who killed Jenna?" Her eyes bulge as they look me over. "No fucking way. It is you, isn't it? Well, go ahead and hit me with shit on a stick. I thought they gave you the needle?"

Unexpectedly, she throws her arms around my neck before I can answer, squeezes me tight. Even more unexpectedly, she plants a wet kiss against my cheek. I get a mouthful of stale body odor and marijuana smoke.

"Fuck me," she breathes in my ear. "I thought you were dead." She hugs some more. Then she pulls her face away just enough to meet my gaze. "This is for real, isn't it? I'm not hallucinating you, am I? Wouldn't be the first time."

"No, Ruby. It's really me. I qualified for an early release, six months ago. And here I am."

"No fucking way." She isn't letting go, still has me locked in her embrace, still staring at me through dilated pupils.

"It's nice to see you, too, Ruby."

"Yeah. I bet. Like contracting hepatitis."

Ruby Dickinson.

Back in the day, Ruby was Jenna's best friend. She wasn't mine. In fact, I couldn't stand Ruby. In my eyes she was a leech and a bad influence on Jenna. What made matters worse was the fact the pair of them were as inseparable as best friends seem to be at that age. Pajama parties and beauty nights galore. Gossip and giggles. Girlie girls in every sense of the words. I didn't buy it. They might have been Siamese twins had they not looked so radically different. As far as anyone could tell, Ruby and Jenna shared the same interests and attended the same extracurricular activities. I always had the impression Ruby wanted to be Jenna. She would buy the same clothes, voice the same likes, and hold the same opinions. In every sense, she was Jenna's wannabe. But where Jenna was princess-cut, Ruby was unpolished. In the right light she was unarguably attractive, but she was rough around the edges—the kind of roughness that runs to the core. And no amount of polishing can hide those flaws.

"I can't believe they didn't give you the needle," she murmurs again as she finally disengages. "Now that would've been a real travesty, for sure. Waste of chemicals, right? Listen, I was just thinking of getting a drink. You coming with? You'll have to excuse the untidiness; my housemaid hasn't called this century."

I follow Ruby down a short hallway and into a living room.

Her forewarning holds true: the place is a mess. Clothes and bric-a-brac scattered everywhere. Towers of old newspapers form an uneven skyline across the front window. A halogen heater is working overtime, blazing like the sun, trying to keep the room just above freezing. The rest of the house is probably abandoned and cold. A pile of blankets and a pillow are on the back of one couch, attesting to the fact that Ruby never ventures very far from this room. There's a sense of despair in here, emphasized by a print of Tretchikoff's famous blue-faced *Chinese Girl* hanging over a mantel-piece, projecting eternal sadness.

"So what happened with the needle?" she asks conversationally as I make myself a space on a cluttered chair. The fabric is worn, threadbare, like its owner.

"Minnesota hasn't had the death penalty for over a century."

"You're shitting me, right? I had no idea they abolished it."

"Well, even if it wasn't, I'm not sure third-degree murder quali-fies anyway."

She settles onto the couch, facing me. "That's criminal. Lucky for you, though, right? I can name several people on one finger who should get it. Starting with the people running Harper for instance, and working backward from there."

Despite her words, there's no malice in her tone. If anything, she sounds blasé. She could be commenting on foreign affairs or something equally insignificant to her. It's the weed, I know. It relaxes reality. Ruby is a hard candy with a soft center. Deliberately, I don't get into the whole capital punishment debate or how the rest of my sentence was commuted on the grounds of good behavior. My case was exceptional. I was arrested as a juvenile and sentenced to twenty-five years for murder without proof of a dead body. It doesn't happen very often. But it does happen. But by no means am I another Donald Blom.

"All the same," she continues, puffing out smoke, "and I don't mean this personally, Jake Olson, so please don't take it that way, but I can't believe they didn't ice you. I mean, come on. You were the number one suspect. They had you dead to rights."

"Except I didn't kill her."

"Sure. Never stopped them killing an innocent guy, though, right? You know, I never believed all that hype about you killing Jenna. Wasn't for me. But they believed it—all those God-fearing townsfolk." Her eyes examine me, like she's able to see through my own hard outer shell. "Jesus, you were one weedy kid back then. No kidding. And no insult intended. For the life of me I never knew what Jenna saw in you. I bet you broke a sweat pulling up your own socks."

I keep my smile polite. "Thanks for the vote of confidence, Ruby. It's good to know you're in my corner." She means no harm and I've been hit with harder sticks and stones. "So that's my life story, in a nutshell. What about you? How've you been?"

A flicker of unease passes over her face. She sucks on the cigarette and blows out smoke. "Okay, you know? I stay afloat, tread water. It's not exactly the high life, but we're not all meant for champagne and caviar."

Life has been hard on Ruby Dickinson. It's visible. And all by her own poor choices. Back in St. Paul, my research revealed Ruby had never married, nor had she birthed any children. Since her late teens, she'd seen more than her fair share of the judicial system, specifically for public disorder offenses, drug-related charges, and arrests for lewd behavior. She'd defaulted on fines and avoided community service work orders, which all contradicted the Ruby of my youth. In school, Ruby was one of the brightest sparks, top of her class. A promising future and the potential to go all the way. But then something had gotten hold of her and hadn't let go, something that had dulled her luminescence and enslaved her.

Intelligence isn't a barometer for addiction.

She pulls a long breath through her cigarette, eyes narrowing, holding in the sweet-smelling smoke and going for the oxygen rush.

Everything on paper says Ruby Dickinson is a bad egg, that her wires are fried and her mind is cracked. But I know firsthand that the truth can sometimes get scrambled.

"The truth is," she says tightly, still holding it in, "I've never been better. No complaints here. There's a roof over my head and food in the fridge. Life's good, you know?" She exhales and seems to sink into the couch as a result.

Strangely enough, I believe her. To everyone on the outside, Ruby's life must appear in a state of utter shambles. She is up to her eyeballs in trash and probably debt, maybe surviving on handouts, and hasn't worked an honest day in her whole life. She's a junkie through and through, one of society's forgotten, but she seems genuinely content with her place. She really does—as though her aims were never higher than a step up from the gutter.

She holds out the reefer. "Want a drag?"

"No, thank you. I quit six months back."

"Shame. It's our vices that make getting out of bed worth it." She stares at me with big pupils. "So, Jake Olson, freeman of Harper, how long you planning on sticking around this time?"

"I'm not sure. I haven't thought that far ahead."

"Be cool to get to know one another. I don't see anyone from the old days, you know? It would be nice to have a friend from the past come visit. Everybody's either moved out or moved on. This was my parents' place until they passed. Now it's just me and my monkeys. You have someplace to bed down, Jake Olson?"

"My father's house."

She nods, then smiles, flashing uneven yellow teeth. There's a gap in the crooked bottom row, food wedged in it. "Well, I was about to say you're welcome to crash here, if you need the company, that is. I'm guessing there are people in town—probably *those* people, those finger-pointing people—who wish you harm. No one will think of looking for you here. This is the leper's house and everyone keeps their distance. Good riddance, I say. I can't promise much in the way of food, just vodka and nibbles. But the pot is first rate and hardly anybody comes calling."

"Thanks, Ruby, but I'll pass this time."

"Suit yourself. The offer's there, whenever you need it." She puts her elbows on her bare knees and leans forward a little, gazes at me through swirling smoke. The top three buttons of her summer dress are undone, and she knows it. "Say, would you like a drink with me, Jake Olson? We can celebrate the old times, see where it gets us. It can't have been easy on you being locked up all these years without female company." She reaches out and touches bitten fingertips against my knee. "Maybe I can help with that."

"Ruby . . ."

The hand withdraws with a snap. "I'm just saying, is all. Don't crucify me. Everybody needs a friend sometimes."

"And I appreciate the offer. Honestly."

"But you're otherwise engaged."

"Something like that."

She takes another drag on the smoke. Her eyes work me over, as though she's noticed my outline is blurred. "You after blood, Jake Olson?"

Her question catches me unprepared.

What am I after? I have spent a lifetime thinking about being back here in Harper, free to clear my name to the ninety-nine percent of the population who believe I am guilty. But what does that mean, exactly, for me or Jenna's real killer?

All my mental energies are focused on unearthing the truth, with none of it reserved to serve up any kind of vigilante justice. I am not the angry, mixed-up kid I was when Jenna went missing. Sure, I tried holding on to my fiery pain as long as I could without getting burned. That's what we do. We cling onto the hurt because it keeps it real and alive. I kept Jenna in my heart for months, maybe years, doing exactly that, with her cherished memory smoldering away, warming me at night. It kept me going, adjusting. It made my hell bearable, or almost. But time gobbled up all its fuel, slowly lessening the flame until the heat went out of my urgency for revenge.

"I know finding Jenna's killer won't bring her back," I say slowly. "But if I can at least expose him, make him confess, then my name will be cleared and I can move on."

"And then what?"

Good question. Everything beyond finding Jenna's real killer is nonexistent, suspended in limbo, with nothing planned.

"A clean slate, I guess—in whatever shape that takes."

"You'll settle in Harper?"

"It's my home."

"So what makes you think you'll even find him after all these years? I mean, let's be brutally realistic here. He could be six feet under or living on the other side of the planet."

"I have to start somewhere."

She thinks about it, then nods. "Good for you, Jake Olson. You do know you'll get no help from the dumbass authorities, or the good people of Harper?"

"I do. That's why I've taken a job at the paper."

She pulls back a little more. It's a natural reaction when some-body thinks about Lars Grossinger. "You're working for him? Shit, is that wise under the circumstances?"

"He's in his eighties. Harmless."

"Yeah, for sure. And an old snake still has venom. Take my advice and quit while you're ahead. That shit will end up giving you a nasty bite."

Ruby goes straight for the kill. Her words may be blunt, but her mind is still as sharp as a surgeon's scalpel.

I take out my phone and bring up the picture of the human bones lodged in the tree roots. "Ruby, there's something you should know. They found her. Jenna. This morning. Or what was left of her. Up at Hangman Falls."

Ruby's eyes widen fully for the first time, enough to show the whites and all the veins. "Now you really are fucking with me, Jake Olson!"

"I was up there myself, with the police. All the heavy snowfall we've been having, it pulled down Hangman's Tree, upturned it. She was underneath. Some hunters stumbled across her on their way down from the lake."

She exhales blue smoke. "No fucking way! They actually found her after all this time? This definitely calls for a drink!"

Before I can object or show her the picture, she skips to her feet and scuttles over to a table in a corner, comes back armed with a bottle of vodka, two-thirds gone.

"This is turning out to be one heck of a weird day of surprises, Jake Olson. First you show up, then Jenna. I mean—Jesus!" She unscrews the cap and takes a hearty glug. Her eyes roll back and she's caught for a moment between heaven and hell. Then she comes back to earth with a bang, licks at a sore in the crack of her lips, and tilts the bottle my way. "Sure you won't join me? It's good stuff."

I shake my head. "I'd like to ask you a few questions and record your responses, if you don't mind."

"For the paper? Sure, okay. Shoot." She takes another swig.

I put the phone on audio-record. "Interview with Ruby Dickinson, Saturday, January twenty-four. Ruby, can you tell me what you remember about the time Jenna disappeared?"

"Before or after?"

"Both, but preferably before, on the run-up, if you can recall it."

"You're asking a lot, you know?"

I smile. "I know. Just take your time."

"My brain is still muddled from the news they found her." She tips more vodka into her mouth. "Fuck me. Okay. Do you want me to close my eyes, like I'm in therapy?"

"If it helps."

91

"Okay." She rests her head against the back of the couch and her eyelids drop. Ruby has eighteen years of misty memories to trawl back through. Most of them will be blurry, incomplete, misplaced. Drugs do that. Long-term misuse affects everything. I'm not expecting any revelations here.

"You know, Jake Olson, when I look back, we were young and naïve. If only we knew back then what we know now."

"Every generation shares the same complaint."

Her eyes move under her eyelids, as though she is in REM sleep. A few seconds later she says: "I remember, in those last few weeks, Jenna was a royal pain in the ass."

"How so?"

"Well, for starters, she kept canceling plans at the last minute. Thinking about it, she was rude and inconsiderate. I loved her like a sister, you know? But I hated her like one, too."

"And that wasn't like her, canceling plans?"

Ruby opens one eye. "Did she cancel any on you?"

Now it's my turn to think about it. Jenna and I were seeing each other for just a few months before her disappearance. Maybe one or two evenings through the week, but mainly at the weekends. Either way, plenty of free time for both of us to do our own things.

A quiet grunt sneaks through my lips. "Not that I remember."

"True love," Ruby snickers.

"Did she say why she kept canceling?"

Ruby sits up. Her smoke's gone out. She puts down the vodka and relights the reefer, sucks on it, checks the end is lit, sucks some more. "Truth is, she never said anything at first. In fact, she avoided even talking about it. I had to keep pushing for answers. She didn't even give me an excuse, just a '*Sorry, hon, I can't make it.*' When I pushed a little too hard she told me to butt out."

"That's not like her."

"Yeah, you figure? Anyway, she said she was seeing you and I was to leave her alone. But she wasn't seeing you. Not those times she canceled."

I sit up a little straighter. "How do you know?"

Smoke trickles from her nostrils. "Because I followed her."

"You followed her?"

"Jesus, it made a change from her following me!" She cocks a crooked eyebrow at my sudden frown. "Do you need me to explain?"

"Please."

"I'm thinking you didn't know the real Jenna. Not the Jenna I knew. You only knew the nice Jenna. The false smiles and sweet-lipped Jenna. You know, the Jenna she wanted you and everybody else to see?"

My frown stays put. "What are you saying?"

"That you were love-blind back then. You had those big puppy dog eyes going on, the kind that can't see the wood for the trees. Jenna was an angel, wasn't she?"

"Sure."

"Wrong! She was anything but angelic! The Jenna I knew could raise hell. Don't you get it, Jake Olson? She only let you see the side of her she wanted you to see. It was all a game with her. She played you, the same way she played everybody else in her life. Jenna was a social chameleon. I heard that term on Lifetime, so I know it's true. She did whatever it took to get what she wanted. And I mean whatever."

My pulse is elevated. "I don't understand."

"That's because she fooled you. I mean, I should know; no one was closer to Jenna than I was, right? Believe me when I say that girl had manipulation and convincing down to a fine art. Don't feel bad. She didn't just fool you. She fooled everybody. I spent most of my life with her tagging along."

"That's not the way I remember it."

93

"That's because you bought into the façade. Trust me, Jenna was exhausting. Everything I got, she had to have. She copied my styles, my tastes in music, even every boy I was interested in, she had to swear her undying love to."

"Including me?" It comes out automatically.

Ruby's lips form an amused slant. "No, Jake Olson, not including you. Jenna chose you for some other reason. Maybe if you looked the way you do now, back then, who knows?" She makes a suggestive face.

My heart is racing. These aren't my memories, my impressions. "How do I know you're not lying?"

"You don't. But I've nothing to gain from not being totally on the level with you. I'm not trying to score points or even my next fix here. I'm just saying it like it is."

"But you were the best of friends."

"True enough." She sucks the cigarette, then blows out smoke. "Don't get me wrong, I liked Jenna. She was fun when she wasn't being clingy. She had this crazy sense of humor. She was wicked. But she was a leech, and sometimes I couldn't get rid of her."

I am stunned and made slightly uncomfortable by Ruby's announcement. It's like I've lived my whole life in a bubble and Ruby has just popped it. "So, you followed her?"

"I did. I tailed the bitch. One night, after she canceled for maybe the third time. The thing is, I hated being jerked around back then, and Jenna was beginning to piss me off by that point. Normally, we didn't keep secrets. We shared just about everything. Then she started giving me the brush off and lying about her reasons. So I followed her. And that's when I learned her dark secret." She sucks on the hand-rolled and holds the smoke in again. "The fucking bitch."

I sit forward, heart thudding. "What secret?"

"You won't believe it. I couldn't believe she'd hidden it from me, for months, and we went everywhere together." She lets out the smoke. "I challenged her about it and we had this huge fight, ironically the day before she went missing. My last words to her were '*go rot in hell, bitch*' and I guess she did."

I am hooked by Ruby's bait, hypnotized. "What was she doing, Ruby? Where did she go?"

Suddenly, Ruby's expression flat-lines and a somberness settles, offsetting the effects of the marijuana. She nods at the phone in my hand. "Stop the recording, Jake Olson, or this conversation ends here and now."

I think about it, think better of it, then slip the phone back in my coat pocket. I don't hit the *Stop* icon on the way in.

Ruby draws a deep breath, leans forward and places her fingertips back on my knee. "Can I trust you, Jake Olson?"

"Implicitly."

"But I don't even know you."

I put a hand on hers. "Ruby, you can trust me."

She stares at me, unmoving, for long seconds, as though she has x-ray vision and is able to see my thorny sparks. "Okay. But whichever way this pans out, it doesn't come from me, right? I'm serious. I want no record of this. No one knows I said anything. What I'm about to tell you can get me killed. Do you understand? Don't tell anyone I told you. I mean it. Not a soul."

I squeeze her hand, say nothing. My heart is in my mouth.

Ruby pulls her hand out from under mine. She glances around us, as though we're being observed. "Do you remember Six Pack?" Her voice is barely above a paranoid whisper.

I frown again. It's the last thing I'm expecting her to say. "Sure, although I haven't heard that name in a very long time."

"What do you remember about it?"

"Not much. Just the usual. I know Chief Krauss was a member."

Six Pack was a members-only group of a half dozen handpicked Harper men who met regularly for hunting weekends out in the

Superior National Forest. All testosterone and egos. Lyle Cody, the founder, owned a hunting lodge squirreled away deep in the wooded hills somewhere north of the lake. The talk in the playground was that its masked members practiced devil worship up there in those hills, that they even made blood sacrifices to the gods. But no one had any hard evidence to corroborate the claim, and no one was completely sure of the truth, but the rumors abounded nevertheless. Kids scaring the bejesus out of each other, no doubt. The stuff of local legend. Ghost stories whispered around campfires. One or two braver souls had tried proving the theory—essentially by sneaking up on the property—only to be caught nosing around and promptly sent back to town with their tails between their legs. As far as everybody at school was concerned, Six Pack was a secret society. Only its members knew exactly what, if any, controversial practices were conducted in the privacy of the hunting lodge. Probably none. Probably just an innocent hunting club whose members had instigated the scare stories in the first place, to stop kids like us from intruding on their fun.

"It was a couple of days before Jenna disappeared," Ruby continues, refocusing my attention. "Abigail Tilley—you won't remember her, the redhead with the ears?—she was throwing a birthday party. Girls only, you know? And Jenna sure liked to party. The deal was we'd go together."

"But she pulled out?"

"She did, and it was the final straw. Like I say, she was pissing me off. I was determined to find out what she was up to. So I tailed her. It was dark. She didn't see me. We were on foot. I followed her to the big house at the end of Morgan. You know the one I mean?"

"Lyle Cody's place." My neck muscles are stiff and my pulse is tapping in my throat. When we were kids, Lyle Cody had a reputation for being a player, and I don't like where this is headed.

"Like I say, it was nighttime. The house lights were on. Jenna went inside. I hung back, mainly because I didn't want to get caught snooping around, not there. I nearly lost my nerve, even started walking away. But eventually I mustered up the courage to sneak up to a window." Ruby gulps down a mouthful vodka, then scans the room for invisible onlookers.

Anticipation pulls me even closer. "Ruby. What did you see at Cody's place?"

Her gaze finds mine and freezes. "I saw four men in a room with Jenna and another girl. They were all buck naked and doing, you know, stuff."

The tapping in my throat turns to thuds. I ask the single most stupid question: "What were they doing?"

Ruby gapes at me like I'm from Mars. "Fuck me, Jake Olson, do you need me to draw you a diagram? They were taking it in turns, that's what they were doing! One after the other. Sometimes two or three at the same time!"

My throat is tight, constricted. Steam is rising in my head. "They were *raping* her?" The words come out like a rasp. For the first time in a long time rage boils in my belly, and something else, too. Something like fear.

"No," Ruby answers with a shake of her head. "You got it all wrong. It wasn't like that. I wish it was; it would be easier to understand maybe, to accept, you know? No, they weren't raping her. Jenna was a willing participant. And she was enjoying it. I mean, she was begging for it. The other girl, too. That's why she was there. That's what she was doing all those times she canceled on me. She was screwing around behind your back and mine."

"She was having orgies with older men?"

Ruby picks at the food lodged in her teeth, then spits it out. "Get with the program, Jake Olson. Jenna Luckman was a harlot. A whore. And I'm willing to bet your life on it that's what got her killed."

Chapter Twelve

Seventeen years ago, when trying to explain my obsession with Jenna, a psychiatrist told me that I block out all the bad and only see the good. She even got me to perform a picture-association test to prove it. The end result was that I idealize those people who are nice to me and never think twice about those who aren't. I always thought it made me sound pathological.

In the blink of an eye, Ruby's revelation makes me question everything I know about Jenna. Just like that.

For almost two decades her golden memory has remained untarnished, radiant. A pristine picture of first love. I never planned it that way. In lockup, inmates do whatever it takes to survive. Visualizing her angelic image kept me alive. I believed in Jenna. I believed in what we had together, that it was real and founded in trust. It was all I had. Now Ruby has turned my world on its head, like that damned tree up at The Falls. Flipped my heart inside-out and got me in a spin. It's nauseating, confusing. A bombshell. Memories turned to rust. If she is right, what else did Jenna keep from me and why didn't I see it?

The answer: puppy love eyes.

But I need to keep some kind of perspective here. Although Ruby has no outward reason to spin a lie about Jenna, I must remember she is a drug addict whose perceptions of reality can be warped. For all I know, every word spouted from her lips could be untrue. Projecting her own failings on another, as my psychologist would say. And yet it doesn't feel like a tall tale. It seems too believable to have been conjured up on the spur of the moment. I have spent eighteen years in the company of liars, cheats, addicts. I recognize the signs, the traits, the plays. Ruby displays none of them. She is a tattered book, but she's an open one.

"Did you tell the police this story, after she disappeared?" I ask her before leaving, while the tape still rolls in my pocket and the panic is yet to flood my veins.

Ruby nods. "You bet. I told the chief everything. Just like I told you."

"So Chief Krauss knew?"

"No, not the chief back then. The new chief, now."

"Meeks? You told Meeks? Why him?"

"Because he was the one who came asking the questions."

She doesn't add the word *Duh* but I hear it nonetheless.

"What did Meeks do about it?"

Ruby snickers at the memory. "He said I should shut my dirty mouth and stop trying to throw slurs on good reputations. He went on to tell me I had a sick imagination and if I told anyone else what I'd told him, he'd charge me with slander, or worse."

It sounds like Meeks.

"So what happened next?"

"What do you think? I thought *fuck this* and did as I was told. You have to remember how things were back then. I didn't want no trouble. I'd seen stuff I shouldn't have seen. These were powerful men. For all I knew, Shane Meeks was one of those guys having sex with Jenna. I didn't want no comeback. Meeks is a bully, but Gavin's a psycho."

"Jenna's brother?"

She nods. "He was with Meeks when he questioned me. He said if I told anyone about his sister he'd do very bad things to me."

I haven't thought much at all about Gavin Luckman in a long time. I knew he and Meeks were in cahoots from an early age and that the deadly duo were notorious troublemakers in town. But the age difference between them and me meant we moved in different circles. Aside from general memories of their bullying, I remember stumbling across them in the woods, one springtime. They were at a creek, playing baseball with frogs. The cracks of bone and the sickening squelch of ruptured flesh echoing across the calm water.

"So I didn't tell a soul," Ruby continues, refocusing me. "Pretty soon it was moot anyway. You were accused of her murder, Jake Olson, and I didn't mention it to anyone else after that. In fact, aside from those two freaks, you're the only person I've ever told. How fucked-up is that?"

I replay Ruby's shocking statement as I leave her home and pick up the main route back into town. The arthritic Bronco is warming to the frozen roads, and the stench of Marlboro Reds isn't as suffocating. I listen to her words on the recording on my phone, my thoughts all shuffled up and scattered, like a deck of cards thrown in the air.

I can't quite process the information. As far as it's gotten me, I have always tried to be open-minded and nonjudgmental. My counselors taught me to always try to wear another's shoes, but only figuratively. If the argument has merit, I can be persuaded to believe it. Right up until ten minutes ago, I believed I knew Jenna as well as anyone knew Jenna. I knew her intimately, in ways others didn't. We were as close as two halves of a clamshell, with something delicious between us. I know I romanticize, but I am not stupid;

I know time can warp memories, make them fonder, warmer than they actually were. But mine were kept in focus by reliving them every moment of my imprisonment. Ruby's damning accusation flies in the face of everything I know. I have spent the greater part of my life savoring Jenna's sweetness. Now there is a bitter taste in my mouth. Instinctively, I want to protect Jenna, even after all this time, but the thought of her screwing around with men old enough to be her dad isn't just uncomfortable, it's horrible.

Puppy love eyes.

Rightly or wrongly, I'd put Jenna on a pedestal all these years. The girl I knew wasn't promiscuous. The girl I knew liked fluffy slippers and nights in front of the TV, watching Comedy Central and finding funny in the absurd. The Jenna I knew didn't keep secrets, especially from me.

And yet, according to Ruby, she had.

Who else has been keeping things from me?

Prison has made me paranoid, and survival has sharpened my senses. Nowadays, I notice things ordinary people overlook.

A glance in the rearview mirror confirms I'm being followed.

During my first week inside, one of my fellow inmates had warned me: "You want to survive this place? You need to grow eyes in the back of your head and keep one of them open when you sleep. Trust me, bro, your enemies will always come at you from behind."

The advice saved my life more than once.

The vehicle in pursuit is a black pickup, with tinted windows—even the windshield, which I know is prohibited. The owner has mounted a pair of bull horns on the radiator grille, right above a nasty-looking bull bar. I first noticed the truck as I left Ruby's street, keeping the same distance behind. To test my theory, I took a circuitous route into town. The pickup followed. Now I'm holding on a red, waiting to take the left, and the pickup is creeping up from behind, about twenty yards back, engine thrumming. It's the kind of strange behavior that doesn't go unnoticed. The driver is hidden behind the tinted windshield. I can hear the dull stampede of percussion instruments trampling brain cells. It sounds like rock music, maybe something by Guns 'n' Roses.

Without warning, I throw the Bronco in reverse and back up at speed. It takes a few seconds for the pickup to perform the same swift maneuver. Then we're both reversing at a pace. Luckily, there's no other traffic in our lane, or even on the road as a whole. I keep the Bronco in reverse until I'm alongside the opening to an alley, then hit the brakes and swing hard left, throw it in drive and floor it through icy puddles.

A glance in the rearview mirror shows my tail is no longer following.

I continue onto Main Street, looking for signs of the black pickup, but it seems to have given up the chase. For now.

The town is busier than it was first thing this morning; more people wrapped up against the chill and watching their step on the slippery sidewalks. More traffic taking it easy. Gray snow clinging to the curbsides.

I park the Bronco at an angle outside Occam's Razor—a barbershop directly across the street from Merrill's—and climb out.

Varney's Bait & Tackle is Harper's prestige hunting store. It's every visitor's starting point before venturing into the wild unknown. Mine, too, it seems.

As I make my way inside, I start the audio-recorder on my phone.

The air is thick with competing smells, but it's predominantly oil and fish that assault the senses. Greased guns and bait worms. The lighting is deliberately dim, to make it feel like a shadowy grotto. I haven't stepped foot in here in twenty years. Unbelievably, the place is unchanged: bait tubs breaking up the floor space; racks of hunting paraphernalia; fishing poles crisscrossing the ceiling.

Everything a hunter needs to bait a trap or kill a prey. Soft country music undulates from a darkened corner. It sounds like Johnny Cash is walking the line again.

An internally lit glass counter-cabinet stretches across the back of the store. Inside is an assortment of handguns, blades, binoculars, and scopes. A treasure trove of killing devices. The whole of the wall behind the counter is lined with rifles, shotguns, and boxed cartridges. Enough ammunition to wage a small war.

The proprietor hears the bell jangle against the glass as I enter and comes out of the back office to investigate.

"You kill me," he laughs to somebody out of sight. "Hold that thought; I'll be right back." He closes the internal door and turns my way.

He's a short guy with a big gut and a handlebar moustache. The last time I saw Ben Varney he sported a thick mop of curly black hair and the kind of beach-boy physique sculpted from obsessive gym work. He was the only guy in town to have a suntan all year round, and that's saying something in these parts. This older version has drifted out to sea. Muscles replaced by fat, with most of it gathered in a limp belly overhanging his waistband. He still sports a mop of black hair, but it's clearly a wig and a bad one at that.

He takes one look at me and reaches behind the counter. A second later his hands reappear holding a double-barreled shotgun, which he promptly points at me.

"Hold it right there, Olson," he says in a no-nonsense tone. "That's far enough. Any closer and you're ground meat."

It sounds like he's watched one too many gangster movies. I'm not deterred by his fake bravado. There's a security camera behind the counter, watching us, and I'm unarmed. He can't use the excuse I was robbing his store to fill me with buckshot. I take a cautious step forward, arms spread, shoulders relaxed, and all of it non-confrontational.

All the same, he raises the gun. "Don't force my hand, Olson. I was warned you were back in town. You've got some sick balls coming back to Harper after what you did. You should have stayed in the Cities. Kept the hell away. No one wants you here. People haven't forgotten what you did, or forgiven."

My hands are still hoisted. "Ben, I'm not looking for any trouble. I just want to talk, that's all. You know me. I used to be in here all the time, messing up the merchandise. You even let me shoot empty cans out back the summer I turned fifteen."

His eyes are mere slits. He's trying to look mean, dangerous, but I can tell by his hunched posture and by the sweat running from under his hairpiece that he's unsettled by my appearance. The gun looks too heavy for him, bigger than he is. I doubt he keeps it prepped for shooting when it's under the counter. Harper may be a frontier town but it isn't a city ghetto.

He waves the weapon dismissively. "So do yourself a favor and turn the hell around, get out of my store. I've been warned not to engage in any dialogue with you. We have nothing to talk about."

I stand my ground. I don't believe for one second Ben will purposely shoot me. He's too proud of his store and too precious about the stock to risk getting blood everywhere. Although the fish might like it, brains in the bait isn't good for business. "Ben, hear me out. I promise, this won't take a minute. I have just one question I need you to answer."

He nods over the barrel of the gun. "Make it a quick."

"You were in Six Pack, back in the day."

Dread rises his face. "So what if I was? That was a long time ago. Nobody speaks about it anymore. What's your question?"

"I'm doing a story for the paper."

"About the club?"

"Not exactly. There's a crossover. I take it you heard the news this morning? They found Jenna's remains, up at Hangman Falls."

His gaze is locked along the length of the barrel. "You sick son of a bitch. What's this—your way of gloating? I ought to do the world a favor and put you down right here."

It's an empty threat and I don't make a bolt for the door. "Ben, listen to me. I'm not here to start a fight. I'm here because I need your help. New information has come to light and I've uncovered a link between Six Pack and Jenna. I think it might have something to do with her disappearance. I only know the names of half its members: Chief Krauss, Lyle Cody, and you. I need you to tell me who the other three are."

Suddenly, the shotgun comes level with my face. "Go to hell, Olson. I'm not saying anything. You're way out of line coming in here like this and throwing around wild accusations after what you did. Everyone in town knows you're a murderer."

"All I need are the names, Ben, for the story. I'm working for Grossinger now."

"Yeah? And I don't give a shiny shit if you're working for the president of the United States. You're not welcome here. Now get out of my store."

Chapter Thirteen

In a nation built on godly virtues, people find it hard to forgive. I backpedal out of Varney's Bait & Tackle and shake myself down before crossing the street. I need to follow Ruby's story to its conclusion if I want to get to the bottom of what really happened with Jenna the evening she disappeared. Six Pack could hold the answers. But when it comes to interrogating the three remaining members, I don't have great expectations, not after my encounter with Ben. Mistakenly, I was hopeful that Ben might have softened with age, like his belly, and that he might have been prepared to let bygones be bygones. After all, he is one of my uncle's closest pals. I would have expected Owen to talk him around to the idea of my innocence after all these years. But now I see that Ben's sealed-lips response is likely to be repeated throughout town, and I have to remember that most of Harper think I killed one of their own. It's going to involve a continent-sized shift in perspective to alter that world view.

I push open the glass door of the diner and wince under a blast of hot air coming from an overhead heater.

With happy hour swiftly approaching, Merrill's is busier than it was at seven this morning: a scattering of regulars imbibing the freshly ground coffee and salivating over Merrill's special pastries;

a few tourists in the corner, here for the snowmobiling, laughing about their James Bond antics; a cook whistling tunelessly in back.

No sign of Krauss.

I strip off my coat and hat, then slide into a booth by the window. It's the same booth I sat in earlier, with Lars. The same booth Jenna and I claimed every Saturday morning as ours.

The TV on the wall is still broadcasting its worldly woes. I keep my gaze diverted.

The young girl from the breakfast shift has been replaced by an older veteran of the hospitality service. I recognize her from an earlier age, but she doesn't recognize me—not because I've changed so radically, but because she doesn't once make eye contact.

She wipes a hand over the tabletop, brushing away a freckling of sugar granules left behind by a clumsy customer. "My name's Maggie," she tells me in a bored monotone, "and I'll be your server today. Can I get you started with something to drink and maybe a slice of one of our special homemade pies?"

"One root beer and one pop," I say, getting out my phone. "I'm expecting company."

"Sure thing, honey. Which pop?" She runs off a list of every kind of soda imaginable.

"Mello Yello."

"Sure thing. Mello Yello coming right up. There's a menu card by the window if you change your mind about the pies. The special today is the blueberry swirl, and it's a real knockout."

She drifts away, humming tunelessly to herself as she goes.

The time on my phone reads five minutes after four. Krauss is late. Not like her. But then what do I know about the new Krauss?

Outside, the snow has stopped falling and an early winter dusk is muddying the overcast sky. Street lights popping on again. Storefronts brightening, like illuminated billboards propped up along the sidewalk.

I avoid my ghostly reflection in the window as it takes shape, thinking instead about Ruby's revelation. Her words have left me with a sickly feeling deep down, like I've eaten something bad and it's indigestible. Not for the first time I go through all the arguments against her being right about Jenna, trying to reason it away or at the very least make it feel more palatable. In prison, my psychiatrist told me I overcompensate for Jenna's loss by only ever thinking of her in perfect terms and excluding all memories that are less than immaculate. Even so, Ruby's claim is the last thing I expected to hear. None of my research into that turbulent time has unearthed a link between Jenna and Six Pack and yet, in one cannabis-smelling breath, Ruby has blown away the silt from my eyes and shown me Jenna in a different light.

"Hello there, stranger."

I look round to see Krauss walking toward the booth. She's wearing a thick roll-neck fisherman's sweater over faded jeans and hiking boots. A big padded jacket is bundled under her arm—one of those silver bubble coats that makes the wearer look like an astronaut.

"Hi, Kim. You're late and out of uniform."

She slides into the booth. "One, it's the weekend and the other is a girl's prerogative."

"And yet you're still wearing your gun."

"Comes with me everywhere I go. We're on the threshold of the great untamed outdoors and I never leave home without it. I'm a crack shot, you know?"

"Really?"

"One of the best in town."

"I seem to remember you had an aversion to firearms."

"Well, I had to toughen up if I wanted to wear the badge. Would you like to see my permit to carry?"

"No, just the food options." I hand her a menu.

She smiles and opens it up.

The waitress returns with our drinks. Krauss's eyes light up when she spies her pop. She winks at me, then proceeds to share polite pleasantries with the waitress: how the weather's warmed up a little; how the January business is slacker than usual; how Krauss's dad must be feeling the chill up there at the lake. I tune it out, scanning the menu card instead.

Finally, Krauss orders the BLT on rye. "It's as good as it's always been," she assures me and I go along with her recommendation.

"You kids enjoy," the waitress says and leaves us to it.

Krauss bats her eyelids at me. "Jake, you remembered."

"Is Mello Yello still your favorite?"

"You bet!" She takes a hearty slurp on her drinking straw. "Hard to beat that caffeine rush. Thank you."

"My pleasure."

She leans back in the booth and gazes around us. "Well, I know this is different for me, but it must be weird for you being back here."

"A little."

"Is that why you look like you've seen a ghost?"

"I do?"

"Yes, you surely do. Or is it because Chief Meeks paid you a visit?"

"Ah. You know about that?"

"It's a small town; news travels at the speed of a sled. I thought he'd at least let you settle in before trying to turf you out."

"Meeks is just doing his job."

"And there's no harm in doing it with a tad more subtlety either."

"He's not the world's most diplomatic person."

She smiles. "You figure?" She takes another slurp at her pop. "So how'd it go, the interrogation with the big chief?"

I shrug a lip. "Not quite a train wreck. Basically, he wanted to remind me of my place in the food chain. My dos and my don'ts.

I guess if this was back during Harper's founding days he would have tanned my hide with a whip and run me out of town."

"He's such an asshole."

"Some things never change." Now it's my turn to smile. It draws one from Krauss's lips. Her whole face brightens with it. She has blossomed in womanhood, I realize. Never the proverbial ugly duckling and not quite the swan now, but she is unquestionably attractive. Surprisingly, it feels easy sitting here with her after all this time; two old friends reacquainting and reattaching, not quite sure if that includes testing the waters.

"Rest assured I'll speak with him about it," she says, twiddling her drinking straw. "Politely remind him which lines he shouldn't cross."

"Kim, there really is no need; I can handle Meeks."

"He used to bully you all the time!"

"I'm wiser now, older."

"Don't forget bigger." Her smile inflates into a grin. "In a nice way, of course. Anyway, I promise I won't make things any worse for you than they already are. I can be very persuasive, you know?"

"No doubt."

When we were in the third grade, Krauss had me believing hers was a royal bloodline stretching back to a principality in Europe. She had me treating her like a princess for a week until her mom laughed it aside and Krauss dropped the pretense.

She taps me on the back of the hand, "Hey, do you remember we used to be in here all the time? This was our booth. Saturday mornings. We'd sit right here in these very seats, drinking milkshakes and putting imaginary speech bubbles on passersby."

I dive deep for the memory, sifting through years of suspended silt, but resurface empty-handed. The only images I have of this place are with Jenna. Then again, virtually all of my more prominent Harper memories feature her and her alone.

The expression on Krauss's face tells me she's a little crestfallen with my inability to pluck out the pearl. "Oh, Jake. You don't remember, do you?"

"Vaguely." I think harder, but the memory simply doesn't exist. The truth is, prison life is acidic. It corrodes those memories least able to withstand the weathering.

"Do you at least remember it was here you first decided to be a reporter?"

I do. But again the memory is with Jenna, not Krauss.

Everything's mixed up.

This time she doesn't wait for me to catch up. "Let me jog your memory. We were fifteen. It was spring break. On a whim, you dragged me to the printing press and practically begged Lars to give you a weekend job at the paper. I remember he was furious with us for barging in like that, right in the middle of a print run. I'm sure he had steam coming out of his ears."

"Not helped by the fact I virtually chained myself to his beloved press."

"That's right!" Krauss shakes her head. "He had to drag you out by your ear and throw you on the sidewalk."

"It stung for about a week. When my father found out he locked me in the old bomb shelter in the backyard the whole of the weekend. I had to sit it out with the dank and my grandfather's rusting junk."

Krauss's nose wrinkles at the thought. "You know, I'd completely forgotten about that place in your backyard until you mentioned it this morning. Mostly, I remember it smelled like a sewer."

"That's because my grandfather built it next to the septic tank. I think his reasoning was that if the Russians dropped the bomb at least my family could still go to the toilet."

Krauss's grin grows into a giggle. "We did some crazy spur-of-the-moment stuff back then, didn't we?"

"We were kids."

"Yeah, and by all accounts, totally shameless."

For a moment we reminisce, enjoying each other's company. Retuning to our favorite frequency and feeling the rhythm.

Krauss and I have a lot to talk about. Years of our lives following different routes, exploring separate social landscapes. Before my arrest, I knew everything there was to know about the teenage Kimberly Krauss. I knew she liked horror movies and books by Stephen King. I knew she favored pasta over pizza. I knew she wanted to be a hot-shot lawyer and that all her favorite songs were sung by Meatloaf. Our divergence means I know practically nothing about this adult version. She's as good as a stranger to me, as I am to her. But I can feel there's something still here between us, connective. Something invisible, bonding us together. Something more than memories.

Krauss slurps more pop. "So how's it shaping up—the story? Knowing Lars, he'll be expecting a first draft on his desk come Monday morning, followed by an earth-shattering exposé by midweek."

I lean back in the booth and shrug. "Lars can expect all he likes. He'll get his pound of flesh when I'm ready, if at all."

All at once Krauss scrutinizes me the way somebody studies a piece of modern art they can't quite wrap their mind around. It's a look I've seen regularly since my release from prison. She's wondering how things have been for me, all these years cooped up with other men, shielded from the world, my horizons pulled in and my worldview shrunken. She's wondering what happened to me in jail, how much of it was bad or even detrimental to my psyche. She's curious to know to what extent my experiences have altered who I was and shaped me into what I am: the unknown quantity she's struggling to pigeonhole.

"You've changed," she concludes. "You've toughened up and become a bit of a bad boy. I think I like it."

But she's undecided if it's truly for the better. Ideally, she wants to believe the boy she grew up with is still in here, the drip of a boy she connected with on so many levels. He is, just like the studious teenage Krauss is deep within her, under her complex layers of experience. We have both grown thicker skins while we've been apart, become bigger than what we were.

She reaches out to touch my hand. "Seriously, though, Jake, I missed our conversations. You and I used to talk until the cows came home. There was never a dull moment. Always something juicy to get our teeth into. When they took you away, I missed our friendship, our hanging out together. Most of all I missed you." She holds my gaze, emphasizing her last three words.

In any other moment, with any other woman, this might feel awkward. It doesn't. Holding hands with Krauss is as natural as breathing, and it's nothing new.

"The thing is, Jake, I wasn't born yesterday. I've been around the block a few times. I don't expect miracles. We've been apart for so long. I don't know what you expect from me and the feeling's mutual. I know it's going to take time to get back to where we left off, to be proper friends again. That's if you want to."

"Kim, you never stopped being my friend."

"And that makes me feel incredibly guilty."

"Why, because you didn't visit me in Stillwater?" I squeeze her hand. "Kim, we were kids. You had school and then college to think about. After that, a life to make. You had plenty of distractions, and I knew that. I never once held it against you. Sure, I missed you. But the last thing I wanted was for you to keep making the long trek to the Cities instead of moving on. It wouldn't have been fair. Besides, you visited me plenty before the trial and I'm really grateful for that."

"All the same . . ."

"We're here now. And that's what's important. Isn't it?"

A rueful smile graces her lips. "Who knows what might have happened had things turned out differently for us, right?"

For a moment I wonder what our lives might have looked like had I not been convicted of Jenna's murder. Would Krauss and I have ended up together, romantically? When it comes to our feminine emotions, men are generally detached from them; the thought has never occurred to me—not because the idea of being with Krauss is repugnant, but because I just never thought of her in that way, the way I thought of Jenna, the way I *lusted* after Jenna. Krauss was more like the sister I never had. Undeniably, we were creatures hurried by hormones, but mine were racing to catch another.

I roll my thumb across the diamond ring on her finger. "Looks like you're already one leap ahead of me, Kim. You got engaged. So who's the lucky guy?"

"An asshole."

"I doubt it."

"Seriously."

"Sure. I don't believe for one second you'd make that kind of mistake. You're the definition of level-headed."

"Yeah, and human, too. And with it comes fallibility. Let's just say I've made one or two questionable choices over the years, and there won't be any wedding anytime soon. That ship has definitely sailed."

She withdraws her hand, and now it's my turn to study her enigmatic portrait.

Neither of us are the same naïve teenagers we were when we last drank at this watering hole. Our fresh springs have run into deeper waters, carrying with them the accumulation of our journeys.

"Maybe there's more than one reason you're back," she adds. "Maybe this is our time to shine."

But she's unaware of the deadly undercurrent running through me. The swirling blackness. If her intention is to cause ripples, she's out of her depth.

Before I can ask her more about her engagement, somebody bangs a fist against the window pane, breaking our eye contact. He's a wiry guy in his early forties, with a blond hairline rapidly receding from a capsized face. A snarl is rolling up his lip.

Gavin Luckman.

"You're a dead man, Olson!" he growls through the glass, loud enough for us and everybody else in the diner to hear. It's the same empty threat left on my father's answering machine, made by the same disaffected person.

Krauss shoos him away with a hand. "Move along, Luckman, or I'll arrest you for disturbing the peace."

His lip continues its upward curl. "Go screw yourself, Krauss. This is none of your business. This is man stuff. Strictly between duckweed and me."

I begin to rise in my seat, automatically, but Krauss pulls me back down. "Jake, it's okay. I'm a big girl; I can look out for myself." She gives Luckman a damning stare. "I said take a hike, Luckman. Now!"

He thinks about it, then bangs his fist against the glass one more time before backpedaling across the sidewalk, spiteful eyes fixed on me. "Catch you later, Olson," he shouts. "You got a come-uppance coming."

Krauss slaps the palm of her hand against the pane. Luckman gives us the finger and crosses the street. I watch him climb into a black pickup parked alongside my father's red Bronco. It's the same truck that followed me earlier.

"Numb nuts," Krauss breathes as we watch him drive away, tires screeching. "If he gives you an ounce of trouble, you be sure and let me know. We have a holding cell with his name on it. It'll be my pleasure to lock him up for the weekend."

Across the street, a woman is talking with a young boy. Both are wrapped up against the cold. She's in her mid-thirties, with long blonde hair flowing out from beneath a knitted hat. Her son looks to be around ten and is clutching a snowboard under one arm. He's listening intently to whatever piece of parental advice she's imparting. I can guess it has something to do with black ice and dangerous driving. He nods; he's heard it a million times. She pecks him on the nose and they move on. As they reach the corner, she glances my way and I feel a hot flush of adrenalin rush through my stomach.

Jenna?

The glance lasts for a split second, no more, but it's enough to squeeze the life out of my chest. She is Jenna's spitting image—or an aged version, a version I have imagined—and suddenly my heart is racing, trying to keep pace with my speeding thoughts. I go to sit up straighter, to get a better look, but the woman has already turned away, and the pair disappear down a side street, gone.

The waitress brings our food. Krauss pushes her pop aside and makes a start.

I glance through the window again, hoping to catch sight of Jenna's lookalike, but she is nowhere to be seen, lost in the advancing shadows. What greets my eyes instead is a police cruiser tearing down the street with its red-and-blues flashing vividly. It slams to a sliding stop outside Varney's Bait & Tackle and Meeks leaps out. His body language is stiff and adrenalized. A thickset guy in a trapper hat intercepts him on the sidewalk. Even in the twilight I can see the guy's face is blanched. He starts making dramatic arm gestures and yelling something at Meeks, pointing behind him at the store.

"Looks like Ben's shortchanged somebody again," Krauss comments through a mouthful of food.

Meeks says something to the guy in the trapper hat, points at the sidewalk, then disappears inside the bait shop. The guy starts flagging down passersby and waving at people to come join him, like he has something juicy to share. Several pause to hear his story, one or two cross the street out of mild curiosity. He gesticulates wildly toward the bait shop and some of the Saturday strollers get out their phones.

An uneasy feeling starts to spread through my stomach.

Meeks reappears a moment later, looking equally blanched. He rushes over to the curb, folds at the waist and sucks on air.

"That's different," Krauss murmurs, sitting up.

Meeks shakes himself like a wet dog, then straightens himself out. He forces his way through the gathering crowd until he engages with the trapper hat guy again. The guy is looking less scared now and more like the center of attention. I see him nod once, twice, then point directly at the diner. Meeks looks over. Even at this distance I can see he means business. More flashing lights race in from the opposite direction: a fire department EMS vehicle, followed by another police cruiser. The medics jump out and grab their kits from the back. The accompanying police officer leaves his cruiser slantwise across the roadway, lights blinking, then joins his chief on the sidewalk. Meeks deals out orders and the officer starts to corral the crowd, ushering them down the sidewalk, away from the bait shop. Meeks hitches up his pants and begins to cross the street toward us.

I hear Krauss slide out of the booth.

"Stay here," she says as grabs up her coat.

Already, onlookers are appearing in store doorways and converging from all directions, drawn like moths to the pretty lights. It's Saturday and the town is as busy as it gets this time of year. They have no idea what's happening, but it's clear this is the biggest show since New Year's Eve.

Through the window I see Krauss skipping over icy puddles. She intercepts Meeks midway across the street, speaks to him. Meeks growls something back at her, something that makes Krauss's jaw drop. Then they both look toward the diner, at the window I'm staring through, at me, and I experience that sinking feeling when you know you're in trouble. Instinctively, I slip out of the booth and get to my feet.

By now, every patron in the diner is peering through the windows. One or two are murmuring their curiosity out loud. One or two glancing at the thuggish-looking guy in their midst, wearing the guilty face.

Krauss starts to protest as Meeks gets out his firearm and marches toward the diner's entrance. She is tight on his heels, still protesting as Meeks throws open the diner's door, scattering Merrill's patrons.

"Everybody out!" he yells.

Everybody obeys, stampeding for the exit. The snowmobilers go first, followed by the locals, the waitress, and finally the chef, tut-tutting while the food spoils.

Not me. I stay put, looking relaxed despite the tension building in my belly. I know he doesn't mean me. I know when my number's called, and this isn't it.

Face thunderous, Meeks approaches, his gun taking the lead. There is something like festering rage bubbling away in his eyes. The color is coming back to his cheeks, all of it blood-red.

"Hands where I can see them," he barks.

They already are, but I raise them level with my head, palms facing out. I know the drill.

Krauss is bobbing on his shoulder. Her expression is a monochrome snapshot of concern versus consternation, whereas Meeks's face is a rough tombstone with the words *you're a dead man* chiseled into it.

He motions with the gun. "On your knees, Olson. No funny business. Just do as you're told and you won't leave here in a body bag."

"What's going on?" I ask.

"Isn't that obvious? You're under arrest for murder."

Chapter Fourteen

Those who have never experienced incarceration think that the first night in prison is probably the worst. It isn't. The first night is a blur. Your mind is too busy reeling from trying to make sense of the inconceivable to fully process the reality of your surroundings. A deadly drive-by with only one victim: you. It's the second night that's the worst, followed by every night after that.

Psychologists call it *the caged animal effect*.

It's akin to cabin fever. A stream of steadily rising panic fed by claustrophobia. Four walls pressing in, like one of those booby traps in a mummy movie. Under such duress, I have seen grown men break down into uncontrollable tears and curl up in corners. Witnessed others claw at the enclosing walls until their bloodied fingers have worn to the bone. When locked in a box with no way out, we all experience the same caged animal effect to some degree or another. For my own sanity I'd learned to phase it out a long time ago, but not before losing my dignity once or twice.

The jail cell in the Harper police station is located below ground level, down a short flight of stone steps, and is shouldered by storage closets and an odorous washroom. It's a plain gray-painted box with traditional steel bars separating it from the hallway. A long aluminum bench is bolted to the rear wall, with metal hoops for attaching handcuffs. There are no windows—just a solitary strip light set into the ceiling, out of reach.

This isn't my first visit.

Eighteen years ago, I sat on this same cool bench, with the same nervous feeling poking holes in my gut. The cell doesn't look like it's seen a lick of paint in the meantime. Unlike then, I have yet to be fingerprinted and photographed, but I have been swabbed for gunshot residue.

Beyond the bars, up the steps and down the hall a little, Krauss and Meeks are throwing fire at each other. It's impossible to pick up every word they're saying, but I get the gist of it. Krauss is defending me and Meeks is having none of it. He's beating down her flames with hot air, but she's sucking in oxygen and raging fiercely.

"Exactly who is it I'm supposed to have murdered?" I asked Meeks, back in the diner, as he tossed a pair of handcuffs onto the table and instructed Krauss to manacle my wrists.

"You know who. Ben Varney."

It was one of those *wait, what?* moments that prickled my cheeks with heat. "You're kidding me, right?"

But Krauss's complexion was snow white, her expression deadly serious. "It's true, Jake. Ben's dead. Killed with his own shotgun."

"And I'm the prime suspect, by virtue of the fact I have a record?" I was genuinely shocked. "What possible motive do I have for killing Ben?"

At that point, Krauss hadn't picked up the handcuffs, and I hadn't dropped to my knees. Meeks wasn't happy about either.

"I'm not getting into the whole debate, Olson," he said.

"Even though I didn't kill him?"

"You're going to say that. Besides, we have a reliable eyewitness saying the opposite."

"Yeah? And who might that be?"

"Someone who will testify you were the last person to see Ben alive."

I nodded toward the diner's window. "You mean the guy in the trapper hat, the one over there, selling his story to anyone who'll listen? Yeah, he looks like the reliable type. Good luck with that, Meeks."

Meeks's eyes became spiteful slits.

He was itching to put a bullet in me, for old time's sake. I wasn't sure if he'd actually ever shot and killed another human being in his life before. But there was always a first time, and I didn't put it past him. He expected me to curl into a ball and cave in. Bullies are like that. They thrive on fear and intimidation. But Meeks didn't know the grown-up me. No longer was I the spineless little kid he used as a punching bag. He held a position of power in the town but he had no authority over me.

Krauss turned to Meeks, her face even paler than normal. "Are we absolutely sure about this?"

"It's a slam-dunk," he said, without taking his eyes off me. "Olson here was seen coming out of Ben's store five minutes before Ben was found with his head blown off. And your friend here didn't raise the alarm, which means Ben wasn't dead when he went in there. According to the eyewitness, no one came in or out in the meantime. It doesn't take a rocket scientist to do the math."

Krauss faced me, blue eyes scrutinizing. "Is this true, Jake? Did you pay Ben a visit right before coming in here? Did you kill Ben?"

Krauss was never one to beat around the bush.

Before I could answer, Meeks interjected: "Kim, it doesn't matter what he says. He's a convicted murderer. His word isn't worth shit. We have a credible eyewitness. Now put the cuffs on him. That's an order."

But Krauss stayed where she was, her gaze burning into me like Superman's heat vision.

"Kim, do you really believe I'd kill Ben?" I asked. "Right now I don't know what's happened, but it looks like Meeks here is trying to frame me. Again."

Krauss turned her heat ray on Meeks and started arguing my innocence. It was a glimpse of the snappy defense attorney she'd dreamed of becoming. But her words were seeds falling on hard ground. Meeks wasn't interested in whether or not I killed Ben Varney. He was only interested in erasing me from the equation and removing me from Harper.

Fifteen minutes later, and back at the police station, she is still defending my case. Down the hall and up the steps, Meeks is telling her to back off, to get the hell out of his face. It's out of his hands now; he's notified the U.S. Marshals and they'll be here first thing in the morning to take me back to Stillwater. Krauss tells him he's overreacted, that he's an asshole and he should test the water before jumping in feet first. Meeks warns her she's walking on thin ice. Krauss tells him to go play with himself and comes clattering down the stone steps toward me.

I meet her at the bars.

Her face is flushed and she's radiating heat. "I swear that man is such an asshole."

"Kim, it's okay."

"No, Jake, it's anything but okay. He's adamant you killed Ben and there's no getting through to him."

"So, he's wrong. We'll figure this out."

"Like last time? He was wrong about you then and it didn't stop you from going to prison. It's like déjà vu." She blows out hot breath and grinds her teeth.

"Okay. So let's think about this. I'm innocent. Which means somebody else isn't. What are we going to do about it?"

Her fiery gaze meets mine. "Everything in my power to get you out of here, that's what. But first I need to know why you paid Ben a visit in the first place."

I let out my own heated breath. "I was chasing down a lead."

"For the paper or for your manhunt?"

"Both, I guess."

"What kind of a lead?"

"That's where things get difficult; I made a promise not to say anything."

Krauss snickers through her anger. "Look at you: already the intrepid reporter protecting his sources."

"Seriously, Kim, it could bring bad repercussions down on her."

Krauss makes a wounded expression. "Jake, and it's me you're talking to here. You can trust me with your life, remember? Plus, look where you are. If this information can help clear your name and get you out of jail, why hold back?"

Suddenly, I am torn between loyalties. "All right. But this is just between you and me, right?"

"My lips are sealed."

"If she finds out I've told someone . . ."

"Jake, I promise it won't go any further."

"Okay. You remember Ruby Dickinson, Jenna's best friend?"

"Sure. She's the town's most colorful drug addict, with a soft spot for hallucinogens, right between her ears."

"Very funny."

"It's true. You wouldn't believe how many times she's stood right where you are now, completely spaced out and professing her innocence."

"Ruby's a lost soul. She means no harm."

"That may be. But I wouldn't trust anything she has to say. She'd convince you black is white if it benefited her addiction. I'm assuming you called on her, too?"

"Earlier, before talking with Ben. You remember what it was like when Jenna went missing? Everything happened way too fast; I didn't get the opportunity to speak with her back then."

"So you wanted to know what she remembered."

I nod. "I needed to see if anything sparked. You know how close the two of them were. Ruby knew Jenna better than all of us, including me. If anyone knows anything, it's Ruby."

"Okay, that's logical. So how does Ben factor into all this?"

"Because of Six Pack."

Krauss frowns.

I lean a little closer to the bars, keeping my voice to a minimum. "Kim, this is awkward. Promise me you won't lose your cool or tell anybody else about this?"

She brings her face closer to mine. "Now you've really got me wondering. I guess it all depends on what *this* is. Just let me warn you in advance: if it's something illegal, I have a sworn duty to investigate."

Our lips are an inch apart, close enough to share more than words.

In hushed tones I recount Ruby's revelation: that Jenna was no angel, how Ruby became suspicious of her activities, that she followed Jenna one night, how she saw Jenna and another girl engaged in sexual relations with four older men.

By the time I finish, Krauss's frown has become a mask of disgust.

"Oh my God, Jake, that's nauseating! Surely you can't believe her?"

"Kim, trust me, I'm having a hard time reconciling the thought of Jenna having sex with a bunch of older men. It's difficult to digest, I know. Not because it's impossible, but because me and Jenna were dating for months and we never passed second base."

"You didn't?"

"Don't sound so surprised."

"I can't help it, Jake. I am. Everybody thought the two of you had it all going on. I'm so sorry. If it's any consolation, the odds are Ruby's making the whole thing up."

"Except for the fact she has nothing to gain from concocting a story."

"You mean aside from her being a drug addict? Jake, the first rule about users and abusers is they lie through their teeth, for any number of reasons—including to get attention. She'd swear she's never tried drugs if you offered her a free hit."

I can't blame Krauss for trying to derail Ruby's train. Ruby's addiction automatically puts her in the untrustworthy camp. In my experience, addicts lie without realizing they're doing it. The whole fabric of their reality is woven with untruths. But there's something else here. Something more than disgust that's causing Krauss to question Ruby's story. It isn't just the thought of Jenna sleeping around with men old enough to be her father that's repugnant, that's causing Krauss to withdraw from my words. It's the fact her dad was a member of Six Pack, and probably still is for all I know.

I reach a hand through the bars and squeeze her arm. "Kim, your dad was the chief back then. As you know, we didn't exactly hit it off. He didn't like me and I didn't like him. But I do believe he's an honorable man. And I don't believe for one second he'd condone sex orgies with young girls."

She shakes her head vehemently. "No, no he absolutely wouldn't. Not for one second. Not if he knew about it. My dad's no saint, but he'd never be party to something like that."

"But he was in Six Pack."

She stares at me like I'm digging for dirt. "Jake, I can assure you he didn't know about it." Her lips form a defensive line. "Fact."

It's the first time I've seen Krauss worked up since the week I was arrested the first time around. Krauss doesn't get agitated easily. Normally, she's the epitome of calm and collected.

"My dad was married to the job," she continues, defending him in the same way he always defended her. "Sure, he was an active member of the club, but I remember he declined a lot of their exploits. Something like that, sex parties with teenage girls, he'd have shut the whole thing down had he found out about it. I mean, it's sick, Jake. Really sick. Has Ruby told anybody else about this?"

"No. Only Meeks and Gavin Luckman."

One of her blonde eyebrows hikes up her brow.

"It was back during the investigation into Jenna's disappearance," I explain. "Meeks was collecting statements with Gavin in tow. Ruby tried telling him what she saw that night but he closed her down. Told her she had a dirty mouth and it would be in her best interest to keep it shut, or else."

"He's such an asshole. Gavin, too, for that matter. Ruby's statement in itself opens up reasonable doubt. It could have gotten you off the hook."

"Yet one more reason I don't like the guy."

She wraps her fingers around mine on the iron bars. "Jake, I'm sorry."

"Kim, it's not your fault."

"It is. I should have made them believe you had an alibi, convinced them."

"You tried your best."

"Not nearly good enough, as it turned out. I promise to make it up to you—even if takes another eighteen years." The fingers squeeze. Her touch is warm, reassuring. "All the same, Meeks probably did Ruby a favor."

"How do you figure that?"

"Because if it had come out at the time, who knows what they would have done to keep her quiet. These are influential people she's talking about. She shouldn't mention it to anyone else. And neither should you. People take those kind of allegations extremely seriously."

"And that's why I need a favor, Kim. You're a cop. You know how these things work. A premeditated murder needs a motive. Everybody loved Jenna. I've spent years trying to figure out who harbored a grudge big enough to want to do her mortal harm. Have you any idea how many names are on my list?"

"Surprise me."

"None. I came up with nobody, Kim. Not one. A few jealous types, sure, but none crazy enough to kill her over it."

"So now you're thinking one of the six club members killed her."

Krauss is a quick study, always was. While I am mashing up thumbs, she hits the nail on the head with the first blow.

"I think it's a possibility we can't ignore. I've exhausted every other avenue. If Ruby's story holds true it changes everything. Jenna was a schoolgirl. These were married men with good reputations to protect. It's like putting a spark in a powder keg."

Krauss nods. "It's motive, all right, that's for sure. Even so, they would have known the risks beforehand. They must have really trusted her, Jake. Known she wouldn't talk, no matter what. So why kill her?"

"I don't know. Maybe something happened to change her mind. Maybe she got cold feet and came to the realization she was in too deep and wanted out."

I'm taking shots in the dark, but Krauss is still nodding.

"I guess I can run with that. Jenna could be feisty at times. I can imagine her getting too hot to handle and somebody not wanting to get burned. Her speaking out would have wrecked marriages for sure, and sent people to prison. It's plenty of reason to get her killed. And now your coming back is threatening to expose that dirty little secret all over again. I know if I were the person who killed Jenna I'd make it my mission to silence anyone who could point the finger of blame at me. Wouldn't you?"

"If I'm the crazy type, yeah. It also means Ben would still be alive if I hadn't come back." It's a sobering thought.

Krauss reaches through the bars and turns my face to hers. "Jake, it's not your fault. By the sounds of things, Ben was involved in some pretty immoral stuff. Sooner or later that kind of thing is going to come back and bite you on the ass."

"He didn't deserve to die."

"And you didn't deserve to lose eighteen years of your life for a murder you didn't commit."

Krauss has always been able to pan the gold from my muddy waters.

"Kim, if we're right about this and somebody is out to keep people from talking—especially to me—then we need to warn the remaining members."

"We?"

"Okay. You."

A wry smile pinches at her lips. "Well, that could prove easier said than done. The founder, Lyle Cody, was found swinging from a tree the same year you left town. As far as I know, the club disbanded shortly after."

"Lyle hanged himself?"

"I know what you're thinking: did Lyle Cody kill Jenna and then, overwhelmed with guilt, did he take his own life? It's one theory. My guess is no one made the connection at the time because you'd already been convicted of the crime. What it doesn't account for is the fact somebody is cleaning up today."

"That's if we're right."

"What do you think?"

"I think the only other thing I can come up with to explain Ben's murder is that somebody is trying to get me sent back to Stillwater."

"You mean to frame you? So far, it's working."

I smile, shakily.

"But I think your gut feeling is right. I think the killer knows you're back in town and asking awkward questions. I think they're out to cover their tracks at any cost."

"Okay, so who else was in the club?"

"Aside from Ben and my dad, barbershop Chuck is the only other person I know who was a member from the start."

"Ryan Hendry's dad?"

"You remember Chuck Hendry?"

"I remember Ryan, the son. He was seriously screwed up in the head. Got in trouble for skinning a cat, then later confessed to cutting wings off birds while they were still alive. When he wasn't doing community service he used to hang out with Jenna's brother and Meeks. The three stooges. He was one angry kid, with the IQ of a log."

My remark brings Krauss's smile back. "Barbershop Chuck and my dad were drinking buddies. They used to see how many shots they could stomach before passing out. Liver cancer took Chuck a few years back."

"So that rules him out and leaves us with two remaining members. Any ideas who?"

Krauss shrugs. "If the theory's right, it makes one of them the last victim and one of them the suspect."

"Last man standing is the killer."

Kim winks. "We should let them duke it out. Do my job for me."

I let her see my disapproval.

She lets out a sigh. "Okay, so, those four men Ruby saw that night—did she identify anyone else other than Ben?"

"No. According to her they were all wearing weird animal masks, even the girls. Don't ask. She only knew it was Ben because she recognized the wolf tattoo on his forearm. And that's why I went to the bait shop, to speak with him."

A police officer comes down the steps and gives Krauss a nod before going into the restroom.

"I need to get to work on getting you out of here," she breathes.

She goes to pull away, but I keep my fingers on hers, preventing her from leaving. "Kim, please, be careful. If Ruby's right and Jenna was killed to stop someone's sordid little secret from getting out, and that same someone has now killed Ben, there's no way he'll take your snooping lightly."

Krauss smiles at my concern. "Jake, don't worry about me. I'm a big girl now; I can take care of myself. Plus, I'm a cop and that comes with a gun and the full arm of the law. I'll be okay. If anyone tries anything, they'll wish they hadn't."

"One last thing," I say before she leaves. "There was somebody else in the bait shop, in the back office, out of sight. I heard Ben talking to them as I entered. Ben has a security camera over the counter. It might be worth a look."

"Okay, I'll do that. I'm also going to speak with Ruby, take her a strong coffee and see if she remembers anything with a little more meat on the bones. Maybe she'll undergo an acid flashback and come up with an identity for the other girl. But first I need to clear you of Ben's murder, so hold tight; I'll be back just as soon as I can. In the meantime, for Pete's sake, don't do anything to antagonize Meeks."

I'm not sure I can hold my breath that long.

Chapter Fifteen

When Tolstoy thought of himself it never came with the label *contract killer*—even though he had killed at the behest of others, and in return for financial remuneration. He preferred to think of himself as a Good Samaritan: a trusted friend with helping hands—albeit ones able to punch through cinderblocks—whose services were enlisted when dirty work needed handling.

Over the years, he'd worked his magic for many employers, both here in Harper and in the neighboring towns. Debt collection agencies, landlords, loan sharks. Tolstoy prided himself on his discretion, his loyalty, and his commitment to the cause. His hit rate was first class. In fact, his record of achievement was flawless, perfect. In any other industry he'd have awards and promotions coming out of his ears. Not so, when you operated on the edge of the law.

For five decades now he'd been cleaning up other people's messes, in which time he had rubbed shoulders with those he did label *contract killers*. Thankfully, he'd found he was nothing like them. Most were paid mercenaries with little regard for either the craft of coercion or for human life, and certainly with no respect for the etiquette of negotiation. More often than not their idea of brokering a settlement came through brute force and lilies at a funeral. No appreciation for the art of positive persuasion.

In his opinion, incentivized people made for better payers.

Give them the right motivation and they would sell their souls.

It was all about leverage and weakness. Find a person's Achilles heel, apply pressure, and then watch them cooperate. You didn't always need to resort to chopping out a man's tongue to get him to cough up.

But sometimes killing was the only option.

Tolstoy thought about the Olson kid as he watched Sergeant Kimberly Krauss of the Harper PD leave the police station and drive away into the deepening dusk.

Chapter Sixteen

The truth is all we have. It shapes us, defines us.

Lars's words take me back to Stillwater, where uncovering the truth behind Jenna's disappearance ate away at me for years. It was a hunger that refocused, a mechanism that kept me centered, on target, distracted from an otherwise mundane existence.

Each night, as I stared at the featureless ceiling of my cell, I went over the same plan in my head, going through it step by step until I had it all worked out in meticulous detail: where I would go once I got out of prison; how I would hunt down Jenna's real killer; what I would do to put things right when I found him.

But nothing ever turns out how we think it will.

As the years passed, I lost the youthful energy that compels us to straighten the world's axis. When my release finally arrived, the passion for revenge had conceded to age and to wisdom. Retribution was no longer my driving force. Answers were.

Somebody had killed Jenna.

I had no idea if that somebody still lived in Harper, or if the person responsible for her death was even still alive.

Frustratingly, my release came with restraints. A conditional freedom that chained me to the Minneapolis-St. Paul area for the next twelve months. Parole wasn't a pardon. It was the sum of good behavior and penitence added to time served and then subtracted from the original sentencing. In other words, it was a hall pass.

"Want some advice?" a lipless clerk in the Probation Unit asked on the first day of my supervised freedom, as I sat filling out one form after another, hand aching. "You see any signs of trouble, anything at all, you turn yourself around and you run as fast as you can in the opposite direction. You got a boat load of baggage now. Dragging it behind you like a ball and a chain. People notice something like that, and they don't take kindly to it; they see you for what you are, which in their eyes is nothing short of trouble. You thought life was hard on the inside. It's ten times harder out here. In the real world you're as good as dead meat. Worthless. I'm not kidding with you. It's tough. You need to put in ten times the effort. Anything less and you won't make it. The world will eat you up and spit you out."

The cheery clerk found me employment in the form of cleaning tables at the Maplewood Mall food court. It wasn't the most glamorous job in the world, but it was a steady income and a stepping stone. I got to sweep up the mess made by impolite teenagers. I knew there should have been an element of irony in that, but it escaped me. The clerk assigned me lodgings in the shape of a bunk at a hostel in Whittier, close by the College of Art and Design in St. Paul. No privacy, but then I wasn't used to precious me-time anyway. I got to share with a guy who worried about me suffocating him with a pillow when the lights went out.

For the next year, my life would consist of reporting directly to Denis Flannigan, my parole officer, on a regular basis.

"Don't you be thinking of giving me any shit now, Olson," he warned me, the very first time we met. He drew my attention to a wall chart. It contained a graph, depicting successful reintegrated parolees versus reoffenders. The imbalance in favor of failure was staggering. "If you so much as sneeze out of place I'll ship you straight back to

Stillwater. It's there in black and white. Happens all the time. So don't get your hopes up. Way I see it you got yourself two options: First is, you get your act together, you get yourself cleaned up, you keep your nose out of any trouble, you get a chance of making it, I sign you off, and you start a new life. Easy, right? Wrong. Most likely you'll go with option two: where you play the victim, you get knocked back, your head goes down, you fall in with the wrong crowd, you go back to your old ways, and before you can say *you're shitting me* you're back in the block, serving out the rest of your sentence and then some.

"This isn't personal, Olson. I see it with my own eyes. Every damn day of the week. Doesn't make a bit of difference to me which option you choose; I get paid no matter what you decide. I will say this, though: you only get out of this what you're willing to put in. Do this the wrong way and I guarantee you'll go back to prison; do this the right way and you get a chance to live a decent life again. Who doesn't want that, right? It's more than can be said for the fucking girl you killed."

Flannigan was a bucketful of joy and hope.

At first, the thought of being pinned down to the Twin Cities, while my home and Jenna's killer were over two hundred miles away in Harper, was a setback. I'd waited eighteen years to uncover the truth, only to find myself held back and on a short leash.

But my hands weren't completely tied.

The Internet had come of age while I was hibernating. Everything I needed to know was now online: births, deaths, marriages, phone numbers, addresses, employment records, newspaper articles, police reports, court archives. I used the public computers in the St. Paul Library to navigate a sea of data. My research was done remotely, through ninety-minute time slots. I was under no illusions. Finding someone who had a motive to do Jenna harm might prove impossible.

I kept telling myself: Jenna was popular. As such, she had an abundance of friends, followers, admirers. Within that broad disk of light there existed nothing but warmth and good wishes. But on the darker periphery the jealous ones orbited. They scratched and they gnawed away at the edges, trying to take a bite and hopefully taste a little of what they desired.

That's what happened when you were popular: you attracted hate.

My goal was to find the hater. The one person who had despised Jenna so badly that they'd wanted her dead. Long ago, I had ruled out accidental death by man or by animal. Harper had its fair share of predators, both human and beast, but predators prey, habitually. No one had gone missing in Harper either before or after Jenna's disappearance, which ruled out some crazy local abducting young women and having his wicked way with them before disposing of the evidence. Of course, it had occurred to me that some anonymous visitor to the town could have killed Jenna at random, but my gut had always told me otherwise.

Jenna's murder was deliberate. I could feel it.

Somebody knew something.

Eighteen years was a generation. It might as well have been a century. People drifted, relocated, died. Memories faded, changed, vanished altogether. I knew that finding more than a handful of people who knew Jenna personally, remembered the events leading up to her disappearance, and still lived in Harper, wasn't just hopeful, it was wishful.

Once out of Stillwater and six months in, and for all my digging, I'd turned up no dirt. I needed to be home. I needed to be in the reality and not merely dreaming about it. Then the telephone call came, informing me about my father and his critical condition, and suddenly I was on my way home to Harper. Just like that.

It was like divine intervention.

"By any flaming means," Flannigan warned me in his thick Irish accent as I prepared to ship out and thumb a ride home, "don't you get to thinking this is a Get Out of Jail Free card. The conditions of your parole still apply, regardless of where you pitch your tent." He handed me a card with a number on it. I recognized it as belonging to the Harper Police Department. "Now, I've spoken with the chief up there. He's not happy about the arrangement, but he's agreed to monitor your release restrictions and report back to me in a timely manner. You be sure about checking in with him the minute you get there, you hear? This is your big chance, Olson. You have something to prove, and especially back in your home community. Don't fuck it up."

Flannigan's final words are still resonating in my head when Meeks comes barreling down the steps into the basement, followed by another officer brandishing a pump-action shotgun. The shotgun keeps Meeks covered as he rattles keys into the lock on my cage and swings back the gate.

"Move it, Olson. The show's over; it's time to go."

I stay seated on the aluminum bench, fingers hooked around the handcuff loops. "Where?"

Krauss has been gone less than a couple of hours, and I trust Meeks just about as much as he trusts me.

"We're handing you over. Let's move it."

"Kim said the U.S. Marshals would be here in the morning."

"Yeah, well, Sergeant Krauss doesn't make the decisions around here. Now move it, Olson, before I get Fickes to shoot you in the foot for resisting a police officer."

To demonstrate his eagerness to carry out the threat, Officer Fickes smiles cockily and aims the weapon at my feet. He's just a kid, with one of those thin faces that makes his eyes look too big for their sockets. Still wet behind the ears and willing to go the whole nine yards to make a good impression. He motions with the weapon: *get up, move out, no trouble; I know how to use this baby.*

"I didn't kill Ben," I tell Meeks as I pull on my coat.

"Wrists," he says.

I thrust out my hands. He clasps them in cuffs.

"Kim's out there, right now, clearing my name."

Meeks pushes me out of the cage. He isn't getting into it with me. To him, I'm vermin and conversation isn't an option. With Fickes holding the rear, he escorts me up the steps and through the police station. It's early evening, Saturday, and the place is empty.

"I'll take it from here," he tells Fickes as we reach the main entrance.

Fickes doesn't hide his disappointment, but he knows better than to voice it to his superior. Dutifully, he stands aside, keeping the shotgun aimed as we leave the building.

It's dark out, bitterly cold. Street lights illuminating snow. Large breaks in the cloud cover, showing stars. Meeks's police cruiser is parked out front with the engine running and the lights on. He opens up the back door and gives me the nod to climb inside.

I hesitate. "We're not meeting up with the US Marshalls, are we?"

"Don't be paranoid. Just get in."

I grab the edge of the car door with my manacled hands. "I know my rights. You owe me a phone call."

"I owe you squat, Olson. Besides, you have nothing but enemies here. Who on earth would you call?"

"Grossinger."

Meeks balks. Lars might be a frail old man, but he still pulls most of the bigger punches in town. I stand my ground. Meeks bars his teeth and puts a hand on his gun. Stalemate. I'm too big for him to physically manhandle into the back of the Mustang all by himself. Forcing the issue will cause a scene. And bullies don't like audiences.

"Where were you when Ben was killed?" I ask.

Meeks stares at me like I'm speaking in a foreign language.

"You were Chief Krauss's sidekick, back in the day. One of your best buddies was Ryan Hendry. His dad was in Six Pack. Were you in Six Pack, too?"

Meeks goes to say something, then bites down on it as a silver Prius slides to a stop next to us and Krauss jumps out.

"What's going on here? Where are you two going? And why wasn't I invited?"

"Stay out of this, Sergeant," Meeks warns, still trying to force me into the cruiser with his stare alone. "This is no longer your concern."

Krauss pushes herself between us and squares up to her boss. "Let's call a truce here. Before you go jumping the gun and making a complete fool of yourself, just hear me out. You're making a big mistake. Jake didn't kill Ben."

Meeks sighs through clenched teeth. "It's getting old, Sergeant."

"I have evidence proving his innocence."

"So tell it to the judge." He tries to step around her.

But Krauss blocks his way. "Shane, listen to me. I'm not making any of this up. And I don't want you to do something you'll later regret. I have a video proving Jake didn't kill Ben."

Meeks's venomous stare moves from me to her.

"There's a webcam outside of Merrill's," she explains. "They installed it a few years ago as an online tourist attraction. The last twenty-four hours is backed up to a hard drive, on a loop. Indirectly, it faces the bait shop." She gets out her smart phone, taps the screen and holds it so that we can all see the picture. "Here's what it recorded this afternoon."

The video shows a dusky view of the main street, on an angle, so that the frame captures most of the antique and specialty boutiques across from the diner, including the barbershop, all lit up against the approaching night. Cars parked on the diagonal, including my father's Bronco. People wrapped up against the cold, walking along the sidewalk or going in and out of stores. Everything normal. It could be a scene from any small town in any northern state, wintertime. In the top left-hand corner is Varney's Bait & Tackle, with its neon signage glowing brightly behind the plate glass. Nothing out of the ordinary.

A rumble grows in Meeks's throat. "Sergeant, you're wasting my time. This doesn't prove a thing."

"Wait and watch. I promise it gets more interesting, real fast." Krauss pinch-zooms the top corner of the image so that the bait shop fills the screen. The picture is fuzzier but not enough to blur details too much.

The bait shop door opens inward and a well-built guy in a heavy winter coat backs out onto the sidewalk. He looks like trouble. It's the first time I've seen myself on camera and I realize I fit the stereotypical ex-con image to a tee: the shuffling body language, the slightly hunched frame, the overall shifty appearance. Consciously, I straighten my spine and puff out my chest. On screen, I see my stubbly face glance up and down the street, suspiciously, before shaking myself down and heading for the diner.

"Looks like you just made my case for me," Meeks comments as my image disappears from view. "It corroborates with our eyewitness testimony. If that doesn't prove Olson's guilt, I don't know what will."

Krauss sighs. "We're not done here yet. Will you please be patient and watch?"

Telling Meeks to have patience is like asking a rabid Doberman to please drop the family bunny and roll over. He's not happy with

Krauss's intervention. He'd rather whisk me away unseen, get me as far from Harper as he can before anyone notices I'm gone. I can feel his restless tension. He's about to dismiss Krauss's defense altogether when something flashes on the screen. It's too fast to make out properly and is gone in the blink of an eye.

"There! Did you see it?"

Meeks releases an irritated breath. "No."

"So pay attention this time." Krauss rewinds the video by a few seconds, then taps the screen again.

The neon sign glows brightly in the bait store window. Behind it, the store is darker, cave-like. No movement. Exasperation rumbles in Meeks's throat. Then one half of the image whitens slightly, softly, pixelated, for a split second, as though a ghostly apparition has strayed across the image and disappeared in a heartbeat.

"It's muzzle flash," Krauss explains.

"I know what it looks like," Meeks growls. "But it could also be a passing vehicle reflected in the window. What it doesn't show is somebody else actually shooting Ben. And it doesn't change the fact Olson is our prime suspect."

Krauss's mouth opens but no words come out. She came to the table with a full house, believing it was good for a win, but Meeks's straight flush has beaten her hands down.

"Looks like muzzle flash to me," I add.

"No one's talking to you, Olson."

Krauss rewinds the video again and pauses it on the flash itself. To the untrained eye it looks like a reflection in the glass.

"Firearms are my specialty, remember? I know my stuff. This is definitely muzzle flash, and that's definitely Ben's shotgun discharging."

Meeks has a mocking expression inching up his face. "Since when can you identify individual shotguns just by their muzzle flash?"

"You're not making this easy."

"I'm the chief; it's my job to get the facts right."

"Either way, Ben's Ruger was found with his body. I could smell cordite on the muzzle, which meant it had been discharged recently." She taps a nail against the screen. "And here's the proof. Okay, so it might not show us who actually pulled the trigger, but it does prove the gun was discharged after Jake left the building."

Meeks doesn't look happy. Bullies never take too kindly to being proven wrong. His smirk is slowly fading away.

"Shane, all I'm asking is you take a step back and think about it. Don't rush in and make the same mistake twice. We both know the original evidence against Jake was circumstantial, and we both know the evidence you did have was cooked up to make it easier to swallow. Jake didn't kill Jenna, and he didn't kill Ben; I just showed you reasonable doubt. So instead of turning him over to the marshals, do the right thing, here, for once, for me. I'm betting you've taken GSR swabs. If the results come back proving Jake fired Ben's shotgun then I'll bring him in myself. You have my word. But you no longer have sufficient cause to hold him, and that's a fact."

⌣

Just like her police SUV, Krauss's Prius smells of mango and leather. I roll down the passenger window just enough to allow the freezing night air to circulate.

Through the side mirror I can see a simmering Chief Meeks still standing on the sidewalk under a streetlight, watching us depart at speed.

"So I went over the bait store crime scene," Krauss says, pulling my attention back inside. "It looks like whoever killed Ben wanted us to think he committed suicide."

"Suicide?" The thought doesn't seem to fit. "Meeks was adamant it was a homicide."

"Only because he jumped to conclusions the moment he heard you were the last person out of the bait store. Had you not been in town today—and especially not visiting Ben minutes before he was found dead—I think his death might have been viewed as self-inflicted, at least until we had all the evidence and knew otherwise."

I thought it over. "That's all well and good, Kim, but anyone who knows Ben knows he's too vain to take his own life. He's the kind of guy who can't pass his own reflection without blowing it a kiss."

Krauss titters. "Maybe the old Ben—or should I say the younger Ben?—but word is he's been suffering from depression recently. He was even talking about selling up so that he could spend more time with his grandchildren."

Now I feel even worse for Ben.

With one hand on the wheel, she hands me her phone. "I took pictures of the crime scene. I thought you might like to see what you were wrongly accused of."

Out of morbid curiosity, I swipe through the snapshots. The flash-frozen images show various angles taken inside the bait shop. Everything appears to be in place apart from Ben Varney's head, which is fragmented and splattered all over the gun racks behind the counter. Blood and bits of brain matter dribbling down gun barrels and dripping off the ceiling. Pellets peppering the wall. The man himself is sprawled on the floor behind the glass cabinet, in a pool of bright blood, with most of his head missing.

It's a grisly scene and not easy on the senses. Nothing like you see on TV. Dealing with violent death calls for a cast-iron constitution.

I pause on a photo of his lower torso. It shows the double-barreled shotgun resting loosely in his hands, a thumb still hooked in the trigger guard, the muzzle directed toward his missing face. It's the same shotgun he pointed menacingly at me a couple of hours earlier. At a glance it certainly looks like he took his own life.

"Do you see it, Jake—the mistake that proves it's a homicide? It's the shotgun. The positioning's all wrong. Had Ben pulled the trigger, the gun would've kicked out of his hands. Landed away from the body. Shotguns are heavy, powerful. You try holding one at arm's length sometime, and the wrong way round. They're cumbersome and difficult to shoot like that. No matter which way you try and hold onto it, the recoil throws it in the opposite direction."

"Every action comes with an equal and opposite reaction."

"See, you were only pretending to be asleep in science class."

I zoom in on the picture so that his hands fill the screen. "Ben was a fitness freak. I remember he had a bone-crushing handshake. When we were kids he'd show off by doing finger push-ups, for what seemed like hours at a time. If anyone could hold onto that gun, Ben's your man."

"Maybe once, but not lately. I heard he had autoimmune issues, hence the depression. Besides, even accounting for blowback, there's little chance of blasting away your entire head by putting the muzzle in your mouth. What you see there is the kind of effect you'd expect if the gun was discharged at close range, from say two or three feet away. Ben wasn't known for his long reach. But there it is, in his grasp. You'd need six-foot-long arms to pull that off. I'm thinking the killer wanted us to believe he committed suicide so that we wouldn't go snooping any further."

It sounded no less feasible than all the other theories we were coming up with. "Okay. So what about the security camera, behind the counter?"

"A dummy. That's why I scanned through the footage from Merrill's webcam. Before your visit, everyone who went in the bait shop came out again."

"The killer entered through the back and left the same way."

"Stands to reason."

I look at her. "Which means the person in the back office, the one he was talking with when I went in there—"

"Was probably the killer."

"And Ben knew him."

We cut down a side street and enter a quiet residential area in the western part of Harper, moving through alternating pools of light and dark.

I hand back her phone. "Did you have any luck finding out who the two remaining members are?"

"No. I spoke with Ruby—or at least tried to—but she was out of it and high as a kite. Pretty useless really."

"What about your dad?"

"I tried calling him, but his phone is either off or out of range. Cell reception is intermittent up there at best. That's why I insisted on us both having a multi-use radio."

We pull onto a driveway. Headlights reveal a large two-story house with an icicle-fringed basketball hoop above a double-garage door.

Krauss kills the engine and we climb out.

"We can call him from here," she says.

"This your place, Kim?"

She smiles lopsidedly. "Home sweet home."

We leave our boots to mildew on the porch and go inside. Krauss pops on the lights. It's a pleasant place, tastefully decorated in warm tones and dark wood.

"Nice."

"Thanks."

"How long have you lived here?"

"Since the engagement."

We drape our coats over ornate hooks and peel off gloves.

"You moved in together? I thought the wedding was called off?"

"It was, and it's a long story I'd rather not get into right now. Beer?"
I nod. "Sure."

Krauss heads down the hallway, waving a hand behind her as she goes. "Don't just stand there. Go through and make yourself comfortable; I won't be a minute."

The living room is awash with autumnal colors and heavy fabrics, pleasing on the eye. Matching couches face each other over a mahogany coffee table. An alabaster chess set sits on the surface, the pieces abandoned in mid-battle. I wander over to a wooden bookcase crammed with monthlies and paperbacks. The magazines are mostly *Guns & Ammo*, going back decades, some outdoorsy stuff. The books are all horror, with broken spines and chafed skins. I run fingertips over bloodcurdling titles until I come to Stephen King's *Misery*, gently work it free from its resting place. It's the only book out of a hundred that isn't bruised and battered. In fact, it's perfect.

"I must have read it at least a dozen times," Krauss says as she comes up alongside me, silently. She leans against my arm, taking a peek at the immaculate cover. "You wouldn't think so by looking at it, would you?"

"I can't believe you still have it."

She looks up at me. "Why wouldn't I? It's the one and only thing you ever bought me, Jake Olson. So lay off with those big clumsy thumbs of yours."

Obediently, I slide the book back in its cavity.

She hands me a beer, then raises her own bottle in salutation. "To new beginnings."

I tap my beer against hers.

But we don't get to guzzle it. Unexpectedly, Krauss raises herself up and plants her lips against mine. For a second it's just the kind of kiss that friends give one another—we've done this a thousand times before, harmlessly, a simple congenial peck, with no agenda and no expectations—but a second later there's a difference, because our lips haven't parted. A second after that and something stirs deep within, something urgent and with a life of its own, and suddenly we're kissing like long-lost lovers, deep and forceful, with no thought to either consequence or conclusion.

Krauss curls a hand behind my neck and holds on tight. I slip a hand behind her waist and draw her close, feel her contours melt into mine. We have embraced before, but not like this, not with such primal desire. I let the kiss take its own natural course, weaving in and out, venturing into previously unchartered territory, realizing I have never properly kissed before or been kissed.

"I'm going upstairs," Krauss whispers as our lips part. "You coming with?"

All at once I want to, desperately. My thundering heart and speeding hormones tell me I need to. But my head—my cold institutionalized head—warns me I am about to cross a line that cannot be uncrossed.

"Kim," I begin softly, "you're in a relationship. What about your fiancé?"

Krauss takes my hand in hers and freezes me with her gaze. "Trust me, Jake. This is okay. The wedding plans were shelved a long time ago and there hasn't been any intimacy in years. Living under the same roof is just a means to an end and actually a whole lot smoother since we decided to quit. So it's just you and me. And it's okay."

Gently, she pulls me deeper into no-man's land. Weakly, pathetically, I offer no resistance.

Life is all about choices and learning to live with them. Choose the wrong path and we can spend the rest of our lives trying to avoid pitfalls.

As a teenager, sleeping with Krauss never occurred to me. The younger version of her was more like a doting sister. Time, age, and our separation have changed all that, I realize. Being sexually intimate with Krauss doesn't just feel natural, if feels right.

But she is engaged to another man—albeit it loosely—and I should feel some degree of guilt. And yet, for some inexplicable reason, I don't. And it concerns me.

"Was contacting your dad on the radio a pretext to get me here?" I call to her as I smooth down the bed linens and plump the pillows. She's in the bathroom, freshening up after our lovemaking. I can hear her splashing around in the sink, happy as a lark. I've never seen her smile so much. As for me, my head is spinning and my body still quakes from an unforgettable experience. Eighteen years of pent-up emotion bursting forth like the Fourth of July fireworks, with Krauss pushing the buttons.

"Partly," she calls back. "If I'm being brutally honest it did cross my mind. Didn't I more than make up for any sleight of hand, though?"

"You did. And you're forgiven."

"Thank you. Listen, I'll be a couple more minutes here. The radio's downstairs, in the den, if you want to try calling him."

My clothes smell of Krauss. I pull them on and head downstairs, balance slightly askew.

The den is part office, part storage room, with a computer desk and a swivel chair tucked under a window. A two-way radio sits on the corner of the desk, emitting a constant stream of static, turned low. The needle in the little yellow signal window is fluctuating, but only slightly. I sit down, crank up the volume, and then press the transmit button on the desk microphone.

"Chief Krauss, you copy?"

Static.

"This is Jake Olson. I'm calling from Kim's place. We need to talk. You there, Chief?"

More static.

"This is urgent. If you can hear me, please come back."

Just mush.

Expecting the old police chief to answer my call is probably expecting a little too much, given the fact we hadn't exactly parted on pleasantries:

Eighteen years ago, as I was led out of the courtroom in the wake of a guilty verdict, he promised me, "You're going away for a very long time, Olson. I hope you rot in jail for what you did to Jenna."

"I didn't kill her," I whimpered back. It was the same pitiful one-liner I'd been spouting since the first inquisition and as a rebuttal to every accusation leveled at me throughout the one-sided trial.

His sneer stretched from ear to ear. He didn't believe me, just like everybody else in the courthouse thought I'd murdered my girlfriend. Verdict unanimous. He leaned close as I passed him by, whispered, "Listen up: if you do ever come back to Harper, I'll kill you myself. God's honest truth."

I settle in the swivel chair and reflect. I know Krauss loves her dad, but feelings make us biased. At the time of my arrest, Chief Krauss was a member of Six Pack. During his investigation into Jenna's disappearance, he didn't refute the evidence Meeks brought to the table, ostensibly proving I killed Jenna. If anything, he endorsed it. A torn sweater with a trace of blood. Guilty. Many times I have wondered who had a vested interest in driving the case against me. Each time I convinced myself that Meeks was behind the wheel. After all, he had eyes for Jenna and he despised me for being with her. It was clear he wanted Jenna for himself. But Ruby's revelation has opened up a whole new can of worms, and I have to consider the possibility of not only Chief Krauss being involved in the sex games but also of him being Jenna's killer.

I try the radio one more time without success.

149

It's then that I notice the framed photograph on the desk, next to the radio, and pick it up for a closer look. It's a picture of Krauss and her fiancé, taken on a sunny day up at the lake. They're kneeling either side of a slain deer, both grinning, both high from the kill. My stomach turns. Not because of the great white hunter mentality, but because I know the man who Krauss is engaged to.

"I was going to tell you."

I turn to see Krauss standing in the doorway, dressed in a black silk kimono and looking rosy-cheeked.

Unsuccessfully, I try to prevent my jaw from dropping. "You're engaged to Meeks?"

It's a bombshell. It's not so much the age difference that surprises me, it's more the fact Meeks was born an asshole and the Krauss I know was smarter than that.

Her nose wrinkles. "Now I feel compelled to explain."

"Kim, you don't need to. I'm just shocked, is all."

"And that's perfectly understandable." She takes a step into the den. "But, please, let me explain. You and I were always open with each other, and that's one of the things I valued about us." She draws a deep breath. "Believe me, I didn't plan on getting into bed with Shane. Not at first, anyway. The truth is, after you left I wasn't planning on hooking up with anybody. Then things got super-stressful at home. I was going through a rough patch supporting mom with her recovery. You were gone and I had no one to confide in. I'm not superhuman; I needed someone to offload onto. Out of everybody, Shane was there for me when things got really difficult. He was supportive when I needed it the most. Our relationship wasn't planned. It just happened."

"It sounds like he took advantage." The comment is harsh, unsympathetic, and I shouldn't have said it. I have no right commenting on any of Krauss's life choices. We all make mistakes and we all expect forgiveness.

"And from the outside it probably looks that way. But that's not how it was. Shane was good to me. I know that sounds bizarre, but he really was. You only know one side of him, Jake. Once you get past all the machismo bullshit he's different. He gave me time when I needed it. He listened, and he never once stepped out of line. If anyone took advantage it was me."

"Kim, you don't need to explain."

"Yes, I do. After what's just happened between you and me, I have no choice." She comes fully into the den and kneels in front of me. "Jake, I was already working for the department at the time. Shane and me, we got close and one thing led to another. It was fun at first. A welcome distraction. No strings attached. Then things got serious. We got engaged and moved in here."

"So what stopped you guys from going all the way?"

Krauss releases an uneasy breath. "Let's just say things didn't work out as planned."

I want to probe further, demand to know why she still wears his ring and still shares a house with him, but I can see my reaction is already torture for her, and I am not that person.

She cups my face in her hands, looks me directly in the eyes. "Jake, listen to me. What we just did, together, was special. Beautiful. Please don't hold my past against me. I was going to tell you back in the diner, but the turn in events carried us away."

Distantly, in another room, a phone begins to play a synthesized melody.

"That's yours," I say.

"So let it ring. If it's urgent, they'll call back."

"It might be your dad."

For moment she holds my gaze—hurt and frustration firing in her eyes—then she disengages and leaves the den.

I turn back to the photograph on the desk. The image of Meeks grins at me: *Got there before you, Olson.*

151

I am about to put the picture face-down on the desk when Krauss returns, looking ashen.

"That was my contact at the Sheriff's Office," she says slowly. "They processed the Hangman Falls crime scene this afternoon. During the recovery they found a purse. It was buried in the patch of soil exposed by the fallen tree. There was an ID in it." Suddenly there are tears in her eyes and a worrying rasp to her voice. "Jake, I'm so sorry."

I leap to my feet and go to her, hold her. "Kim, what is it?"

"We were wrong, Jake. We shouldn't have jumped to conclusions. The remains up at Hangman Falls, they aren't Jenna's."

"Not Jenna's?" The words cut through my chest like hot blades. "But that doesn't make any sense. It has to be Jenna. No one else has gone missing."

But Krauss is shaking her head and trembling in my arms. "No, Jake. They're adamant about it. It's definitely not Jenna."

I am stunned, astounded. "So whose remains are they?"

Krauss stares at me with eyes magnified by tears. "They're your mom's."

Chapter Seventeen

J okingly, my brother once said that everybody dies from shortness of breath. If that were the case, then right now I am banging on death's door.

A mixture of fear and disbelief sends me rushing outside, desperate to replace the fire in my lungs with frigid winter air. Krauss's words have wrapped themselves around my throat and all at once I am unable to breathe or even to think coherently.

"Jake, I'm so sorry," she repeats as she follows me outside. "I don't know what else to say. It's unbelievable."

"It's not her." My vision is pulsating, everything spinning.

"And I didn't believe it myself, until I saw this." She thrusts out her phone, the bright screen facing my way.

Blazing away is the photograph of a Minnesota driver's license. Clearly visible is the headshot of a young woman with rich mahogany hair and eyes like mine.

Erin Olson.

The blades in my chest slice deeper.

"See, Jake, there's no mistake. This is your mom's ID. They found it with the remains. It's her, not Jenna. They're treating it as a homicide."

"She was murdered?" My heartbeat thuds in my throat, banging in my ears. "When?"

"The ME puts the rate of decay at around thirty years."

Another blazing surge of internal fire sweeps through me. My mind whirls again with the thought of my mother being dead for the past three decades. If the Medical Examiner has his sums right, then the horrible realization is, my mother died younger than I am today, and probably within days of her leaving home. All my life I have believed she ran away with another man, that she left Harper and possibly Minnesota for good and never came back, that she was elsewhere, alive and healthy, living her new life with a new husband and maybe even a new family. I was seven when she walked out on my father, on us, on me. At first I missed her terribly, crying myself to sleep at night, pleading with God to make her come back, promising I would do everything she asked and never give her any cause to leave me again. But she never returned. As time passed, the hole formed from loss started to fill up with hurt. And eventually the hurt hardened into hate. By the time I realized she was never coming back I was glad she wasn't. What kind of mother does that to her child?

Now I know: the dead kind.

Krauss pulls me into her arms and holds me close. "Jake, I'm so sorry."

And the dam bursts. Thirty years of bottled-up denial breaching the dike, spilling over, physically unstoppable. First the surges, then the floods of tears, repressed childhood pain unleashed at last.

Krauss clings on, absorbing my tremors. "Let's go back inside," she whispers. "We'll catch our deaths out here."

We do. I am not embarrassed about being outwardly emotional in front of Krauss. There is no judging, no thoughts of weakness or of how pathetic it is for a grown man to sob like a little girl. I am not in Stillwater where my tears will be used as a weapon against the weakness. Krauss doesn't force me to talk about my oppressed feelings, but I do. They gush out, more than they have in any therapy session. For a moment I am back in her bedroom, at her parents' house, in the aftermath of Jenna's disappearance, spilling my guts and bearing all. It's as though everything has come full circle. Coming back to Harper has exhumed my past and shaken me to the core. Stirred up my darkness and ignited its thorns. Something has changed in me. An awakening. A revival. Roused by my return.

"Kim, I have to go," I insist, finally, when I am run dry.

She brushes a loose tear from my chin. "You don't need to go. You can stay the night."

I'd be a liar if I said I am not tempted by her offer. But I can't. It's not just the news of my mother's death that has unearthed emotions in me, I realize; our lovemaking has rekindled a fire, and the heat of it is seductive, irresistible. I can't be here when Meeks arrives home.

"If you're worried about Shane," she says, as if reading my mind, "I'll tell him to spend the night in a hotel. This is more important than anything else right now. *Anything*. You shouldn't be alone tonight. I mean it."

"Kim, I'll be okay. I need be at home, in familiar surroundings."

"So let me come with you. Spend the night there, together."

She wants to. I can see it in her eyes. Krauss is as hooked by our newfound physical connection as I am.

But it's all happening too fast and I don't want to spoil our chances by rushing in headlong, mindlessly trampling over anyone else's feelings, including our own.

I slip from her grasp and get to my feet. "Kim, don't think for one minute I regret you and me, because I don't. I just need to get my head together. And I need to do it on my own."

Krauss kisses me on the cheek. "Call me?"

"I promise."

Then I pull on my coat and make my way out into the starry night for the long walk home, knowing that the news of my mother being dead these past thirty years comes with two definite consequences:

All my childhood emotional wrangling was for nothing.

And she didn't die of natural causes.

Chapter Eighteen

Whereas you going to get it through your thick skull she's never coming home again? She's gone, thanks to you. Cleared out. Doesn't matter how much you cry about it, she won't be coming back. So stop your whimpering, you sniveling little brat. Don't you understand? You'll never see her again. Sooner you get used to the idea, the sooner you can stop acting like a crybaby and give me some blessed peace. Now get out of my sight and leave me the hell alone."

From the doorway of his bedroom, I gazed at my father through eyes blurred by tears.

It was my eighth birthday and no one had thrown a surprise party. No friends on their way with gifts and cheer. No magician booked. No finger-food and cake in the kitchen. Just the same tense emptiness as always, and the knowledge that things would get worse as the day wore on.

I was a needful child, hurting, and yet my father had no sympathy for me. Anger consumed him. He was too embroiled in hate to even consider my feelings, or that I had any. He offered nothing to mitigate the torment knotting up my belly, no calming words, no hope. Nothing to blow away the black smoke churning away deep inside me.

It was midday and he was still in bed. Weeks of the same. Only ever rising when he needed to fill his bladder or empty it. The bedroom stank of sweated alcohol. Garments strewn on the floor and piled in the corners. The whole of the house was like this now: a mess. This way for months, slowly accumulating, suffocating. My father was a mess, too. When he wasn't in bed, feeling sorry for himself, he wandered aimlessly around the house like a zombie, unshaven and in week-old underwear, with a twitch in his eye and a curse on his tongue. Sleep and drink. Drink and sleep. Come the weekends he'd make an effort, when his social services were more in demand. He'd wear a heavenly face for those that mattered more than I. He'd rake nicotine-yellowed fingers through greasy hair, drag a razor over tight jaw muscles, shake out the creases in last week's clothes. Then he'd preach about wrongs and rights to anyone within earshot. Of course, he only did so because he was duty-bound and unable to opt out, not because he wanted to. What he really wanted was to get his hands on my mother's throat and squeeze the life out of her for leaving him.

"He's right about one thing," my brother told me as I caught up with him in the yard, where he was raking autumn leaves into a big golden mound. "Mom's gone, Jake. Doesn't matter how much you cry about it, it won't bring her back. We just have to get on with things without her."

I dragged a damp sleeve across my face, wiping away snot.

Aaron was my hero. Since our mother had walked out, he'd been a rock. I hadn't seen him shed a single tear in public or in my presence. He knuckled down and got on with things. I wasn't that good at pretending, not then. But I would be.

At that point I was simply too young and too mixed up to fully understand most of what was happening. I didn't understand complex relationships. I couldn't work through the reasons why. I wasn't aware of repercussions. I knew my father blamed me but I didn't understand why. Unconnected synapses struggling to spark. I had no idea what I'd done to earn my father's hatred, or the part I'd played in forcing my mother from the family home. The sad part was, even if I had all the information at hand I wouldn't have known what to do with it. The rational pathways in my eight-year-old brain simply didn't exist. It left me confused, upset, and unable to process.

Frequently, I sought solitude in my darkness, then fled it when the thorns began to prickle.

The kids at school knew my mother had left. It was the hottest topic of conversation for the whole of one day—my first day back after her leaving—before something juicier came along to occupy their tongues. Meanwhile, to mollify the hurt and to quash the gossip, I made up my own stories and sold them to disinterested ears, making excuses for her walking out: *she'd landed herself a prime photography assignment with one of the big magazines on the other side of the country, maybe oversees, she'd be gone a while and nobody knew when she'd be back.* A day later her departure was old news and no one at school ever spoke of her again, not even my teachers, not even me.

But my father made a point of reminding me that she was gone whenever our paths crossed, sometimes with brute force.

For my own well-being, from the moment she walked out, I learned how to compartmentalize, to divide my mind into two halves, to contain the fallout from the loss. I learned how to keep the pain separate from my day-to-day activities. It helped me get through. Unexpectedly, the damage limitation had a beneficial effect on my father. With my withdrawal, his slurs and raised fists turned into cool indifference. His cold-shoulder treatment stung just as much as the back of his hand and his spiteful words, but

I could live with it, adapt. I learned to keep a wary distance between us. I learned to keep everything in, locked away, pushed down in the darkness. I learned that displaying emotion was a weakness.

Now, thirty years later, I discover my mother's true fate and it brings everything home to roost. It's all I've ever known: that my mother abandoned me. Suddenly, I am being compelled to rethink a premise that has underpinned my entire life so far and influenced the way I have viewed the world, and the way those perceptions have changed me.

My mother didn't leave me.

She was killed.

While the seven-year-old me was sobbing into his pillow at night, silently pleading with his mother to return to him, she was already dead and decomposing.

It's enough to break the seals on Pandora's Box.

Still dazed, I hunker into my coat, switch down a dark side street, and almost lose my footing on black ice. An incandescent moon hangs in a sky salted with stars. Everything's still. Everything not already frozen is freezing—including me. I watch my step and cross the street.

Cold Harper isn't a hotbed of crime. When it isn't hibernating for the winter, it serves as a busy tourist destination. Visitors respect the laws and go about their business peacefully. Aside from Jenna's disappearance, there are no other known killings out here on the edge of the National Forest. None, it would seem, until now.

Could the person responsible for killing Jenna be the same person who killed my mother, all those years ago?

After all, what are the chances of there being two killers living in tiny Harper?

Is it my father?

I dig in my heels, suddenly reeling from the thought. Every dark memory I have of my parents together is bitter, stained in blood. My father abused my mother, the same way he abused me. It doesn't stretch the imagination to think that he chased after her the day she left, possessed by rage, to unleash his own brand of biblical retribution on her.

But why would he kill Jenna?

A black pickup swings dangerously into the curb next to me, braking hard and throwing up a wave of snowmelt. Before I can step aside, the passenger door springs open and a short, chubby guy with a ginger beard jumps out onto the sidewalk. Despite the inclement weather he's wearing cargo shorts and board shoes.

"Get in," he commands.

I know him. He's an older version of Ryan Hendry, the son of barbershop Chuck, the former town barber and deceased member of Six Pack. He holds a handgun, aimed at me.

"I said get in, Olson. Or as God is my witness I'll put a bullet in your balls."

But even if I wanted to I am not given the chance to do as instructed. Something like a wrecking ball slams into the back of my skull and white-hot fire explodes through my brain. My knees buckle and the sidewalk comes up and cuffs me on the chin. I roll onto my side, senses scurrying from the pain, flashbulbs popping in my vision. Something equally unkind slams into my stomach, and more fire purges the air from my lungs.

"Told you you're a dead man," comes a voice I recognize.

It belongs to Gavin Luckman. Through acid tears I see him looming over me—weasel-thin, with blond hair shaven into a fuzz—wielding a tire iron.

"Time to pay the piper, duckweed."

Another boot slams into my burning belly and my lungs pancake.

"Wait," I gasp.

But they aren't interested in striking up a conversation, only retribution.

A leg swings and a boot connects with my forehead. It's like being hit by a bolt of lightning. Another boot stamps. Then it's open season and the pair go at me, unrestrained, kicking and whooping with delight. No holding back. I try to curl into a ball, to roll with the blows, to protect my head and face as burning pain rains down. My mind takes refuge in its safe place, in the sanctuary decked out like the shrine of a seven-year-old boy, and sits out the storm in darkness.

"Hush now. They can't hurt you here."

Then the world fractures like a smashed mirror and the shards tumble into blackness.

Chapter Nineteen

Occasionally, the nature of Tolstoy's job meant following his target until it was practical to approach. In his opinion, engaging a person in public was both unprofessional and bad practice. Often, it would attract unwanted attention, sometimes from the authorities, and sometimes with negative consequences. Experience had shown him that the majority of those he chased down responded more positively to home visits, where he could demonstrate the error of their ways in an environment in which they felt secure. Rarely, he followed them around town all day.

But he had spent the best part of twelve hours tailing Jake Olson from one location to another, all over Harper, reporting his movements back to his employer.

Three hours ago, after sitting patiently outside the Harper police station, he'd followed Olson to the house shared by two of the town's police professionals, then sat in wait, again, at a discreet distance down the street, trying not to think about the broken glass tumbling around in his bladder. Two hours after that, Jake Olson had ventured back outside, leaving on foot.

To his own error, Tolstoy had made an assumption that had lost him his target.

It had appeared that Olson was headed across town, and it had occurred to Tolstoy that Olson was making his way back to collect his father's pickup truck from where it had been left outside Occam's Razor earlier in the day. From experience, Tolstoy knew that following someone on foot while he was in his vehicle came with all sorts of impracticalities. And so he'd made his own way to the middle of town ahead of Olson, to park up down the side of Merrill's, to wait for Olson to show up.

But he hadn't.

He'd given him plenty of time.

But Jake Olson had vanished without a trace.

And now Tolstoy was driving around town, in the dark, annoyed with himself, his bladder screaming for relief, while he peered down one deserted alleyway after another, clueless as to Jake Olson's whereabouts.

Fearing the worst, he had already powered up his police scanner.

Chapter Twenty

The glassy splinters reattach and a dreamlike scene resolves out of the darkness, as real as if it is happening in real time:

I am a boy again, standing in the lake, with cool water lapping at my ribs, feeling the soft mud squelch between my toes. The surface teems with flies. They congregate around the blood caked on my hands, forming dark, moving mittens. Behind me, the sun is low in the sky, almost set, turning the lake into liquid bronze. I am alone, and the only sounds are those of my ragged breathing and the constant buzzing of the insects.

Slowly, I lower my hands into the molten surface. The flies go into a frenzy as the water dilutes the blood, sucking it away to form purple clouds. They bounce and scatter across the surface like hail falling on ice. I push deeper with my arms until the water level touches my chin, further dissipating the blood until it becomes part of the lake itself.

Then I submerge myself completely, letting its silken touch cleanse, remaining immersed for long silent seconds, suspended, drifting, until my lungs ache, forcing me to resurface and gasp for air.

A sound in the sky causes me to look up.

A rent has opened up in the twilit heavens, right above me. A black hole, high up, shaped like a mouth. A deafening scream is issuing from its cavernous throat. I watch, mesmerized, as a water-fall of blood spews out of the sky-fracture, becoming a glistening red torrent plunging to earth. It hits the lake with an almighty roar and drowns me in bubbling blood.

Noise and pain.

Both vie for sensory dominance in waves crashing against the shores of my consciousness. They roll in and out, muddying my thoughts and pounding at my brain.

Disoriented, I fall back into reality on the backseat of Luckman's pickup, propped up against the door frame behind the driver's seat. I have no idea how long I have been unconscious. Long enough it seems for my captors to bundle me in the truck and begin the journey to whatever secluded destination they have in mind to finish what they started.

From under a swelling eyelid I see Luckman doing the driving, and doing it erratically. I assume he's pumped after pummeling me into the pavement. Hendry is in the passenger seat, thick head rocking to a heavy metal stampede coming from the stereo. We're moving along an unlit road, with snow-heavy trees rising up on both sides, headlights guiding the way. No other traffic. Looks like the northeast route heading away from town and deep into the Superior National Forest.

Tentatively, and without drawing their attention, I evaluate my predicament. It's not sunny. The outlook is plenty of scattered pain, with bruises developing later. My mouth tastes like I've been sucking coins, and the worst headache since leaving Stillwater is pushing at the insides of my skull. My abductors have worked me over good, kicked and battered, but nothing feels broken.

Zip ties bind my wrists together.

Something Krauss told me a lifetime ago, the day Jenna first vocalized her interest in me, comes to mind:

"Trust me, Jake. Dating the queen bee is the quickest way to make enemies. They'll forever hate you for it and make your life a total misery."

She wasn't wrong.

Jenna was beautiful and brimming with life. Heads turned in her wake—boys and girls alike, but for very different reasons. I knew my viewpoint was prejudiced, but no one could dispute the fact that Jenna was the prettiest at the ball by far. Exactly why she'd chosen me was unclear. I was nothing special, even less to look at. I didn't come with a prestigious pedigree. Nothing to offer. Prospects equally uncertain. I was moderately intelligent, humorous in the right company. But I was shy and withdrawn among strangers. Jenna could have had her pick of the boys. But she was the one who had made the first move, and flattery was a huge ego-booster to a seventeen-year-old hormonal male with confidence issues.

"You actually want to date?" I asked her, stupidly, with an equally stupid expression flattening out my face.

We were on a lunch break, and the school grounds were knotted with noisy students soaking up the early spring sunshine. Dozens of curious glances, all rotating our way.

"I'd like to, if you want to. See how it goes."

"Why me?" Another stupid question.

"Because I like you, Jake. You're different, interesting." She laughed lightheartedly. "Wait a minute. I'm not making a mistake here, am I? You are into girls, right?"

"Sure, so long as they're female."

Another giggle. "So what's with the hesitation?"

"Surprise, I guess. And worry that maybe you've taken a knock to your head, or I have."

Her laugh became playful and she batted long blonde lashes at me. "See, quirkiness. That's exactly why I'm drawn to you."

Naïvely, I felt like I'd won the state lottery.

Things like that didn't happen to a scrawny kid from Harper, and especially not to one who didn't have the balls to gamble.

I remember gaping at Jenna with big, stupid, unblinking eyes, my heart hammering out the tune from *Love Story*. Tragic, I know.

Then and there it was less important to know why Jenna was interested in me than it was to bask in the warmth of the moment, even if it later proved to be short-lived.

"I'm telling you, Jake," Krauss said after Jenna and I had arranged to meet at Merrill's for milkshakes, "this can only end one way, and that's in tears."

Almost twenty years later she's still not wrong.

"Check he's breathing," Luckman shouts from up front.

Hendry twists in his seat, props the handgun on the armrest, and looks me over. "Seems pretty banged up to me, dude," he shouts over the deafening music. "You want me to put a hole in him, see if he squeals?"

"Just check, okay? I need him alive and conscious when I take him to pieces."

"You mean when we take him to pieces. We're in this together, remember? Never skinned a human before." Chuckling, Hendry scoots up in his seat, leans over the gun, and reaches out two meaty fingers to press against my throat.

I don't let them touch.

I loop my bound wrists over his head, grab the back of his fat neck, push down as hard as I can. The move takes him completely by surprise. It forces Hendry into the gap between the two front seats, facedown, before he can react and before he can yelp a warning. He's big and it's a tight fit. The hand holding the gun is crushed under him and the other is wedged against the backseat.

Luckman glances around. The pickup fishtails. Using Hendry as a vault, I throw myself forward and head-butt Luckman in the side of his face. It's the last thing he's expecting and his hands fly off the steering wheel. Hendry squirms under my knuckles, a yowl rumbling in his compressed chest. I plant a knee on the back of his neck, pinning him down, then loop my bound wrists over Luckman's dazed head, hook them around his throat and pull backward with all my might. Frantic hands claw at mine. With no one driving, the pickup fishtails again, this time dangerously. Luckman emits a high-pitched scream. I lean back, strangling him, putting all my weight on Hendry. Luckman's foot stamps on the gas. The truck swerves perilously across the road, a fender scrapes the bank of plowed snow. Metal whines. Snow and ice spray up across the hood and windshield. The impact bounces us around. Uncontrolled, the truck rebounds. Luckman's thrashing feet hit the gas and the brake, alternately. The pickup lurches, swerves on a tighter angle, and hits the snowy barrier on the opposite side of the pavement, this time head-on. The bull bar buries itself in the snow and the impact throws me into the back of the driver's seat. I disengage from Luckman, fumble open the door with gloved fingers, and leap out.

The pickup is dug in deep, tail-lights blazing.

I gather my bearings, then I run, on shaky legs, sucking in freezing night air and blowing out crystallizing clouds, leaving the din of rock music behind.

———⌣———

I put a hundred yards between us before pulling out my phone and dialing Krauss's number. The connection is dead. No signal. I keep running. It's over a mile to the outskirts of town, all downhill; I can make it. But it's slippery underfoot; I tumble twice and scuff off skin before shortening my stride. The beating has left me with a wobbly gait, aches and creaks everywhere, but adrenaline is burning through and evaporating the pain. I can make it. At some point I'll get a phone signal and Krauss will come pick me up.

When she does, Luckman and Hendry will be facing some pretty stern questions. And I will be pressing charges.

I keep to the shadows, following a snowy rut cut by multiple wheel impressions. No obvious sounds of my abductors coming back for more. No other traffic on the highway.

Some concerted effort will be needed to extract the pickup from the snow bank, I know, and Hendry is way too fat to give serious chase on foot. Luckman, on the other hand, is wiry, and wiry guys fed by hate can run like headless chickens.

The safest and shortest route to town is through the snow-choked woods, but it would sap energy and take forever to navigate the darkened terrain. Even with a flashlight the going will be tough. The highway is the straight-line option and with fewer obstacles. If I keep my head down I can be back in Harper in fifteen minutes, at a push. Running is keeping me warm, but I've never been any good at it. Not like Aaron. I get breathless, quickly, and as soon as I slow, the unremitting cold rushes in and flails me bare.

I'm about five minutes out from the crash site when I see a pair of high beams in the distance, illuminating a tunnel through the overhanging trees. Aside from Luckman's pickup it's the first vehicle I've seen out here. I straddle the median and wave mana-cled hands over my head. The vehicle slows as it nears, pulls over, headlights blinding. A door opens, then the silhouetted shape of a man moves through the brilliance. He's wearing a Harper PD parka and a mystified expression.

"Meeks? Never thought I'd be glad to see you."

He emerges from the glare. "Olson? What are you doing out here, and what the hell happened to your face?"

I wipe tacky blood from my busted lips with the back of a glove, blink swollen eyes. "Gavin Luckman and Ryan Hendry. They jumped me back in town, then bundled me into Luckman's truck and brought me out here to finish the job."

"No kidding?" He shakes his head. "So what happened—you escaped?"

"I forced Luckman to wreck the truck. About a half mile back."

"Anyone seriously injured?"

"Who cares?" My tone is sharp, cut by wheezing lungs. "We weren't on our way to a picnic, Meeks. They were out to lynch me. You need to go back up there and arrest them for kidnapping—unless vigilante justice is your kind of law."

A familiar sneer creeps up his face. It looks like there might be a toxic retort lingering on the tip of his tongue, but he keeps it in check. "Okay, get in. Let's go finish this."

I thrust out my wrists, revealing the bloodied zip ties.

"After I confirm your story," he says.

"Meeks."

"After. It's not open for debate."

The police Mustang still reeks of cheap cologne. Meeks cranks up the heater and pops on the turret lights. Red-and-blue specters skitter across the surrounding trees. He pushes my gloved hands to my bleeding lips. "Please, no blood on the leather." Then he squints at the bruising developing on my face. "Looks like they roughed you up pretty good, Olson. Broke your nose. You feel as bad as you look?"

"I survived Stillwater."

"That you did. But Harper's a whole different ball game." He puts the cruiser in drive and we set off, heading back the way I've come. "So let me get a handle on this. You say they jumped you back in town?"

"Yeah."

"Whereabouts?"

"Does it matter?"

"Maybe not to you. But it's my job to determine if there were any witnesses, to corroborate your story."

I lift up my shackled wrists. "So what's this—fantasy role-playing? Meeks, you can see with your own eyes what they've done to me. Luckman was talking about chopping me into little pieces and Hendry was salivating at the thought of skinning me first."

"Those two are born idiots."

We round a bend. The red-lit backend of Luckman's truck comes into view at the limit of the high beams. Meeks hits a switch and the police sirens let loose a short squawk. Up ahead, Luckman drops out of the truck, one hand massaging his neck while the other shields his eyes against the oncoming light. A second later he's joined by Hendry, who is breathing out huge clouds of condensing moisture, looking pissed, still brandishing the handgun.

"You might want to call for back-up," I say.

Meeks snorts. "I think I can handle these two." He slows the cruiser and brings it to a standstill several yards short. "Now stay here. Let me do the talking. I'll fix this." He climbs out and closes the door behind him.

He joins my abductors in the glare of the headlights. Neither Luckman nor Hendry look apologetic. Far from it. They're hot with rage and eager to get on with my lynching. The trio engage in a heated discussion, muffled by the buzzing in my ears and the rock music still bellowing from Luckman's pickup: Meeks with his hands on hips, Luckman gesticulating wildly, Hendry with the gun pointing my way.

It sounds like they're justifying their actions. I can imagine what they're saying:

They were out for an innocent drive. I appeared from nowhere and flagged them down. I commandeered their vehicle. My wounds are the result of their fighting back. Luckman ditched the truck off-road to take back control and I took off, in fear of being caught. I'm a convicted felon when all's said. A murderer, right? My word isn't worth jack over theirs.

It doesn't explain how the zip ties got on my wrists.

Meeks glances over his shoulder, at me, his eyes narrowed against the glare of the headlights. He hasn't instructed Hendry to put away his weapon, hasn't told Luckman to back off and calm down. It doesn't look like he's about to arrest anybody. If anything, it looks like they sold him a sob story and he bought it.

In situations like this, a hundred miles from civilization, with tempers riled and intentions deadly, it all comes down to loyalties and a small-town mentality.

And Meeks isn't in any hurry to do anything.

The keys are still in the ignition, I notice, engine running. Instinctively, I reach for the electronic door-lock button and push it. The bolts snap into place with a muffled *thwunk*.

Three pairs of eyes turn my way.

"What do you think you're doing there, Olson?" Meeks calls.

"Buying life insurance," I shout back. "I thought you were going to arrest them, Meeks?"

He gestures with his hand. "Unlock the doors."

I don't move.

He places the palm of the hand on the hood and the other on the butt of his firearm. "I'm not fooling around here, Olson. This a police vehicle and you're very close to violating your parole. Now do as I say and unlock the doors before you make me do something you'll regret."

Still, I don't move. Not yet.

I'm not exactly flavor of the month. If things head south for me here no one will come looking for me. Meeks will spin a very convincing story about me skipping town: *He's gone back to the Cities or wherever. Who cares? Good riddance, I say. Harper is safer without him.* Meeks is the law around here. His word is golden. No one will dispute him. Luckman and Hendry will get away with murder, my murder, scot-free. Meeks will be complicit. But I don't think that will bother him in the slightest.

Meeks leans his weight on the hood. "Last warning, Olson. I mean it. Don't make this any worse for you than it already is. I will use deadly force to eject you. Now open the doors."

"Arrest them, first."

Meeks bangs a fist against the hood. "This isn't open to debate, Olson! I said open the doors!" His face is suddenly flushed, eyes flaring.

Luckman and Hendry edge nearer, either side of the car, expressions hardening as they come. Hendry's gun is pointed directly at my face.

Meeks gets out his own firearm and waggles it in my direction. "You have two seconds, and then I'm getting serious."

I don't take my eyes off him.

Sometimes in life we go down a one-way street the wrong way. We don't stop and turn around. Not because we fail to recognize our mistake, but because we are committed and there's no going back.

It's three against one. Their word against mine. And Stillwater has programmed me to *survive*.

I grab the steering wheel with both manacled hands and haul myself over the center console and into the driver's seat.

The movement is like putting a lit match to Meeks's short fuse. He barges Luckman aside and rushes round to the driver's door, bangs a fist against the glass. "Open this door, Olson! You're making a big fucking mistake here. Open this door!"

He rattles at the door handle, thumps at the glass.

I throw the Mustang in reverse and stand on the pedal.

The wing mirror clips him, spinning him on the spot.

Then the cruiser is wheel-spinning on the icy asphalt, slewing backward and gathering speed. Luckman makes a futile grab at the hood as the vehicle backs away. Hendry stands his ground, raises his handgun and squeezes off a shot. One half of the windshield becomes a maze of crisscrossing cracks. The impact reverberates through the metalwork. I keep the pedal floored, head dipped, as the muzzle of Hendry's gun lights up again and a loud clang sounds from under the hood. I spin the steering wheel. The Mustang turns through an arc. Another clang as another bullet hits its mark. I press the brake to straighten up the car, and the second it's facing the opposite direction, I lean on the gas again and hear the responsive engine roar. In the same instant, the rear window blows inward, showering the cabin in glass crumbs.

It doesn't look like Meeks has any intention of ordering Hendry to stand down.

Put distance between us. This is my first thought. My second is to reach Krauss and let her know exactly what's happened here.

On the dash, the police radio is spitting out hiss. I snatch up the microphone and hold it against the wheel. "This is Jake Olson. I'm out on the highway northeast of town. This is an emergency. To anyone who's listening, I need your help."

Something bangs inside the engine. The Mustang bucks, yanking the wheel from my fingertips. I drop the microphone and hold on. My foot is jammed hard on the accelerator pedal but the cruiser is slowing, losing power. Another metallic thud sounds and the dashboard lights go out. Unbelievably, the Mustang rolls to a stop—dead, killed by one of Hendry's lucky bullets—less than a quarter mile from Meeks and my abductors who, according to the rearview mirror, have seen the Mustang die and are now sprinting my way.

Waiting for them to catch up would be like signing my own death warrant. I have no choice but to abandon the car and run, feet pounding against the sparkling roadway. Adrenaline spurting as I head down the gradient at a pace.

Behind me someone hollers *"Stop!"* and something too small to see skips past me on the pavement, followed a second later by a whip-cracking gunshot. Out here on the highway I'm a sitting duck, I realize, and certainly no match for two guns and three angry pursuers.

Without slowing, I switch tack, aiming for the woods sloping downhill toward town. Something shrills past my face, cutting me off. Another bullet, followed by another crack of the whip. The tiny projectile *thunks* into a tree at the side of the road, splintering wood. I skid to a stop, then dart the opposite way, cutting across the pavement and hurdling the three-foot-high ridge of plowed snow on the other side road.

Despite the full moon, it's dark in the woods. I don't let it stop me. I pound on, wading through crisp snow, shielding my face from branches keen to claw out my eyes. It's the wrong side of the road, heading away from town, but there's no turning back now. I head uphill, leaving great gouges in the snow as I go. Even at night my footprints are easy to track, but there's nothing I can do about it. I know that beyond this rise lies the lake. And summer cabins are scattered around its shoreline. At least one of those cabins will have a working radio, or even some crazy trapper hibernating away the winter. If I can reach one of those lake houses, a telephone, or even a hunting rifle, I know I'll stand a better chance of surviving the night.

As I climb, a memory pushes to the surface. It's of Luckman visiting me in Duluth, eighteen years ago, as I sat out my pretrial wait from behind bars:

"This isn't a social visit, duckweed," he said with such force that his spittle pebbled the glass partition between us. "It's a warning. You come back to Harper, you die. Simple as that."

We glared at each other, neither of us giving an inch.

At that point, the St. Louis County Jail had been my home for several long weeks. Orange becoming my least-favorite color. Solitary confinement was keeping me safe, alive, stewing, but it was driving me crazy. My eighteenth birthday had come and gone without celebration. The lawyer, appointed and paid for by Lars Grossinger, had already informed me I would be tried as a juvenile, but sentenced as an adult. Aside from my Uncle Owen and Kimberly Krauss, Jenna's vitriolic brother was my only other visitor.

"I didn't kill Jenna," I breathed through tight lips, for the third or fourth time and feeling like a cornered rat.

Luckman's thin face was puckered, like he could smell something noxious. "Shut the fuck up, Olson. You can lie all you like. You've proven you're good at it. I'm just saying it like it is, is all. Doesn't matter what you say or how you try to squirm your way out of it. Doesn't change a thing in my mind. I know the truth. I know what you did to my baby sis."

"That's just it—I didn't do anything. I'm innocent."

Luckman came close to the glass, his voice low, angry. "Listen, you little piece of shit, I believe you killed my baby sister and that's all I need to know."

"But I loved her!"

He snickered. "Get a grip. You don't even know what love is. You think screwing around with my little sis for a few months makes you an expert? She couldn't stand you, duckweed. All she spoke about was how the sight of you sickened her."

Now it was my turn to be drawn to the glass. "You're a liar!"

His snicker ballooned into a smirk. "And you're a dead man, Olson. Come back to Harper and I'll take you to pieces."

Eighteen years later, Luckman's threat could be moments away from being realized.

I pause to catch my breath, work out the lay of the land. In every direction, black tree columns divide the sloping snowfield into parallel lines of alternating tone. My breathing is hoarse, brow lacquered in cold sweat. I can barely make out the highway a hundred yards downhill. Even less chance of spying anyone following. I strain my ears, listening for the sounds of men crashing through the woods and calling out death threats, but aside from my own panting it's deathly quiet up here.

I scoop up a handful of snow and pack it against the swelling on my cheek, hold it there until my lungs stop screaming. The cold burns. Then I keep moving upslope, weaving between trees, swiping aside bony branches as I go.

Fifty yards later, a break in the canopy reveals a snowy trail cutting diagonally across my path, glowing in the moonlight. Overlapping wheel impressions forming deep runnels. I follow them on heavy legs until I come to a spatter of elongated footprints climbing into the woods on the opposite side. Then I retrace my own boot imprints from earlier in the day, repeating the steps Krauss and I both took to Hangman Falls.

Chapter Twenty-One

When we were kids we made these woods our own. We carved out tracks from one feature to the next, drawing our own adventure map and redefining the landscape to suit our play. Hangman Falls was at the center of this imaginary realm. A sixty-foot plunge of thundering water, fed by the lake over the hill. To aid our world domination we cleared away loose rubble and tangled undergrowth from the shattered rocks shouldering the falls, creating primitive steps to the top.

I slow to a walk before I get there, stomach knotted, lungs aching.

A circular patch of disturbed soil marks my mother's grave.

In the moonlight I can see the snow is flattened and muddied around it, refrozen. Small piles of black soil where the Sheriff's Office has dug deeper, searching for clues.

While we frolicked in the falls, splashing and laughing on lazy summer days, she was here the whole time, a few feet underground, being invaded by roots and turning to dust.

Back then, I never felt her watching me. But I do now.

Darkness churns within me.

The makeshift steps are overgrown and clogged with snow. I haul myself up, grabbing handfuls of woody shrub in my manacled hands. My gloves are sodden, fingers numb. Barely a few feet to the side, the frozen waterfall drops into a black abyss, treacherous, seemingly bottomless. One misstep and it will be game over. I focus on the ascent, leaving the ghost of my mother behind. Then I'm clambering out into the shallower gully that connects The Falls to the lake, trudging through knee-deep snow, through thinning trees, lungs laboring as the picturesque view of rolling woodlands opens up as far as the eye can see.

Everywhere is still, silent. Gleaming ghostly in the moonlight.

I check my phone. One fluctuating bar on the signal meter. I try Krauss's number. It tries to connect, then drops out. With rubbery fingers I type in a short text, press *Send*, and then copy it to Lars's number. I have no idea if either text will get through.

Pristine snow slopes through a quarter mile to a flat white oval in the distance. The lake is completely iced over and coated in snow, the far side butted up against petrified woodlands that stretch all the way into Canada. A dozen cabins are dotted around this frozen shoreline, I know, but even in the moonlight it's impossible to pick out individual dwellings unless they are internally lit. Luckily for me one of them is; faint lights barely visible, off to my right.

I go for it. But wading through snow is exhausting, and by the time I reach the cabin my legs are sluggish, energy almost spent. The threat of hypothermia knocking at my door. I trudge my way around front, glance up to see a large hand-painted sign hung over the doorway. Black letters against a white background:

Krauss Outfitters

A renewed rush of hot hope fizzes through me.

This is Chief Krauss's place, I realize—home to Grizzly Adams and a two-way radio.

I hammer frozen hands against the door. "Chief, open up! It's Jake Olson. Chief! I need your help!"

With a creak, the door opens to reveal a male figure framed in yellow light.

"Glad you could finally make it," he says.

But it isn't Chief Krauss. And the air goes out of my lungs.

"Meeks? You've got to be kidding me."

He smiles a smile that is anything but welcoming. "Who were you expecting, Santa Claus?" Then he steps back, showing the firearm he's holding at hip level. "For a moment there we were thinking a bear had beaten us to it. We got the truck out," he adds in response to my stunned expression. "Won't you come in? Don't be shy. I promise the party hasn't started without you."

For a second I contemplate running. But I know I won't get very far before Meeks puts a hole in the back of my head. What I need to do is buy myself some time, keep him talking, engaged, hope that my text reaches its destination and Krauss comes to my rescue.

The inside of the cabin has been remodeled into a single cavernous room, lined with stock-filled shelves and racks of equipment. A wooden counter stands to the side, with a cash register at one end. Several colorful kayaks are suspended on wires from the rafters, together with crisscrossing paddles. A ladder at the back leads to the loft space where Krauss's dad calls home. Luckman and Hendry are loitering either side of a stuffed brown bear raised up on its hind legs. Hendry is sporting a big jagged blade and Luckman is holding the tire iron.

"How'd you know I'd come here?"

Meeks closes the door behind us. "Law of averages. Plus, you're not exactly the unpredictable type. The route you took only goes one way. Doesn't take a genius to figure out you'd head for the nearest cabin with signs of occupancy."

"This is the chief's place."

"I'm the chief."

"Whatever floats your boat, Meeks. You know what I mean. So where is he? He was never a fan of mine but he wouldn't subscribe to pack mentality."

Luckman takes a menacing step forward. "Who gives a fuck where he's at? This is none of his business."

"We're in his cabin. I'd say you've just made it his business. And knowing the chief, he won't be happy about it."

Luckman raises the tire iron above his head.

I don't even flinch. He won't take me by surprise this time.

"Hold it," Meeks intervenes. "He's right. Maybe we should do this someplace else."

"Yeah? Like where?" Luckman's eager to meter out eighteen years of revenge and won't be talked down easily.

"Preferably someplace we won't leave trace evidence."

"So we'll burn the place down when we're done."

It makes sense and I can see Meeks knows it.

"Got my vote," Hendry speaks up. "I say we slice and dice him right here." He takes a step toward me, brandishing the blade.

I raise my manacled hands. "Wait. Just wait a second and hear me out. I phoned Kim from the top of the ridge. She's on her way here, right now. She knows everything. Don't make this any worse than it already is."

But Meeks just laughs and pushes me forcibly to the middle of the room. "Nice try, Olson. Pity for you I know there's no cell reception out here in the wintertime. Which means no one's rushing to your rescue." With the gun aimed at my face he forces me to my knees.

Then the three of them surround me like schoolyard bullies.

"You're making a big mistake. All of you. I can prove I didn't kill Jenna. The killer's a member of Six Pack."

Meeks pushes me down with the toe of his boot. "Six Pack doesn't exist anymore."

"Just speak with Ruby Dickinson. She'll confirm I'm telling the truth."

"Ruby's dead."

I look up at Meeks, unable to hide my surprise.

"We received a nine-one-one earlier this evening. I went over there myself, right before I came out here. She overdosed—or at least that's what somebody wanted us to believe. I found a used syringe in her hand. The plunger wasn't fully down. I could see there were no traces of any chemicals in the needle. Ask me and I'd say someone shot her full of fresh air. So where'd you go, Olson, after you left the station with Kim?"

I went back to the house he shares with the woman he'd planned to marry, made love to her in a bed that was once his. It's an airtight alibi, the best, but how do I tell the town bully I slept with his girl without incurring his wrath and a bullet in the head?

"He was at your place." Luckman spits it out before I can compose an alternate story. "We followed them from the station. Waited down the street for over two hours before duckweed here came out. The lights were on and the drapes open the whole time. They spent most of it in the bedroom."

Something like a red mist descends over Meeks's face.

He doesn't ask me if I slept with Krauss; he doesn't need to, my cheeks are burning like hot coals.

"You son of a bitch!" He swings the gun and cuffs me on the side of the head. Electric pain flashes through my brain, vision spangling.

Luckman joins in and plants a boot in my stomach. The blow folds me in half and ignites flames in my lungs. He drops to his haunches, grabs me by the hair, and yanks my head back to face him.

"You know something, you weren't always number one on my hit list. There was a time I thought that dipshit brother of yours killed Jenna."

"Aaron?" It comes out a gasp. The thought is as alien to me as trying to think in Japanese.

For a moment I am catapulted back to The Falls, against my will, immersed in the dream sequence where I am standing at the rim of the ravine, with blood draining from my hands, heart beating so hard it hurts. Aaron is the least aggressive person I have ever known, but his competitive nature meant he never stood down from a challenge. When I lacked the balls to thwart my bullies, he stood strong on my behalf, and yet he never once landed a blow on my account. Aaron was solidly built, athletic, and could wear an unfathomable poker face. To get the job done, all it took was the promise of a swift and overwhelming response and my bully always backed down.

But Aaron isn't here now and I have three to contend with.

Luckman's breath is putrid against my face. "Yeah, he dropped off the radar round about the same time my sis disappeared. Weird, don't you think? At first I thought they'd eloped or something. My sister and your dipshit brother, having a secret affair. How about that, Shane?"

Meeks grunts something unintelligible. He is pissed with me for being in his home, for being with Kim. He's unable to compute the notion of Aaron being with Jenna, the same way he could never come to grips with the fact she was with me.

"But I guess if Olson's dipshit brother did have eyes for Jenna you'd have known about it. Right, Shane?"

"He didn't." Meeks's tone is flat. He's seething, roping it in and then playing it out in his head: me and Krauss, in his home, his bed. *Bastard.* "Let it go. Aaron was never a person of interest. We all know which piece of shit killed your sister."

Luckman's mouth turns down at the edges, his eyes dark with hate. He forces the tire iron under my chin. "So why'd you do it, duckweed? Why'd you kill my baby sister?"

I press against his resistance. "Why don't you ask your friend here the same question? We all know Meeks had a hard-on for Jenna. He was the jealous one. Don't tell me you didn't see it."

Suddenly, Meeks looks like he's got a mouthful of boiling water. "Zip it, Olson."

The pressure on the tire iron slackens off a little and I push home my advantage. "Listen to me, Luckman. Your sister confided in me. She told me she was scared to be alone with Meeks. She told me he tried groping her one night, when you were drunk and out of it. She had to fight him off."

"That's bullshit," Meeks growls.

"What's he talking about?"

"He's trying to deflect, buy himself time."

I push against the tire iron. "She showed me the bruises."

Meeks leans in and slugs me on the jaw. "Shut the hell up!"

Pain crackles and teeth clash.

Meeks recoils, shaking his fist. "You hard-headed son of a bitch!"

I spit out blood, unmoving; I've been hit harder. "Why do you think he was so eager to pin her death on me? This all happened the day before she disappeared. Your best friend here roughed her up. She came to me crying, told me she was afraid of him, that she was in fear for her life. We had an argument about it in school. I wanted her to go to the cops, but she wouldn't. She said Meeks was the cops and he'd make her pay with her life if she told anyone. So go ahead, Luckman, ask him where he was the night Jenna disappeared. I guess if he couldn't have her, no one would. Isn't that right, Meeks?"

Stunned silence fills the cabin.

Then Meeks steps forward and aims his firearm at my face. "That's enough of your bullshit, Olson. It's lights out for you."

For a split second reality drops a gear and falls into slow motion. The whole of my universe revolves around the black hole in the muzzle of Meeks's gun. It dominates the scene, in sharp detail, inches from my face, with everything behind it out of focus: Luckman at one side, doubting eyes directed at Meeks; Hendry on the other, keen to see Meeks blow my head off; and something else, something small and silvery, streaking across the room from the direction of the doorway, blurred by speed. Blink and I will miss it. So I don't blink. I watch the metallic object slice through the scene. It moves in a slight arc, toppling end-over-end, soundlessly, toward Meeks's livid face. I see it connect with the side of his neck, just beneath the ear. I see half of it disappear into his neck. Then the black hole in my vision shifts position. It migrates north, elevated as Meeks tips back on his heels. Lightning bursts from the barrel and thunder booms. I feel my hair part, heat scorch, ears ring, knowing I have escaped death by a whisker. But I am too busy watching his face, Meeks's blood-red face, mesmerized by unfolding events, as his bitter eyes roll up in their sockets like barrels in a slot machine.

Luckman and Hendry are slow to react: Luckman is still trying to grapple with the thought of his best friend harming his sister; Hendry is looking on, jaw slowly dropping as realization dawns. Meeks continues to tilt backward, stiff as a toppling statue. Briefly, his balance is in perfect equilibrium. Nothing moves. Then he crashes to the canvas like a KO'd boxer, and his gun goes skittering across the planking. An arc of frothy blood squirts from his ruptured jugular, spraying across Hendry's stricken face. Luckman is now looking past him, disbelieving eyes picking out the man hulking near the doorway at the back of the room: he's a bald African American as big as a bear, bigger, with both arms pulled back, as if ready to pitch two baseballs, simultaneously, imminently.

Then reality snatches up a gear and everything kicks into real time.

If Luckman or Hendry intend to fight or flee they are given no time to do either. They hesitate, which is always the worst move in any dire situation. The giant near the doorway doesn't. He pitches. Both arms snap forward like highly sprung catapults and two identical slivers of metal cartwheel through the air, hitting their targets with military precision. Luckman and Hendry collapse under controlled demolition, joining Meeks on the floor. The aim is perfect. The strikes swift and fatal.

Still, I don't blink.

The grip of a throwing knife juts out of Luckman's right eye. An identical one is wedged in the nape of Hendry's neck. All three of my attackers are down and ejecting blood at high velocity.

And my heart is banging in my chest.

At the doorway, the black giant produces another knife. This one's a mean-looking combat dagger with a jagged edge. Six inches of carbon steel alloy. Lethal.

Purposefully, he strides toward me.

Chapter Twenty-Two

From his vantage point high in the red elm the hunter had an unprecedented view of the frozen lake nestled within moonlit woods. He could even see an impression of Harper in the far distance, glowing softly in the dark, like campfire embers, but none of the actual buildings themselves.

He'd constructed several of these observation platforms over the years, scattered them throughout the wooded hillsides, each designed to give him eagle-eyed views of the most frequented wildlife trails. Each platform was an arrangement of seasoned planking attached to the tree in the basic form of a chair with a fold-down table, the latter part installed to provide a stable point on which to rest his elbows while sighting out prey. He'd lost track of how many hours he'd sat here or there, perched up one tree or another, patiently waiting like a cop on a stakeout for his quarry to take the bait, only for nothing to happen except for cramp or hunger to set in. But it never stopped him from repeating the performance night after night. Unarguably, there was a certain thrill to be had from hunting, but the real buzz came from being out here, alone, using his own skills to survive, to beat not just the local opposition but also the odds. Essentially, one man pitted against the elements, as though he were the last man on Earth.

He had no time for interlopers.

Although he never left home without his trusted Sako Finnlight mountain rifle, his preference for nighttime hunting was the crossbow, especially in winter. Compared to the springtime, the wintry woods were almost silent, and that silence called for a more stealthy approach. Noisy rifles had their place—there was no better means of taking down a deer at distance than the Sako—but there was nothing quite like the quiet flight of an aluminum bolt as it sailed through the air to catch its prey completely unawares. Couple that with a night vision scope and he was king of all he surveyed.

He had no time for intruders.

He was guzzling hot coffee from a thermos when he noticed the twin balls of light floating along the far shoreline. Typically, during the snowbound winter, nobody came out here after dark. The lack of street lighting, cleared roadways, and the unreliable cell phone reception were enough of a deterrent to keep lovesick kids away from the pitch-black picnic areas. Occasionally, other hunters from Harper and its neighboring towns came out here during the day, left their trucks parked along the lake road, and waded into the woods, looking for game and supper. But most of them were gone by sundown.

He corked the flask and brought up the crossbow. Through the enhanced scope the twin balls of light resolved into car headlights. A truck, bouncing along the far shoreline, headed in the direction of Krauss Outfitters. Out of curiosity, he scanned the sights along the trail until the cabin store filled the lens. In the night vision, the edges of the windows were brighter than the surrounding green-and-black, indicating the lights were on inside.

A mixture of surprise and anger heated up his chest.

He had no time for burglars.

He slung the crossbow over his shoulder and started to climb down the elm, feeling out the foot pegs as he went.

Chapter Twenty-Three

Composure is a weapon. I'm not a blithering wreck; prison fights have hardened me up, taught me the importance of the face-off.

In the early days of my incarceration, I was viewed as new meat for the grinder. As such, I was ground up and left for dead on countless occasions. What else could I expect? I was a pathetic kid convicted of murdering his girlfriend. One rung up the sewer ladder from a child killer. But I didn't let the beatings beat me, never had. I had no intention of dying inside, even though I was. Prison was my present but it wasn't my future. I wanted to survive, had to, for Jenna's sake. So I learned technique—the trick all scrawny fighters use to conquer their mightier foes—and once I pulled my weight and started winning every bout, I never had to prove myself again.

The giant striding toward me is built like a Russian tank: chunky angles and rustproofing. I've seen him before, but not recently—when I was young. Before Jenna.

Light glints off the blade in his hand.

On my knees, with wrists bound in front of me, I am defenseless. Those paddle-sized hands of his can snap my neck between thumb and forefinger before I know what's happening.

He steps over Luckman's twitching body and drops to one knee—still looming—and brings up the knife.

I head-butt him in the face before he can slice me open. It's an upper-cut and a move I've used before, in Stillwater. The top of my brow striking the underside of his chin. It's not a life-threatening blow by any means, but it's enough to daze him momentarily and give me a chance. I hear his teeth clack together as his head snaps back. I grab at the knife and peel it out of his loosened grasp. Then I launch myself again, with another head-butt, same place, and he slams backward onto the wooden boards with a resounding crash. Then I'm on top, straddling his broad chest, with the jagged blade pressed against his throat.

"You're the guy they call Tolstoy."

He blinks up at me. "That's right. The name's Warren Peets, but most folks know me by that nick."

"You were at my house when I was a kid."

Suddenly, I am seven again, impressionable, vulnerable, standing at my bedroom window with my face pressed against the cool glass, hot breath fogging it, occasionally wiping a palm across the pane to clear it. The memory feels completely real, present:

Raised voices are rising up through the floorboards of my bedroom to claw at my ears. The dominant voice belongs to a stranger, to a big black Goliath I have seen lumbering around town. The general belief among my classmates is that he is the last remaining descendant of a race of giants. Eight foot tall in his stocking feet, which are the size of skateboards. The rumor goes that he lives out in the woods and eats children, and so we maintain a respectful distance, scurrying to cross the street whenever he's around.

My seven-year-old cheekbone grinds against the glass.

I hear my father yelling, always yelling; furniture being pushed around; things being thrown against walls, smashed; vile curses and bitter oaths of retribution. My whole life to this point, and worse beyond. It's been this way for as long as I can remember. Lately, the arguments have gotten increasingly worse, with the violence bestowed upon my mother keeping the frightening pace.

Through all the din and destruction I am unable to make out exactly what is being said downstairs. I know it isn't good. It's never good. I press my face harder against the glass, holding my breath, squeezing every last drop of information from the smallest vibration.

Then the giant reappears, his shaven head gleaming in the sunlight like a block of varnished mahogany. Instinctively, I pull back from the pane, still not breathing, not daring to, afraid he might see me and if he does, come for me. He moves down the front walk on redwood legs, three strides and it's done. In one hand is a suitcase, seemingly as small as a book, in the other is my mother's hand, with my mother trailing behind like a ragdoll as he rushes her toward a waiting limousine. She's crying, trying to hold it together, coattails flapping. I hear my father ranting and raving from the doorstep, no doubt shaking a fist and condemning her to hell. But she has been living there for years. This is her escape. My pulse is quickened by excitement and fear. Maybe hope. There is someone inside the car, I notice. His legs are visible through the open door. Definitely a man's legs: black dress pants and polished brogues. I have no idea who they belong to. My mother drops onto the backseat and tucks in her feet. The giant closes the door and then shoehorns himself behind the steering wheel. The car's suspension drops noticeably by several inches. Then it's pulling away, speeding down the road from the house on Prescott. And the last glimpse I have of my mother leaving is through the rear window, her face torn between loyalties, run through with tears and streaked mascara.

"You took my mother," I growl, thirty years later, as I press the knife against the giant's throat.

"That's right."

"You killed her."

His eyes bulge. "Not so. I rescued her. See, I got your momma out of there before your daddy beat her to a pulp. I told him never to lay another finger on her, otherwise I'd snap every one of his in half and feed them down his throat, thumbs included."

A trickle of blood runs round his neck. We both know if he tries to throw me off or knock my hand aside the razor-sharp edge will inflict a lethal cut.

"So how did she end up dead?"

"That's just it. I didn't know she was until I heard it on the police scanner." His voice is deep and calm; if he's in the least bit concerned about my threat to do him harm, he doesn't show it. "And that's the God's honest truth. Same way I heard you were up here and in need of urgent help. Your momma was alive when I left them at Mr. G's place."

"Mr. G?"

"Mr. Grossinger."

With a start, I realize that Lars was the other person in the car that day. My mother ran away with Lars Grossinger. And, according to the ME, she was dead shortly after.

Steam rises in my belly. I lean on the blade. More blood runs. "Did Lars murder my mother?"

Thunder rumbles in his throat, gushing out of his mouth in the form of a laugh. "You got it all wrong, boy! See, Mr. G ain't the killing kind. Heck, he can't even bring himself to swat a fly! Why do you think he needs somebody like me?"

"You work for Lars?"

"Sure thing. And I believe the same goes for you, too. It's the reason I'm here. Mr. G sent me to protect you, boy. Look after his interests, so to speak. Now are you gonna let me loose or do we need to go get ourselves a marriage license?"

I stay put, thoughts tumbling over themselves. "Last question: why was Lars so interested in helping out my mother?"

"You mean aside from her working for the *Horn*, taking all those wonderful pictures of hers? I guess they never told you, did they?"

"Told me what?"

"It ain't none of my business to say, boy."

I press with the knife. "Make it."

"Easy." He wraps a big paw around my forearm and I realize he could snap my bones before I could do anything to stop it. "Mr. G never approved of the way your daddy treated your momma. For years he tried persuading her to leave, but she was married and committed. A headstrong woman, that one. Probably one of the reasons your daddy couldn't cope with her in the first place. Then one day something snapped and she'd had all she could take. She wanted out and Mr. G stepped in."

"But why him, out of everybody?"

"You really don't know, do you?"

"Enlighten me."

With ease, the giant known as Tolstoy lifts my hand away from his throat. "Because your momma and Mr. G were lovers, see, and had been for a long while, even before you were born."

The words sound like notes played off-key, tunelessly clanking one after the other. The thought of my mother having an affair with Lars even more so.

One of my last memories of her reemerges from out of my darkness, overwhelming the here and now:

Her breath is hot, sweet as candy as she leans over me. "Honey, I won't be gone for long," she assures me as I snuggle in my bed the night before she leaves for the last time. She strokes my hair, soft fingertips transmitting love. She often sits at my bedside, watching over me this way, protecting me from the monsters that lurk in the shadows.

"Is it my fault?" I ask tentatively.

"No, honey, it's not your fault at all. And please don't think for one moment that it is. Ever. I mean it, Jake. It's mine. And I'm going to make it up to you, I promise. Mommy and Daddy misbehaving the way we do isn't good and I'm sorry it upsets you. But I will fix things. I promise. I'll make everything better, for you and me. Soon we'll be starting a whole new life together and you won't ever feel this way again."

I wrap little fingers around her arm. "I'm scared; I don't want you to go."

She caresses my forehead. "Shush, cutie pie. It's okay. Don't worry. It'll only be for one day. I'll be back before you know it."

"Can't I come with you?"

Her smile slips but she soon hitches it back up. "Mommy just needs to sort a few things out first. Grown-up stuff, you know? You be a big boy while I'm gone, make sure you remember to take your medication?"

I nod my head against the pillow, against the damp patch from the tears rolling down my cheek.

She leans in and kisses me on the cheek. Her warmth is womb-like, the smell of her skin as uplifting as springtime blossom. I feel secure in her arms, always have, safe from all the world's cruelties, including my father's. "Jake, I promise I'll come back for you. I promise. For Aaron, too. Just hold tight. Can you do that for me? Can you hold tight?"

Another nod.

"I love you, Jake."

"Love you, too, mommy. Please come back."

"I will."

But she never does.

Lifeless, I stand at my bedroom window, day after day, watching for the same black limo to come rolling down the street, bringing her home.

But it never arrives.

I cry myself to sleep at night, smothering my sobs so that my abusive father cannot hear. My tears attract his fists. I keep out of his way, dodging bullets. In my mother's absence he has become a raving lunatic, cursing God and drinking himself into a stupor. Whenever our paths cross he clouts me with the back of his hand and screams obscenities at me.

"Bastard child! I wish you were never born! Get out of my sight!"

I do. But I don't understand any of it. I have already stopped taking my medication in the hope it brings clarity. My father has always been crabby with me, withdrawn, only ever looking at me down the length of his nose, treating me with contempt. This, however, is a whole other level of abuse. For my own well-being, I maintain a low profile, through the painful weeks and the lonely months following my mother's departure. Never a great length of time without one or the other eye blackened. Never far from a vicious beating or a spiteful tirade. Sometimes surrendering to the darkness, my only salvation. Unlike me, Aaron escapes our father's wrath. Aaron is the firstborn and can do no wrong. He is the sun and as such he is untouchable. His warmth protects me, nourishes me, but there are three years between us and we move in different orbits.

"We'll get through this," he promises me, time and again. "It won't always be this way."

But it is. It's unending.

As time passes, I accede to the fact that my mother is never coming back, that she has run away with the man in the limo, that her abandoning me to my maltreating father proves her promises are vaporous, that she has never loved me, that she is a liar. It is a bitter pill to swallow for one so young. But I get over it, eventually. I have to. I have no choice. I learn to adapt. I learn to avoid. I learn to soak up all the darkness and bury the hurt, keep it stowed inside, deep down where it can do the least harm. I learn to close my eyes when my father's fist strikes. I learn the suppleness of submission and the merit in retreat.

Increasingly, I learn to seek refuge in my darkness.

I learn to live without parental love.

I never see my mother again, in the flesh. I dream about her, for years after, about our final moments together, that night in my bedroom, but the dreams warp with time, like unseasoned wood, becoming misshapen and rough at the edges, until they resemble something monstrous, nightmarish. As I grow older the dreams weather and fade until they become figments of my past, a past buried under a mountain of denial. Adulthood further distances her memory, and imprisonment banishes it altogether. Then I learn that the skeletal remains wedged within the roots of an upturned tree are hers, left there almost three decades earlier by the hands of her killer. If that isn't shocking enough, now I learn that my mother loved another man and was probably cheating on my father even before I came along.

All at once I am struck by the unsettling notion that my father isn't my biological father after all, and that Lars is my bloodline. The shock is enough to crack open the chasm within me and let a lifetime of suppressed black smoke start the long rise to the surface.

———

"Was it really necessary to kill them?" I ask Tolstoy as he picks himself up and dusts himself down.

I keep my distance, keep the blade between us, just in case. My thoughts are in disarray, memories clashing and pulse pounding. I am not sure I can trust anything or anyone right now, including myself.

"Would you rather they killed you?"

He has a point.

"But you murdered the Chief of Police. That's not going to go down well."

He shrugs mantelpiece shoulders. "Flesh and blood, is all. Fancy title don't make a man." He wipes a hand over his neck and frowns at his fingertips covered in blood. "You cut me."

"You'll live."

"I wouldn't count on that happening."

"So Lars sent you here?"

"Like I say. When he heard you were back in town, he asked me to keep an eye on you, make sure you came to no harm." His eyes dart to the three slain bodies lying close by. "Case in point. Somehow I don't think they were members of your fan club. Mind if I take back what's mine?" He sees my stance stiffen and adds: "Relax, boy. I'm your guardian angel."

While Tolstoy retrieves his throwing knives, I sever the ties binding my wrists and peel off the wet gloves.

Then I watch, slightly horrified, as he wipes brain matter off the blades, dispassionately, as if he's done it a thousand times. The fact that it was either them or me comes as no consolation. Already, I am worrying what Ned and Nancy will think when their son fails to come home. How will they cope with the news of another child's death? What will they think if they discover my involvement?

Tolstoy picks up Meeks's discarded firearm, wraps a big hand around Hendry's thick neck and hauls him to his feet. "Excuse me while I fix this scene. We don't want anyone pointing the finger of blame in our direction." Then, holding Hendry upright with one arm, he aims the muzzle at Hendry's forehead and pulls the trigger. Just like that. Brains and bone fly out the back of Hendry's head and splatter all over a rack of camping gear. Unlike me, Tolstoy doesn't even blink. He drops Hendry like a bag of wet sand, grabs hold of Luckman's scrawny neck, hefts him into a vertical position and repeats the move, blowing his brains all over the counter.

"Isn't that a little like overkill?" I ask.

Tolstoy drops Luckman to the floor. "Best to make it look like they had a falling out and the chief killed them." He puts the gun in Meeks's limp hand and feeds his index finger behind the trigger guard.

"So who killed Meeks?"

Without evening stopping to think about it, Tolstoy picks up Luckman's tire iron and plunges the straight length into Meeks's chest, cracking through ribs and puncturing a lung. Meeks's body lurches under the force of the blow and a bubble of blood bulges from his mouth.

Tolstoy steps back to admire his handiwork. "Looks to me like the chief was fatally wounded in the scuffle. He fought them off as best he could before bleeding out. As far as I'm concerned the man died a hero. All we need to do now is to cover our tracks and get you back to town, safe and sound."

Tolstoy's idea of covering our tracks is to set the cabin alight.

Mesmerized, I stand stock-still in the ankle-deep snow, watching as the fire takes hold and begins to consume the log cabin. The flames will be visible for miles. They light up the surrounding woodland, throwing a gray pillar of roiling smoke high into the inky sky. Even so, no sleepy firefighters will be rushing out here to douse the flames. Not at this time of night. Not out here. When dawn arrives and they come to investigate, no one will question the burnt evidence showing that Meeks killed Luckman and Hendry—for whatever the reason—before finally succumbing to his own death by their hands. Meeks's abandoned Mustang will be found on the highway, riddled with bullets from Hendry's gun. My tracks will be found snaking up over the ridge and down to the cabin, and be mistaken for his. The investigators will think that Meeks was forced to flee on foot, only to be cornered at the cabin. Two and two will be put together and no one will fail the math test.

They would have killed you, a voice inside me says. *You had no choice. They would have put a bullet in your brain and buried you in the woods.*

"So what's the story with you and Lars?" I ask Tolstoy as he stows the empty gasoline can back in his truck.

"I fix things for Mr. G when things need fixing. Him and me, we go way back. Been over fifty years since we first met down in Louisiana. Mr. G was in town at the time, fishing tuna out in the Gulf. I was eighteen and wet behind the ears. He saw me gutting fish on the dock one day and we got to talking, him and me. Said he was impressed with my skills. Said I could handle a blade like a magician handles his wand. Next thing I know, Mr. G is offering me a job I can't refuse, including full relocation expenses and the promise of a bright future up here in the north. I moved to Harper the following week and never looked back."

"Were you in Six Pack?"

He looks down at me like I've just called his mom a whore. "Let's get something straight: ain't nothing for a man like me in any setup like that. Be easier for a black man to be the King of England than be in that kind of club."

"How about Lars?"

Curiosity thickens his brow. "Why you asking?"

"Because I believe one of its members killed Jenna Luckman."

"And you're trying to clear your name, is that it?"

"Something like that. It's the best lead I have." I don't say it's the only one.

"Well, I reckon I wouldn't be surprised one bit if that turned out to be the case. I hear they got up to some seriously weird stuff out there in Cody's hunting lodge. As far as I know, Mr. G gave it a wide berth. Sure, he likes his fishing and all, but hunting bigger game never appealed to him. Maybe you should be asking that uncle of yours."

"Owen?"

"Far as I remember, he was the big fish in that puddle. Nothing went on in that club without him giving it the yay or the nay first."

Owen? My throat is tight and it shows in my tone. "But Lyle Cody ran the club."

Tolstoy shakes his big head. "See, now that there is a popular misconception. Sure, Mr. Cody started things off back in the day, but it was your uncle who was the real brains behind the scenes. Nothing got by him without his say-so. If anyone knows anything . . ." His words trail off, eyes growing large enough to reflect flames.

"What is it?"

His mouth works wordlessly, then he gasps: "It's my back." And he twists, trying to see over his shoulder, to reach with a hand.

I turn him around and feel adrenaline flood my stomach.

Level with the top of my head is a long thin rod protruding from between his shoulder blades, at a right angle to his spine. Twelve inches of cold aluminum, glimmering in the firelight.

Beyond him, out on the lake, I can just make out the figure of a man in a camouflage jacket. He's standing at the midpoint, on the frozen surface, loading another arrow into a big crossbow. I see him draw back the string, take aim. Instinctively, I grab a handful of Tolstoy's coat and heft him behind the vehicle, just as the second bolt clatters against the hood and buries itself in the snow behind us.

"You've been shot." I tell him. "There's an arrow in your back and a guy out on the lake with a bow. I think it's Chief Krauss."

Tolstoy's breathing sounds ragged: "Think you can pull it out?"

I reach up and put pressure on the metal shaft, trying to lever it free, but it's stuck in tight. Blood squirts over my hand. Tolstoy howls and slumps against the truck.

With a loud clang, another bolt impacts against the metalwork.

I pull the giant upright. It's like raising a felled tree with my bare hands. "Listen to me. We need to leave here, now, or we're both dead. Give me the keys."

With a big paw, Tolstoy pushes me away. "No can do. Mr. G wants you safe and out of harm's way. That means dealing with whatever problem we have here. So don't cramp my style, boy. I'm not done yet; I'll take care of this." He smiles for the first time, showing black blood on white teeth. "Now go. Shoo. Get the hell out of here, fast as you can. I'll handle the chief."

Chapter Twenty-Four

Two months ago, and after almost a year of unremitting abdominal pain, Tolstoy had put aside his distrust of the medical profession, surrendered to his wife's pleas, and sought his physician's professional opinion. He'd exhausted all the over-the-counter medications. Popped enough pills to make him rattle when he walked. Nothing had worked. He'd even obtained some stronger meds from one of the town's more colorful junkies, but the side effects had made him nauseous, and had barely taken the edge off the pain.

Increasingly, when he went to the toilet, what little pee came out was predominantly pink.

The family physician had politely scolded him for not coming to see him sooner:

"These kinds of things are more responsive to treatment the earlier they are detected and dealt with," he'd said. "Persistent and untreated bladder infections have been known to lead to dementia."

Despite raising Tolstoy's blood pressure, the physician had told him not to worry unduly and had taken a urine sample to send off for testing.

"The results of the urinalysis will be back in about five days," he'd told him. "In the meantime, we'll get you started on a strong course of antibiotics, just in case an infection is at the root of everything."

Tolstoy had gone home, to take yet more pills and to put the problem to bed. Being 'big-boned' meant he was all too familiar with aches and pains. He'd had them all his life. Maybe the tummy ache, the weight loss, and the blood in his urine were just another phase he was going through, like getting old. Maybe there was nothing sinister to worry about.

But then the results had come back sooner than anticipated, and the physician had sent him to see a specialist. The urologist had taken more urine and blood samples and had performed a cystoscopy. Tolstoy had ground his teeth as the doctor had inserted a thin telescope into his urethra, poking around and chewing some lip. Then he'd arranged a follow-up appointment and the samples had been sent off for analysis.

"I'm afraid the news isn't the best," the urologist had told him matter-of-factly during the follow-up, without skirting the issue or softening the blow. "The lab detected cancer cells. Given your symptoms, and how long you've had them, it's possible we're looking at bladder cancer."

Tolstoy had been stunned. "I'm going to die?"

"Mr. Peets, we all die. But it's not necessarily your turn right now. These days not everyone diagnosed with cancer dies from the disease. Medical science has come a long way in recent years. Some forms can be successfully treated, even cured."

Nevertheless, Tolstoy had been horrified. "What about this form?"

"It depends on how invasive it is. If the tumor is superficial we can operate on it, remove it, then get you all cleaned up with a dose of intravesical chemotherapy."

"And if it isn't superficial?"

"Now that's a little bit trickier. If the cancer has spread into the surrounding muscles then we'll still operate, but we'll need to remove the bladder itself and put you in chemotherapy before and after. I'd like to get you in for CT scan sooner rather than later, if that's okay? What about tomorrow?"

"Good. Yeah."

In a daze, Tolstoy had gone home, fearful of what the scan might reveal, but even more fearful of telling his wife about the cancer. They'd been inseparable for over fifty years, built a lovely home together, and raised three wonderful children. The thought of putting an end to their perfect life was something he'd rather not think about.

"Men don't deal," a female friend of theirs had once said over lunch, in the aftermath of her own marriage's breakup. "They defer. I say screw them. But not the way they want you to."

The next day, Tolstoy had gone for the scan. He'd been nervous, not knowing what to expect. His sheer size had posed a challenge for the radiologists. They'd had him twisted and at all angles, just to make sure they'd imaged everything needed.

Afterwards, the doctor had called him into his office and had told him to take a seat, which was never a good sign.

"It looks like the bladder cancer might be secondary. There are other masses, mainly in the bowel, but elsewhere, too."

He'd shown Tolstoy several monochrome images on a screen, pointing out various anomalies in the pictures, white patches against gray, as if they'd mean something to him.

"But you can cut them all out, right?"

Solemnly, the doctor had shaken his head.

Tolstoy's stomach had turned over. "So, that's it, then? You're saying there's no hope? How long you giving me, doc?"

"The bad news is, even if you take things easy, you're looking at three months at the most. The good news is we can extend that to six months with intensive chemo. Tell you what we'll do, let me get you hooked up with our oncologist and we'll get the ball rolling."

But Tolstoy had declined. He'd seen the corrosive effects of intensive chemotherapy on his wife's cousin and vowed never to go down that road. In any case, it still led to a dead end.

And so he'd opted for quality over quantity, making the most of what he had left, while he could still enjoy it. He'd spent every waking moment with his family, turning down every job that came his way—all except those from Lars Grossinger. And only because he owed Mr. G his life, everything.

And now that it was coming to an end, he was determined to make his final moments count for something, to make Mr. G proud of him one final time.

You know what needs to be done.

Tolstoy waited until Jake Olson had backed away before hauling himself inside the truck and starting it up. Ignoring the pain slicing though his chest, he slammed his foot against the accelerator pedal. Snow and mud sprayed out from the wheels, rattling the fenders. The vehicle slewed on the unstable surface before grabbing hold and powering toward the frozen shoreline.

The pain in his back was immense—like somebody was using a power drill to bore a hole in his spine. Probably, the bolt had nicked a vertebra. His shoulders were on fire, pain pulsing outward from the point of impact. His breathing had become ragged and erratic, a disconcerting bubbling noise in his throat. Blood on his lips. A metallic taste in his nose and mouth. He wasn't stupid. He knew the arrowhead had buried itself in one of his lungs. He knew it was only a matter of time before the lung filled to the top, then started to aspirate into the other.

The front wheels bounced over the narrow beach, almost jarring the steering wheel from his hands. More unbelievable pain lanced though his chest. Then the truck was leveling out and fishtailing on the frozen lake, tires scrabbling for purchase. Tolstoy wrestled with the wheel and straightened it out. He had the chief in his sights. He could see him hunched slightly forward, aiming the crossbow. There was a loud bang, reverberating through the bodywork, and a fractured hole appeared in the windshield in front of him. More crucifying pain exploded through his chest. The bolt had cut clean through the laminate and burrowed through his shoulder, pinning him to the seat. The truck was doing thirty, forty, on a direct collision course with the man standing calmly in the middle of the frozen expanse. Tolstoy floored it, closing the gap. Another deafening bang sounded. Something flashed by his face, slicing through the flesh of his cheek. Another feathered hole in the windshield.

The chief was ten yards away, standing his ground, reloading the crossbow. No escape. He had him now.

Then the world tilted, suddenly, dramatically, without warning. The steering wheel came up and smacked him in the face, hard enough to knock out teeth. He had no time to react, to save himself from the abrupt impact. Momentum catapulted him out of his seat and threw him into the windshield. His head smashed into the glass and electricity crackled. The front of the truck pitched downward, steeply, lifting the rear end up off the ice and pinning him against the dash.

The truck had broken through the thinner ice at the center of the lake, he realized. It was going under, sinking, taking him with it.

Black water thumped against the windshield, gushing in through the holes left by the bolts. It spurted over his face, icy.

He was jammed in tight, one cheek wedged against the glass. He tried reaching for a door handle, anything to help hoist himself up, but excruciating pain held him back. The truck let out a metallic moan and tilted some more, almost vertical now. Icy water breached the door seals and sprayed into the cabin. The lights flickered and went out. Freezing water showered over him. He couldn't move, couldn't avoid the inevitable, couldn't breathe. Then the black liquid was rushing in, pouring over him, drowning him, and there was nothing he could do.

He grabbed one last bloodied breath as the blackness engulfed him. Then everything was calm. The cabin filled up with icy water, numbing him, taking away the pain, at last.

Suspended in the cold limbo, he thought about his lovely wife as the truck sank into darkness, taking him with it.

Chapter Twenty-Five

Everyone I know or have known, everyone I love or have loved, was either born here or died here. All inside Satan's snow globe.

I wonder if Harper will be my beginning and my end.

On tired legs I follow my own footprints, trudging up the snowy slope, away from the lake and the prospect of being slain like a fleeing deer. I don't look back until I am at the summit of the hill. When I do, all that I see are tire tracks leading to a black hole in the middle of the frozen lake, and no signs of Tolstoy, his truck, or Chief Krauss.

I keep moving.

The walk back into town takes the best part of thirty minutes and the best part of my remaining stamina. Repeatedly, I hold melting snow against the sorest parts of my face, reducing the swelling. I'm not overly concerned; it's been in far worse shape over the years.

Six months into my stretch at Stillwater, a knucklehead attacker had towered over me, wiping my blood off his hands. "Next time you get in my way I'll bite your nose off, bitch," he growled. He was a monster with a shaven scalp veined with tattoos. Sewer breath.

"If you know what's good for you, Olson, you'll do everything I say from now on. Suck my dick if I tell you to. You're my bitch now."

He'd caught me by surprise, in the washroom, smashed me against the tiled wall and then pummeled me to the wet floor with his sledgehammer fists. A mistake. I'd been educating myself, getting survival savvy and familiarizing myself with the body's vital points. And the taller they were the harder they fell.

My first strike was with my toes, curled like a ballerina's, to his testicles. The blow sent electricity discharging though his brain, folding him forward. While he was clutching at his busted balls, I jumped to my feet and knocked him down from behind. Then I planted my heel as hard as I could into the small of his back, from a great height, and shattering vertebrae.

The bully spent the rest of his sentence in a wheelchair.

It was the last time anyone in prison made a mess of my face.

By the time I reach Harper I am cold and wet and uncomfortable in my own skin. Teeth jittering. Hands jammed in my pockets and my head jammed up with thoughts.

According to Tolstoy, my uncle was in Six Pack. And if that isn't surprising enough, it turns out he was its leader, too. I didn't sense Tolstoy was lying, but I can't quite process the idea of Owen running the show. Not because the club participated in blood sports—hunting is in the genes hereabouts—but because of Ruby's revelation. It means Owen would have known about the sex parties and very likely participated in them himself. It's not only difficult to swallow, it's gagging.

I pass through the outskirts of town, keeping to the shadows.

Owen has always played a major role in the town's affairs. As far back as I remember he was an active city councillor, a stalwart of the community, and probably still is. Often, he was the loudest voice of reason against Lars Grossinger's propagandist take on the world. I know we all have our darker sides, but the thought of him excusing or even taking part in orgies with young girls is mind-blowing.

But I can't ignore the possibility just because he's family.

What's more, if Krauss is right and the last two unnamed members are the final victim and his killer, then either it means Owen's life is in mortal danger and I must warn him, or . . . my uncle is the murderer and I must confront him before he kills the final member.

And yet, for the life of me, I can't imagine my uncle being a killer. Owen is gentle, kindhearted, squeamish. Okay, so he has his faults like the rest of us, but the thought of him killing to protect Six Pack is incomprehensible—at least to my biased brain.

But isn't the thought of his participating in the sex orgies just as inconceivable?

My phone vibrates in my pocket. It's a text from Krauss:

Can't sleep. Missing you! Call me, SOON!

Two kisses and a smiley face complete the message.

My stomach sinks; she knows nothing of her fiancé's fate.

I check to see if my earlier cry for help connected. The message shows as a draft, unsent. I delete it.

What to do with Kimberly Krauss?

Krauss is a problem. I haven't decided what to tell her yet, about Meeks, or indeed how to tell her. I have stewed over it all the way back to Harper. Krauss is important to me, always was—even more so in the wake of our coupling. The last thing I want is for tonight's events to come between us. But that's exactly what will happen. It's as inevitable as night following day. Krauss is quick to denounce any feelings for Meeks, but she had them once, in abundance, and that kind of affinity is hard to shake loose. How can I play an instrumental role in the death of her fiancé and not expect a backlash?

The town is in a coma, everything deathly still. Moonlight and snow transforming the world into shards of black and white. I arrive at my destination, glance up and down the sleeping street before

211

moving silently up the long front walk to a darkened house. The door is unlocked. Quietly, I knock slush off my boots before letting myself inside.

The house smells of cooking and candles. I cross the reception hall and go into a spacious living room. In the silvery moonlight coming through the large bay window I can make out the shapes of furniture, couches, bookcases. I fumble my way over to the antique Wurlitzer jukebox standing in the corner and power it up. Garish red-and-yellow neon floods the room. For a moment I press my face against the curved glass, marveling at the carnival lights in the same way I used to when I was a small boy, spellbound, for hours. Purposefully, I select a track. The mechanism springs into life, clicks and does its thing. An arm places the desired vinyl record on the turntable and the needle makes scratchy contact.

Then I sink into a padded armchair, in shadow, with my phone set to audio-record and my fingers tapping along to "The Great Pretender" as its melody meanders through the house.

———

The Platters are deep into the second chorus by the time a light comes on in the reception hall, throwing a yellowy panel across the living room floor. Heavy feet sound against stair treads. Floorboards creak. A hand crawls around the edge of the arched doorframe, feeling for the light switch. The lights come on and a disheveled-looking man in his early seventies wanders into the room, half-asleep, hair mussed, his fleece robe pulled tight over his paunch.

He blinks when he sees me. "What the . . . Jake? That you?"

"Hello, Uncle Owen."

He floats into the room, grinding a fist against one eye socket. "Is everything okay? What are you doing here at this hour? It's after midnight. And what's with the music, for Pete's sake?" He goes to the jukebox and pulls the plug from the wall. The neon lights flicker and die, the music slows, stretching out notes, singers sounding demonic. He waggles a reproving finger at me. "It's a good thing your aunt is at her sister's, otherwise she'd be chewing your ear off right now." He looks me over, noticing my busted lips and broken nose for the first time. "My God, what happened to your face?"

"It's nothing."

"Nothing? You look like you've had a run-in with a windshield. Let me get you some ice." He goes to leave the room.

But my words hold him back: "I know about Six Pack."

He pauses, mid-stride, turns back to face me. "Six Pack? Now there's a blast from the past I haven't heard in a while. They were a pretty wild bunch of guys, if I recall rightly."

I keep my tone business-like. "Please, Owen, don't pretend. Don't make yourself look foolish. I know you were a member."

My disclosure flattens out his face. "Well, sure, I was a member. But that was a long time ago. You caught me off guard, that's all."

"You ran the club."

His head tilts back, so that he's looking at me down the length of his nose. It's the same stance my father adopted, right before he unleashed his rage. "Oh? And who told you that?"

"Warren Peets."

Owen bursts into forced laughter. "Tolstoy? Seriously, Jake? Tolstoy told you? Then there's your mistake. He works for Lars, you know? Which makes his word completely unreliable. Whatever lies he's been spinning, you can rest assured it's all designed to further Lars's cause."

"Ruby told me about the sex parties."

Now his expression buckles, like it's being pulled in from behind.

"She told me everything. She followed Jenna to Lyle Cody's house one night, the week before Jenna disappeared. She snuck up

213

to a window and saw Jenna engaged in sexual activity with four men and another girl. I know for a fact Ben Varney was one of those men, most likely Lyle Cody was, too, considering it was his house. I'm willing to bet Chuck Hendry was also there, given he used to rent out porn movies from in back of the barbershop. Now I'm wondering, Owen, if you were the fourth man."

Slowly, my uncle straightens himself out. All at once his cheer is gone, replaced with a coolness I have never seen in him before— only in his brother, and too many times. "You seem to know a whole lot about stuff you don't know nothing about."

"I know my coming back here has upset the apple cart. I don't think anyone ever thought I would, not for one minute, including you. They thought I'd stay locked up forever. And even if I did come out, the death threats would be enough to keep me away. I know you didn't expect me to come back here. When you heard I'd made parole you sent money so that I could start over again in the Cities."

"I was just trying to help out. Do the family thing."

"But then something unexpected happened: my father had his stroke, and lo and behold I'm the next of kin."

"Only because they couldn't get in touch with your brother. The authorities tried reaching him, but no one has seen or heard from Aaron since he left home. He just upped and vanished, like Erin."

My stomach clenches at the sound of my mother's name. "He's better off where he is."

Owen shrugs. "Maybe. Who knows?"

"So I returned to Harper, to sort out my father's affairs. And that's when the fun began. Whoever killed Jenna thought he was in the clear a long time ago, scot-free. But my coming back spooked him, motivated him to tidy up loose ends before I could learn his true identity."

"Sounds like you've got it all figured out."

"I do. I've been doing a lot of thinking. I've had plenty of time on my hands, remember? My theory is, the real killer never thought I'd come back. But once he knew I was in town, stirring up the pot, he knew I wouldn't stop looking for her real killer. He knew someone would talk, eventually. They always do. He knew I'd find him, expose him. So he silenced Ben and Ruby. Ben knew his killer. You and Ben were thick as thieves. He trusted you. He wouldn't have given your handling his shotgun a second thought."

Owen's eyes are defensive slits. "So you think I killed Ben and then Ruby? Shame on you, Jake. Ben was a good friend. The best. We've been pals since kindergarten. I'm gutted he's dead."

"You don't look it."

He tilts his head back some more. "How dare you come in here making these kinds of accusations. I don't even know where Ruby lives. Sure, she comes into the store every once in a while, but she's never once had a home delivery. I wouldn't know where to start. So how dare you."

"It makes sense."

"From which padded cell is that? This whole story of yours, it's all conjecture. Like one of those tales you used to dream up all the time when you were little. You practically lived in your own world until high school. You've always been a daydreamer, Jake. And you have no proof of anything here. Go ahead and ask me where I was when Ben died. Go on."

I raise my eyebrows.

"I was at the store, in the back office, talking with Walt Krauss."

"The chief?"

A smirk tugs at the corner of his mouth. "You can tell you've been away awhile. No one's called Walt the chief for eighteen years, but yes, he was there when all the commotion kicked off outside the bait shop. And before that I was serving customers, out on the floor, same way I do every Saturday, with witnesses to prove it. Jake, I didn't kill Ben, couldn't have. I didn't even know what had happened until afterward."

"What about Ruby? According to Meeks she was killed early evening. Where were you after you closed the store?"

Owen lets out a tired breath. "Do we really need to do this?"

"Just humor me."

"Okay. If I must. I was at the bar on McLean."

"I thought you were on the wagon?"

"I am. I didn't fall off, if that's what you're thinking. News of Ben's death knocked the wind out of me. I couldn't believe he was dead. With your aunt at her sister's house I didn't want to be alone. So I went to the bar to talk things through with Joe."

"Who's Joe?"

"The fact of the matter is, I wasn't alone. And I can prove it."

"Was the chief with you?"

"You mean Walt? No, not by then. He picked up his supplies and headed out before they loaded Ben on the ambulance. I stayed in the bar all evening and left for home around eleven. I've been in bed since."

"What about Jenna?"

His face scrunches up.

"Where were you the night she disappeared?"

"Why? Do you think I had something to do with that, too?"

"Just answer my question."

"I don't remember; it was a long time ago. I know I wasn't with her that night. And I definitely think I'd remember if I killed her."

I look at my uncle with fresh eyes, every bit of respect I had for him turning to stone. "But you did have sex with her."

"Yes."

Something turns in my stomach. It's an effort not to leap out of the chair and knock him to the ground.

"But it was all consensual. No one forced her to do anything she wasn't happy doing. In fact, she loved the attention, the stuff we bought her."

Now my fists are curled. "She prostituted herself for gifts?"

Owen senses my anger and settles onto the arm of a couch. All at once he looks every bit the frail old man. It isn't easy admitting to this kind of wrongdoing, especially to family and more so to the boyfriend of the girl he slept with.

"I guess it didn't seem that way at the time," he says quietly. "Like I say, no one forced Jenna to do anything she wasn't willing and eager to do herself, or suggest. She seemed so, I don't know, enthusiastic. Like she was exploring her own sexuality."

I feel sick to the pit of my stomach. "If that's the case, why was she going to throw off the lid and expose everything?"

He shrugs, looking genuinely mystified. "If she was, it's news to me. You're thinking that's what got her killed?"

"Consider it a work in progress."

"But there was no conflict. We all liked Jenna. There wasn't a shred of animosity among us."

"What about barbershop Chuck?"

"What about him?"

"For starters, he was into all those hardcore porn movies. What if he had plans on making some of his own, with Jenna, and she wanted out?"

The thought hasn't occurred to me until now, and I can see it has never occurred to my uncle. It should sound ludicrous but it doesn't.

Owen shakes his head. "The Chuck I know wouldn't go down that road. Sure, he liked his porn, but he was real gentlemanly with the girls. What you're talking about there is more like the kind of harebrained scheme Gil would come up with."

I sit forward. "Who's Gil?"

"Chuck's younger brother. You won't remember him. He got a job with a logging company in the Pacific Northwest when you were still just a boy. Gil's the reason we started the parties in the first place. He'd been seeing this girl from Babbitt for a while. She was sixteen. He brought both her and a girlfriend of hers out to Lyle's cabin one weekend. We all got drunk and one thing led to another. The parties became kind of an annual tradition after that."

Gil Hendry is the mysterious sixth member, I realize, which leaves me with no more members of Six Pack to pin Jenna's murder on. My stomach is tense with disgust. "So how many girls were there over the years?"

"I don't recall exactly. No one got hurt."

Teenage girls experimenting with their sexuality with older men, learning how to manipulate, to get what they wanted, fooling the men into thinking they were desirable. None of the girls traumatized in later life, for sure.

"Right from the start your dad told me to stop. But I wouldn't listen."

"My father knew about the girls?"

"It's the main reason we fell out all those years ago, before you were born."

Unquestionably, my father is a bad man—unholy in spite of his self-righteous preaching. But the thought of him knowing about his brother and his friends sleeping with teenage girls, and not exposing them to the authorities, doesn't just fill me with revulsion, it goes against the grain of everything he professed to stand for, to believe in. In his prime, my father was no saint, but turning a blind eye to something like this was beneath even him.

Owen rubs a hand through his thinning hair. "Your mom never forgave him when she found out he was covering for us. They were never the same after that. Arguing all the time."

"That's why she had the affair with Lars?"

"You know about that?"

"Tolstoy told me. He said Lars and my mother were in love and that's why she went away with him. Then she was dead, within days."

He nods. "Walt told me about the remains at Hangman Falls and whose they were. He was up there hunting when the Sheriff's Office were cleaning things up. He recognized your mother's purse. That's why he called into town this afternoon. He wanted me to know they'd found Erin. Jake, I'm sorry. You've got to believe me. I had my suspicions all along, but to get the confirmation was horrible."

Now I am on the edge of my seat. "You knew she was dead? You knew my mother was dead all these years? Oh my God, Owen! And you never once said anything to me when I was a kid! You let me go on believing she'd run away and left me with my abusive father. You let me hate her!"

His complexion is ashen. "Don't hate me for it, Jake. It was only a theory. I never had any proof to back it up. What do you want me to say? You were hurt enough already. Her leaving tore your world apart. Telling you I thought she was dead would have tipped you over the edge for sure. Like I say, I never knew for certain. I just suspected it. The only family your mom had was in Brunswick. After her leaving, your dad was a mess, so I called them several times on his behalf, but she never turned up. Even a year later, no one had seen or heard from her."

"She was with Lars." It comes out like a hiss.

"At first, yes. But not by that time. She only stayed with Lars for a few days, to get her head together. She wanted to come back for you and Aaron, but it wasn't safe."

"My father threatened to kill her."

"If he laid eyes on her again that's what he swore he'd do. All the while he was making threats and smashing things up. He even went to the Grossinger mansion and threw rocks at the windows. Walt told him to desist or he'd lock him up. Eventually, your mom agreed to an arbitration meeting, at Merrill's, to talk things through on neutral ground. Must have been five or six days later, after the fire in your dad's rage had died down a little. I was there, refereeing and trying to get your dad to see sense. So was Walt Krauss. She told your dad it was over and there was no going back. She wanted to move her boys out to Lars's place. Your dad said she could take you but she wasn't taking your brother. He said she was corrosive, a bad influence. He caused a scene. He even grabbed up your mother's purse—the one they found up at Hangman Falls, according to Walt—and tried to bash her skull in with it. Being the chief, Walt intervened and carted him away for the night. The last anyone heard of your mom was she was heading home to pick you boys up."

"Only she never made it."

"No."

Suddenly, my thoughts are whirling again, heart quaking. My mother had intended to come back for me, for us. But something—or someone—had stopped her along the way and changed my life forever.

"Did anyone ever look for her?"

"No. But I wish we had. We all thought she'd had a change of heart and skipped town. There was no evidence of her being abducted, least of all murdered. Like I say, I had my suspicions, but no proof. Your dad didn't want to file a missing persons report. He said she could rot in hell for all he cared. So I guess she just faded away."

Like a Polaroid picture left out in the sun.

All this time I'd hated her for never coming back.

But she'd tried.

The weight of my guilt is crushing.

"Of course, Jake, I did my best to watch over you, through the years, to make up for my brother's failings. You were such a sickly child. Always one malady or another. When your mom disappeared I made a point of spending time with you. We used to go fishing, remember? You loved to go fishing out by the lake. You loved the quiet, the calm. Those were great days, weren't they? You helped out in the store, too, during the holidays. You were always a pleasure to have around. A little introverted, shy, but on the whole well-behaved."

He leans toward me. "We never told you this, but your aunt couldn't conceive. Having you under our feet was good for her, for us. We thought of you as the son we never had. You were so fragile, we just wanted to wrap you up and look after you. When I heard you were being bullied by that upstart Meeks, I spoke with Aaron to make sure he had your back. When your dad was going through his meltdown over your brother and his plans to join the military, I asked Jenna to step up and take your mind off their bickering."

I straighten my spine, blink. "Wait, what? You did what?"

"I asked Jenna to help out. Jake, you have to remember you were absolutely miserable at the time. Worrying over your graduation and what was to come after that. Worried about Aaron leaving home, stranding you with your dad. You became isolated again, the same way you were after your mom left. It was a critical time in your social development. I wanted to cheer you up, make your life a little less grim. Jenna was already on board with the club by that time; it was no big deal to her. Seemed like the perfect fix. I pointed out my little nephew was down in the doldrums and she willingly jumped at the challenge."

Bitter discontent rumbles deep in my larynx. After hearing Ruby's revelation I had begun to foster suspicions about Jenna's true motive for being with me, but to get the confirmation is a double betrayal.

The awful truth is, Jenna had dated me out of obligation, to satisfy my uncle's desires in more ways than one. Not because she was interested in me. Not because she had any feelings for me. It's as though my whole life has been a sham.

"I did it for you," Owen says. "It worked, didn't it? She made you happy, didn't she?"

His words cut into me and I am gutted by them. My uncle has no idea. No concept that his good deed is the cause of all my woes. He makes Jenna's relationship with me sound like a task, or, worse still, a chore.

"Don't hate me for it, Jake. You're my nephew and I love you. We're family. We're all we've got. We need each other. I've only ever had your best interests at heart."

With vomit pluming in my throat, I get to my feet and rush for the door.

"Where're you going?" He calls after me. "Jake! Will you just hear me out? I swear on your aunt's life I didn't kill Jenna. But there is one other person who might know what happened that night. The other girl. She could hold all the answers you're looking for."

I pause with my fingers on the door handle, swallowing back puke. "Who?"

Chapter Twenty-Six

E very which way I turn, ghosts reach out to grab at me from the shadows. They follow at a distance, joining forces, whispering my name, slipping into the dark the moment I glance over my shoulder.

I don't believe Owen is responsible for Jenna's death, not directly, but I do believe his choices helped put the pieces in place for somebody else to kill her.

His closing words hammer through my brain like shots from a nail gun. His recorded confession is enough to blow the rumors about Six Pack out of the water and sink reputations. Their fate, their memories, are now in my hands. Unexpectedly, I don't feel powerful for it, just hollow. Their debauchery comes with consequences, victims: the girls, whose lives will fall under public scrutiny the second this gets out. Most will be wives now, mothers, with good careers, husbands and children, decent lives devoid of debasing sexual misconduct.

But the roar of the wild waits for no man. Right?

Mind racing, I rush along sleeping streets toward the center of town, blindly cutting through snowy alleyways, slipping and sliding over frozen puddles, mindlessly putting distance between me and my uncle's depraved world.

The darkness inside me is stirred, agitated. Monsters moaning in the abyss. Memories clawing their way to the surface.

I stop, gasping for breath, both palms pressed flat against the side of a building, as vomit gushes out onto the snow. Tears spring from my eyes and acid sears at the back of my nose.

"Leave me alone!" I bark at the ghosts lingering in the mouth of the alleyway. "I can handle this!"

My phone rings. A dog barks. I wipe goo from my lips, take a deep breath to settle my nerves, then answer:

"Kim?"

"Jake, where are you? I tried your home number but you didn't answer. Are you close by? I know it's the middle of the night, but I'm missing you like crazy here. Is that wrong of me? What do you think? Anyway, I guess what I'm trying to say is: do you want to come over? Shane isn't here, if that's what's stopping you."

Every fiber in me is suddenly yearning to be near her. Krauss is my keystone, my mainstay, the one person holding the arc of my story together. Whenever my world has been in crisis, Kimberly Krauss has been my savior. I need her to bring focus, to bring coherency to my chaos.

"I'm on my way."

"Hurry."

I reach Main Street and head for the solitary vehicle still parked at an angle outside the bait shop. My father's Bronco starts first time. Headlights illuminate the storefront, revealing a door sealed with yellow-and-black police tape.

The truck spits out fumes as I gun it down the road, heading for Krauss's place.

Chapter Twenty-Seven

When we were young, my brother taught me two valuable life lessons: never wager more than I was willing to lose, and never enter into a fight I couldn't win.

Meeting Krauss, knowing what I do, has me on an uneven keel. How can I explain Meeks's fate and her father's face-off with Tolstoy without condemning myself and getting wounded in the crossfire?

"Hi there, stranger," she says through a broad smile as she pulls open the front door. The silk kimono is gone, replaced by her day clothes.

"You headed someplace, Kim?"

"No." She raises a blonde eyebrow. "What makes you say that?"

"It's two o'clock in the morning and you're dressed for the outdoors."

"So are you, but I'm not asking."

"Except, I'm not wearing a gun."

She laughs her hyena laugh and bats my remark aside with a hand. "Will you stop overthinking everything and get your ass in here? For Pete's sake, you're letting all the heat out."

I step inside.

She closes the door behind us. "Come on. Give me your coat."

I shuck it off.

She hangs it on a hook by the door, then lifts up on her tiptoes and pecks me on the lips. "I missed you. Thanks for coming back. It's warmer in the kitchen and there's fresh coffee in the pot."

Holding me by the hand, she starts to lead me down the hallway. But I resist and swing her back around to face me. "Isn't there something you want to ask me about?"

Parallel lines etch themselves across her brow. "Like what?"

"Aren't you going to ask me what happened?"

The lines deepen. "Happened?"

"Kim, look at me. I'm standing here in your hallway with my face all busted up and you haven't batted an eyelid."

"Oh." Her mouth twists in the way I know it does whenever I catch her being evasive.

"Well?"

"Okay, so I can't lie, Jake. I know what happened, or at least I know the gist of what happened."

I keep hold of her. "How?"

A man's voice echoes from down the hall, in the direction of the kitchen: "Because I told her, Olson."

I turn to see Chief Krauss standing in the doorway. He's cocooned in snow-camouflage gear, a sheen of sweat on his balding pate. In his hands is a hunting rifle, pointed in my direction, white tape wound around its barrel.

I nod a greeting. "Walt. I thought you were dead."

"Sorry to disappoint."

"Sorry about your cabin."

"It's insured."

"So what happened to Tolstoy?"

"What can I say? He insisted on driving his truck straight to the bottom of the lake."

"With your arrows in him, no doubt."

"No doubt. It's the least I could do in return for him burning down my home, don't you think?"

"And now you're going to finish what you started and kill me, too. Is that it?"

He raises the rifle. "Unless you can give me one good reason why I shouldn't."

Kim pulls free and steps between us. "Okay, truce! I won't allow the two men I love the most to fight like this. Not only is it ridiculous, it's entirely unnecessary. Dad, this is Jake here. He's good people, remember? I know you're pissed at him, and I don't blame you, but hasn't there been enough killing for one day?" She turns back to me. "Jake, we just want to talk, that's all. Find out what you were doing up at the cabin. My dad's pretty precious about his business, and has every right to be, but he knows I feel the same way about you."

She doesn't know what happened to Meeks, I realize. Her dad didn't witness the events inside Krauss Outfitters, only those outside and from afar. But he knows Tolstoy and I weren't there to purchase a canoe. He wants to know what I was doing up there with Grossinger's hired hitman, burning down his business. They have no idea what went on inside, and it's to my advantage.

Walt Krauss motions with the rifle. "Okay. Come on. This way. In here. Let's talk this through where it's warmer." He sees my hesitation and adds, "Relax, Olson. Kim doesn't want me to kill you. For some reason she's got an affection for you and that's your saving grace. But I will shoot you if you misbehave."

I have no zip ties on my wrists but my hands are tied.

The three of us go into the kitchen, Kim bringing up the rear. I need to know how much they know, and so I'm happy to play along with their little charade, for now.

Walt waves me to a seat at the breakfast bar. "Sit. It's not a request."

I perch myself on the stool and get out my phone.

Immediately, he swipes it out of my hand and places it face down on the counter. "No phone calls, okay?"

"Sure, Walt."

"So let's get this started, clear up a few mysteries here. I found Gavin Luckman's truck parked round back of my cabin. And on the way down here I passed Shane's patrol car on the side of the highway, with bullet holes in it. I want to know what happened up there tonight and why it ended with my place being razed to the ground."

"Plus, I've tried calling Shane," Kim adds, "a number of times now, and he isn't answering. I know the reception up there is touch and go at best, but something's not right here. You need to help us out, Jake."

The pair of them stare at me through the same cold eyes. Father and daughter, cast from the same mold.

At this point I have a choice: I can level with them, tell them the truth, trust that Walt Krauss has a shred of decency still left in him, trust that he'll see that the killings were in self-defense and on the tail end of an abduction, trust he'll do the right thing; or I can fabricate and see what develops.

I loosen up my shoulders. "Okay. I'll try my best."

"Go right ahead."

"It's simple, really. I was on my way home, from here, from being with Kim, when Gavin Luckman and Ryan Hendry jumped me. As you can see from my face, they knocked me around."

Walt nods. "You're a big boy now, Olson. I'm sure you can handle yourself in a fist fight."

"Only Hendry had a gun on me the whole time. They beat me up and then bundled me into Luckman's truck. From what they were saying, I knew their intention was to take me out into the woods and chop me into little pieces."

"I told that jackass to lay off," Kim says through her teeth. "Jake, I'm sorry I didn't arrest him this afternoon. If I had, none of this would have happened."

I don't say that bad things have a tendency to happen around me no matter what preventive measures are taken.

Her dad nods. "So how does Meeks factor into all this?"

"My guess is he got wind of what they had in mind and came to put a halt to it."

"Meeks intervened?"

"Sure. He pulled them over on the highway right there and got me out. We started back toward town, but Hendry used his gun and shot out Meeks's Mustang. The thing died on the roadway, stranding us."

The chief looks skeptical. "I find that hard to believe."

"Why, because Luckman and Meeks were bosom buddies and so he'd never go up against him? Walt, you're forgetting one thing: they were blinded by rage and drunk on revenge. Plus, Hendry is a real bad influence. He's Harper's resident psychopath, remember? He had Luckman all wired up. They wanted me dead and buried, and they weren't going to let anything or anyone stop that from happening. Besides, their argument wasn't with Meeks. He just happened to get in the way. That's why Hendry only knocked him out cold and left him by the roadside. Then they carted me off to your cabin."

Kim's eyes widen. "Oh my God, is Shane okay?"

"I'll get to that, Kim."

Walt makes a disgruntled noise. "Why my cabin?"

I shrug. "My guess is they wanted to torture me first and needed somewhere secluded to dice me up. They're nut jobs. They attacked the police chief. Who knows what they were thinking?"

Kim looks concerned. "Okay, so what happened with Shane? He wasn't anywhere near the patrol car when my dad passed through. Is he okay?"

Her feelings for Meeks are deeper than she admits. I meet her gaze, keeping my expression blank, hoping she'll buy my story.

I have a nice yarn to sell. If I spin it out slowly, she'll catch the thread and run with it.

"It's like this: we all know Meeks and Luckman were the best of friends. They were a tag team, always were. I bet Luckman couldn't fart on the other side of town without Meeks sniffing it out. My guess is Meeks must have anticipated where they were headed, because the next thing I know he's bursting into the cabin, waving his gun around like Bruce Willis, and subsequently all hell broke loose."

Walt taps the muzzle of the rifle against the granite countertop. "Whoa, slow down there. Backtrack a little. You're saying he abandoned his car and came on foot, past Hangman Falls?"

I nod. "It's the straight line option. By which time Luckman and Hendry had already beaten me to a pulp and were about to start skinning me alive."

"What happened next?"

"They started arguing, the three of them. It got heated, loud. Tempers flared. Hendry came at Meeks with a tire iron."

"Oh my God," Krauss gasps, hand to mouth. "Is he injured somewhere?"

"Worse," I say without any emotion. "Kim, he's dead. Luckman killed him. He thrust the tire iron into his chest." I hit her with the sucker punch, full on, without holding back, without any padding to cushion the blow.

She recoils from it, eyes flaring wide, steadying herself against the kitchen counter.

"He's lying," Walt says. "Something's off here. I don't buy that course of events. Gavin would never hurt Shane. Not in a million years."

"It's the truth, Walt. Those two were acting crazy. Meeks didn't stand a chance. Once that fire's died down, you'll see the evidence will confirm my story." I stare him out, comfortably knowing that prison perfected my poker face.

"Son of a bitch," he breathes.

Now that I have them eating out of my hand, I don't stop there: "To his credit, Meeks managed to fatally shoot Luckman and Hendry before he died. Got to hand it to him, he was a crack shot. Got both of them in the face. It was heroic. And that's when Tolstoy turned up."

Kim looks stunned, teary-eyed. I don't feel sorry for her loss. Meeks was a bully. The world is a safer place without him in it.

Her dad wraps an arm around her shoulders, tries to draw her into him, but she shrugs him off. It's the first time I have ever seen her shun him.

Walt's wounded eyes rotate back to me. "So how'd the fire get started?"

"You can thank Tolstoy for that. I was all banged up. He carried me out of there and then went back and doused the place in gasoline, set it on fire. I have no idea why. Maybe he was following orders. I don't know. You'll have to ask him."

"Very funny, Olson. Doesn't explain why he tried running me over."

"You shot him, fatally, and he knew it. Even if he hadn't gone through the ice he wouldn't have survived. That first bolt pierced his lung and probably a major artery. Either way, you killed him, Walt. The evidence will show that, too."

"Then it's a good thing he's at the bottom of the lake, isn't it?"

"Which leaves you with a dilemma. I'm witness to an unlawful killing by your own hand and you don't know what to do with me, either of you."

Walt nods. "You've got this all figured out, haven't you? Well, I won't hide the fact I've never liked you, Olson. When you were kids, coming over to our place to study, I tolerated you for Kim's sake. God knows what she sees in you. To me, you'll always be that runt kid who ruined his dad's life. If it was up to me I would've put you down the minute you were born."

I force a smile onto my face. "Love you, too, Walt."

"As it is, Kim doesn't want me to do anything. She's all hung up on you the same way she's always been. Even more so now that you and she have gotten to know each other in the biblical way."

I glance at Kim. "You told him?"

She just blinks. Her face is blank, eyes filled with tears. She's still trying to absorb and process the fact her estranged fiancé is not only dead but also cremated, and I played a part in it.

"Kim and me, we've always been upfront with each other," Walt continues. "There are no secrets between us, never have been."

I force the smile again. "Well, I'm happy for you, Walt. Really, I am. You tell each other everything and that's fantastic. It's the way it should be between father and daughter. Congratulations. In that case, I take it she told you she was one of the girls who had regular sex parties with most of the members of Six Pack back in the day?"

———

It's one of those moments when the world stops spinning and people get off.

The statement is seismic in magnitude and the shock instantly shows in their faces. It rocks them on their feet and shakes them to the core, snapping Kim out of her mourning.

"Before you try and deny it or cover it all up again," I say, "let me point out I have it on good authority and from a very reputable source. My Uncle Owen told me everything. All there is to know about Six Pack, about who did what and to whom. I know Kim here was one of two girls who prostituted herself to the club, Jenna being the other."

Kim's diamond-bit eyes drill into me, but her dad is staring at her, face squirming.

"What's this, Walt? Don't tell me you didn't know? I thought you guys shared everything?"

"Stop," Kim breathes.

I don't. "According to Owen, your daughter here attended all the parties. She was Jenna's tag partner. That's right, Walt. She and Jenna were a two-girl team. In fact, I hear Kim organized most of those parties. Even introduced a little S&M to spice things up."

"I said stop."

"Walt, she had sex with all of them: Lyle Cody, Ben Varney, Chuck Hendry, plus my uncle. God forgive him. Everyone except you, of course, because that just wouldn't have been right. According to Owen, you knew about the parties but chose to turn a blind eye. They were your friends, but you didn't want to know. He said it was the only aspect of the club you didn't agree with. Said you never knew Kim was involved and prostituting herself to your closest friends."

"Please. Stop."

"I'm betting you don't know about her exploits today, either. About how she was in the back of the bait shop when I spoke with Ben, advising him to keep his mouth shut if I came asking. About how she blew his head off with his own shotgun after I left, just to make sure. About how she paid Ruby a visit while I was being detained at the police station, and shot her veins full of air to stop her identifying Kim as the other girl."

Walt's mouth is open, like he's in the middle of a scream, but nothing's coming out.

"I have to hand it to you, Walt, your daughter's a smart cookie. She had me and everyone else believing Jenna's killer was a member of Six Pack."

Kim's eyes are hard slits, cheeks florid, lips peeled back in a silent snarl.

"But that's not the case, is it, Kim? You killed Ben and Ruby to keep your involvement in the sex parties a secret. You were the other girl that night, the night Ruby snuck up to the window and saw Jenna with those men. Luckily for you, you were all wearing masks at the time, otherwise your secret would have been out a long time ago."

"Stop. Right now."

"Plus, you didn't want me finding out about your sordid sexploits, because that would have ruined any chances of you and me being together on a permanent basis. And that's what you've wanted all along, isn't it, Kim? I bet you were overjoyed when you heard I was coming back to Harper. Suddenly you had a chance to start a brand new life, with me, take up where things left off a lifetime ago. And yet, how could I be with you when you've been with my uncle? It's disgusting, right? Unthinkable. It makes me sick just knowing it."

Kim's hand moves to her hip and comes back up with her gun in it, aimed at my stomach. "I said stop!"

My next words are aimed at her dad, but my eyes remain locked on hers. "I didn't see it at the time, back when we were seventeen. I was young and blinded by what I thought was true love for Jenna. But Kim wanted to be more than friends, even then. Neither of us were anything to look at. No one was interested in us apart from us. Kim made a point of our spending every waking moment together. We grew close, real close. We were like lovers without the intimacy. I never knew then, but I know now that she wanted our friendship to go the next step."

"Jake! Stop!" Tears are leaking from the corners of Kim's eyes.

"Then Jenna came on the scene and Kim was insanely jealous. Again, she hid it from me and I never even guessed. She wanted me for her own and couldn't live with the idea of Jenna imposing herself on us the way she did, splitting us apart like that. How dare she come along and do such a thing, right? Especially when the two of them were a team elsewhere, during their Six Pack orgies."

The gun shakes in Kim's hand. More tears roll. Her finger curls around the trigger.

"When I started spending more time with Jenna than with her, it was the final straw. I don't know exactly how it happened. One thing that being locked up twenty-three hours a day has given me is a good imagination. I imagine Kim lured Jenna somewhere quiet, secluded, that night she disappeared. Maybe she told her it was something to do with Six Pack. I know she told you she was with me, Walt. At first I thought that was to give me an alibi. But it was to give her one. I imagine she told Jenna what her plans were for her and me, about how she wanted exclusivity, and for her to back off. I can imagine Jenna not being too fond of the idea, especially given the fact she was doing my uncle a favor by dating me. I imagine one thing led to another. Things got out of hand. There was a fight. And then—"

"STOP!"

Thunder booms inside Krauss's kitchen. Lightning flashes and strikes me in the gut, through the flesh just under my ribs, and into the wall behind. At first there is no pain, just a disconnected sensation of spreading warmth. I look down to my side, at the blood starting to spread on my shirt. Then, through disbelieving eyes, I gaze up at Kim, to see my shock reflected in her face.

Behind her, the slightest wisp of vapor rises from the muzzle of her dad's hunting rifle.

"You've said more than enough, Olson," he growls. "One more word from you and the next one's through the heart. Mercy kill."

I smile. "Chief Krauss protecting his daughter, just like always. Willing to kill for her. It's sweet. Now that's the kind of father I'm talking about." I press a hand against the leaking hole in my side. "One last thing, Walt—did you cover things up? Is that why you and Meeks were so keen to pin her death on me? Did you know Kim killed Jenna? Not to protect her secret but to keep me for herself?"

Walt Krauss raises the rifle and aims it at my chest. "One more goddamn word," he breathes.

I snatch up my phone and slide to my feet. "It's been fun catching up." The world spins. I grab at the countertop to steady myself. Kim drops her gun and reaches out. But I push her hands aside, push past her, aiming for the hallway and outside.

"Please, Jake!" she calls as I stagger toward the front door. "Let me explain? Please! Come back!"

But there's no coming back, not from this, for either of us.

I hear her try to rush after me, but her dad grapples with her, holding her back.

I grab my coat and someone else's scarf and burst through the door, out into the starlit night.

Chapter Twenty-Eight

E very window blazes with light in the Grossinger mansion, illuminating the snow-covered grounds and the frozen fountain sitting in the middle of the lollipop driveway. No need to get worked up over a huge electricity bill when you're the richest man in Harper.

I climb out of the Bronco, stiffly, one hand pressing my coat against the bloody patch under my ribs. Walt's bullet is a through-and-through. It's torn a nasty hole in my side, but I don't think it's struck a major organ. I've lost some blood, but I've packed the wound with the scarf, and think I have it covered. I stab a blood-ied thumb against the doorbell, hold it there, annoyingly, while it rings out.

Thirty seconds later, half the double-door opens to reveal the man himself, Harper's homegrown marvel: Lars Grossinger.

He looks me up and down with twinkly blue eyes. "So, the prodigal son returns. And looking worse for wear. Are you okay, son? I got to say you don't look it. Do you need me to call you a doctor?"

"It won't be necessary. Can I come in?"

"Sure." He waves me inside. "Be my guest."

The entrance hall is as big as the house on Prescott. Polished wooden floors, sweeping staircases, and palatial chandeliers.

I follow him into a study. The dimly lit room is warm and wood-paneled, heated by a real log fire crackling away in a stone hearth. Walls crammed with books and souvenirs from foreign expeditions. Artistic black-and-white photographs of Harper, its townsfolk, rural living, all taken by Erin Olson, my mother.

He waves me toward a leather chair. "Please, Jake, sit down. Take the load off your feet. You look like you've done five rounds with Mike Tyson."

"I'll stand, thanks."

"Okay. Have it your way. Can I get you a drink? Something stiff to warm you up?"

"No, thanks."

He sits down behind a big wooden desk, props his elbows on the leather inlay. "So, Jake, it's three o'clock in the morning. Good thing I'm pretty much a total insomniac these days. I take it you've got something for me, and that something is so marvelous it can't wait until Monday."

"It'll put your beloved *Harper Horn* back on the map."

"I'm listening."

I get out my phone. "On here are several taped conversations: one from Ruby about Jenna being sexually involved with Six Pack; one from my uncle, revealing how Six Pack held regular sex parties with teenage girls; and one from Kim and her dad, about her killing Jenna out of jealousy. For the record, I believe she also killed Ben and Ruby to keep her secret safe." I slide it across his desk. "You'll find my own confession on there, too, including the killings up at the lake."

Both of his bushy eyebrows hike themselves up his brow. "More murders?"

Cherry-picking my words, I recount the night's events, culminating in the fire at Krauss Outfitters.

238

"So there's your blessed story, Lars. It's bigger than you expected. Play it right and it'll be statewide within a day and nationwide by the end of the week."

He picks up the phone as though it's a bar of gold. "Son, I'll be honest, I'm at a loss for words. And that's something you don't hear from me every day of the week. Jake, you've done me proud. Great job. I knew you'd come through. I had every faith you would." He pulls open a drawer in his desk, drops the phone inside, then brings out a small metal lockbox. "Here, let me double your retainer. No, triple it."

I hold up a halting hand. "Lars, I don't want your thirty pieces of silver."

He opens the box. "Don't be a martyr, son. You've earned this and more."

"Give it to your favorite charity." I backpedal toward the door, shaking my head as I go. "I don't want your blood money."

He rises to his feet and throws me a questioning frown. "What's going on here? I don't expect you to work for nothing. If your story holds up, then this is going to be huge. Explosive. We're in this together, son. Whichever way you slice it, you and me, we're a winning team."

I stop and stare at him from under a heavy brow. "Jesus, Lars. Were you ever going to tell me?"

"Tell you what, son?" His expression is cast-iron, no give.

He knows exactly what I'm referring to, knows I'd ask this question, eventually, once I was back home and snooping. He's had over thirty years to perfect his reaction, to prepare for this line of enquiry.

"You mean about me and your mother?"

"No, Lars. About you being my biological father."

He raises his hands. "Ah. You got me there."

"That's why my father hated me from the moment I was born. He found out my mother was sleeping with you and knew I wasn't his. That's why I look nothing like the rest of the Olson bloodline. I look like you, don't I? That's why you hired me a hotshot lawyer and tried getting me out of those murder charges. Not because you owed it to my mother's memory, but because you knew I was your son."

His mouth tilts to one side, threatening to let his bone china expression slide off and smash on the floor. "You think you have me dead to rights. But the truth is there was never any confirmation, Jake. Your mother was confident I was your father, but we never got around to a paternity test." He sees my glower darken and adds, "What do you want me to say?"

"That you're sorry."

"For what? For loving your mother and for fathering you? I won't apologize for either."

"No, Lars, for failing to stand up and be counted when I needed you the most. You knew I had issues. You knew what my father was like. You knew my childhood was damaging. You could have stepped in at any point and changed it."

"Except for the fact your mother didn't want me to."

"Bullshit!"

"It's the truth, son."

I snicker. "Here we go again. Same old crazy. Lars and the truth, pitted against the world."

He shakes his head. "It wasn't like that. Your mother wanted to do things in her own time, her way, and I respected her decision. She was a woman of honor, integrity. She meant the world to me. I was devastated when she disappeared."

But not nearly as much as me.

"Didn't you ever wonder what happened to her?"

He sighs. "Son, contrary to popular opinion, I'm not a complete monster. Sure, I can be dogmatic at times. But that's a requirement of my job. Your mother's disappearance hit me hard. It haunted me every damn minute of every damn day, for years. I spent weeks looking for her. Calling in every favor I was owed. I even had every-one in her life investigated, but nothing turned up. Not one thing. It was as though she just vanished into thin air."

"Then I showed you that photo on my phone, of the skeleton up at Hangman Falls, and you knew, didn't you? No wonder you looked like you'd seen a ghost. You knew it was her. And yet you didn't say anything. Not one word. You just let me go on think-ing it was Jenna."

"I wanted to be sure."

"No, Lars. You're a coward. You hide behind the *Horn* and use heavy-handed tactics to get your way. Hiring someone like Tolstoy to do your dirty work proves you're spineless. The real reason you didn't intervene when I was a kid is because it would have interfered in your little megalomaniacal plan for Harper domination. I was dead weight. A hindrance. The last headline you wanted anyone to read was the news you had a bastard child."

My words are fierce, but Lars doesn't cower from them.

Instead, he shakes his head, "I know how it looks, son. But it wasn't like that. Behind the scenes, I did my best for you."

"You did nothing for me. All your money and connections didn't get me off that murder rap. I went away for eighteen years—*for a crime I didn't commit*—while you went about your business printing lies and selling them. You probably never thought about me again."

"Son . . ."

"Don't call me that!" The wound in my side flares with pain. I wince and catch my breath. "I'm not your son. You have no right thinking I am. You want to know the truth, Lars—seeing as how you're so precious about defending it?"

"I'm all ears."

"My father might have abused me and treated me like vermin, but at least he was *there,* which is more than can be said for you.

Do you get that? You abandoned me, Lars, just like my mother did. So print your prized story. Watch it go viral. Make a name for yourself outside of Harper. I hope it's all worth it."

Before he can respond, I turn on my heel and leave.

Even with his cane, he has time to come rushing after me, to call me back, to plead with me to believe his version of the truth one final time, to promise to make amends for his role in my wasted life. But I don't hear another word from him. Nothing. And I climb back inside my father's Bronco, knowing that biology doesn't buy loyalty.

Wheels spew out slush as I gun the truck down the driveway. I have one last thing to do before I can rest, and the thorn-filled darkness within me is almost at the surface.

Chapter Twenty-Nine

While I've been away, the Harper Community Hospital has undergone a major renovation: out with the blue carpet tiles, the teak veneer, and the dowdy pink paintwork—in with the beechwood, chrome fixtures, and high-shine vinyl floors. It's all new, fancy, but it still smells of disinfectant and death.

"Someone left me a message," I tell the silver-haired woman seated behind the horseshoe-shaped reception counter.

We're alone. The place is quiet, dead. Hardly any hospital employees scuttling around at this time of the night. Patients dosed up and dozing. For a second she studies my pulped face—my general thuggish appearance, my pale and sweaty pallor, the dried blood on my collar and down the front of my coat—unsure whether to call security or a nurse.

I smile awkwardly.

"What name is it?" she asks.

"Jake Olson. I think it was a Dr. Townsend who left the message on my answering machine? Maybe a day or two ago? She said she was here, working nights, all weekend, and that I should call and speak with her."

The receptionist's eyes scan a computer screen. "Here we go. Follow the red line down the hall. It's the fifth door on your left. Room one-eleven."

"Thank you."

A woman's voice answers with a *"Come in"* as I rap knuckles against the specified door.

"Dr. Townsend?" I say, entering.

"Yes? Can I help you?"

She's a small brunette with soft features and chestnut eyes. She's sitting behind a desk, inputting patient notes into a computer terminal. She's a few years younger than me, maybe enough for her not to remember the murder of Jenna Luckman and who was convicted for it.

I reach out a hand. "Jake Olson. I got your message. I'm here about my father."

She accepts the handshake. Her fingers are delicate but their grip is strong. "Oh, yes. Thanks for coming over. Nice to meet you, Jake. Please, take a seat. I know it's early, but can I offer you a coffee?"

"No, thanks. I'm good." It's a lie. I look anything but good. I look like somebody with a bullet hole in their belly. She knows it. If she could see the bloodstains beneath my coat she'd have me admitted in a heartbeat.

"Rough night?"

"Something like that."

She nods out of courtesy rather than belief. "You need a stitch or two, on your forehead, near the hairline. Maybe some analgesics?"

"I'll survive."

My words don't persuade her, but she doesn't argue the point. We seat ourselves on opposite sides of her desk. On its busy surface is a coffee mug with the words *I Heart Heart Surgeons* on it.

"Jake, do you want to talk about what happened to your face, and why you look like death warmed up?"

"No."

"Okay. Maybe later, then?"

"Maybe." I shift my weight on the chair, wince at the stabbing pain in my side, one hand pressing at the wound.

"Did the administrator who contacted you in the Cities tell you in any detail about what happened?"

I shake my head. A week ago, the hospital contacted the prison. The prison put them in touch with Denis Flannigan, my PO. He relayed their news, secondhand.

"What I got was sketchy, at best. They mentioned some kind of a stroke?"

She nods. "A ruptured aneurysm, to be exact. It's when a swelling in a blood vessel puts too much pressure on the weakened wall, resulting in a bleed. In your father's case, he suffered what we call an intracranial aneurysm in one of his cerebral arteries. It's a mouthful, I know. The translation is, it's critical. We don't have the facilities here to cope with that kind of an emergency. Your father was airlifted to the Regions Hospital at St. Paul for specialized treatment. He underwent neurosurgery to repair the damage and was returned to us, Friday morning, for convalescence. We would have contacted you sooner, but he didn't have you listed as his next of kin. We tried contacting your brother but were unsuccessful."

My father had spent the best part of last week in St. Paul, within spitting distance of me and my job at the mall, and I never knew.

She leans forward. "Jake, I'll be brutally honest with you, your father's condition isn't rosy. Right now he's stable, but his outlook is very poor. What I am about to say is probably very difficult for you to hear, to accept."

"His insurance ran out."

She looks startled. "No, and I wish that were it. The money isn't an issue here; your father's hospital expenses have all been taken care of by a third party. It's where we go from here that we need to work

245

out. What happens next, after this meeting." She sees the crease dividing my brow and adds, "Maybe it would be best just to show you what I mean."

‿‿‿‿‿‿‿‿‿‿

Great men change the world. Great men win respect and loyalty and make a positive difference in the lives of those around them. Great men are measured by the scale of their good deeds. Great men have nothing in common with my father.

On heavy feet, I follow Dr. Beth Townsend to his dimly lit room at the end of a quiet ward. It smells faintly of him: musky, with traces of Marlboro Red. The only illumination is from silvery moonlight seeping around the edges of the window blind. The reduced lighting makes the readings on his monitors all the more vivid, real. I have not seen my father in eighteen years and my stomach is in knots, but not from excitement.

He is flat on his back in the bed, arms straight at his sides, as though he's standing at attention, lying down. Wires connect him to machines. Soft bleeps and spiking lines. A tube runs from his mouth to a medical ventilator, allowing breathable air to be pumped in and out of his lungs. Under the linens, his chest rises and falls, rhythmically, keeping pace with the mechanical respirator.

His eyelids are closed but I feel his mean stare burning into my soul.

The gravity of his situation draws me closer.

He's aged, radically. The sockets of his eyes are dark-rimmed craters on a lunar landscape, overshadowed by the angular bluntness of his nose. He resembles somebody in the late stages of cancer: gray skin draped over brittle bone. The leftovers from his brain surgery are visible through the prickly gray fuzz coating his scalp. Everything colorless, stiff, like he's carved from a plank of silvered wood.

This is the calmest I have ever seen my father.

Dr. Townsend lingers at the door, voice hushed. "It was a major rupture. Most people don't survive that kind of bleed. They die then and there. He's been in a coma ever since."

"Can he hear us?"

"It's a possibility."

"Will he pull through?"

"No."

I glance at her.

"I'm sorry, Jake. They tried their best. The repair was a success but the damage was already done. I'm afraid this is as good as it gets."

Her words ought to quake me at the knees, make me break down in tears, have me trash the place and plead with God to give my father a second chance, miraculously return him to life so that we can reconcile and finally have the relationship we never had. But he's not that kind of dad and I'm not that kind of son.

"So what happens next?"

"Medically speaking, we have two clear choices: we can keep him on life support indefinitely, providing his organs don't fail, or . . ."

"You unplug him."

She lets out a quiet breath, "Like I say, Jake, I'm sorry. I know this isn't the prognosis you were hoping for. This is the worst news ever, and I hate that I'm having to tell you. There's no immediate rush to make a decision either way. We can accommodate whatever you decide. As I say, the treatment cost is taken care of, but there will come a time when artificially maintaining your father's life becomes counterproductive. As clinicians we have a duty of care to save life, but as realists we know there's a tipping point." She opens the door. "Look, I'll leave you with your dad for a while. I'll be in my office when you're ready."

"Thanks."

She closes the door and suddenly I am on my own with my father, left with the choice between keeping him here inside a living hell or sending him to the real one.

All my life he was more powerful than me, bigger, tougher, stronger. Now he's just a shell, fragile and weak, and I have all the power.

It doesn't make me feel victorious.

I want so much to scream at him, to shake sense into him, to berate him for being a terrible dad, for despising me for my biology and for never finding a morsel of love in his heart for me. But he's just a shadow, almost a ghost, and I can't bring myself to be like him.

Stooped with pain, I pull up a chair and sit at his side, take his hand in mine. His skin is cool to the touch, waxy—not much different than my own. This will be the first and last time I hold his hand. Gently, I squeeze his bony fingers. He doesn't squeeze back. This spindly old man is not my dad, but he's the only one I have ever known.

There's a leather-bound Bible on the trolley-table, gold-edged pages, dog-eared and well-used. Rosary beads curled around it. A *Thinking of You* card with the Virgin Mary on the front, nursing baby Jesus, my uncle's handwriting visible on the inside. Now that I look, there are more cards stuck to the walls behind the bed. A mosaic of color. Dozens of well-wishes, children's paintings, hopes for miracles.

Despite his drinking, my father was a popular pillar of the community, loved, respected, worshipped. In public, he wore his cloth with pride, hiding behind heavenly virtues that were never his. In the privacy of our home he was demonic.

If only they knew him the way I knew him.

I cup his hand in mine and bow my head—but not to pray. No amount of prayer can save his soul, or mine. If God exists then my father will never meet him, and neither will I.

Eighteen years ago, my prison counselor told me to save my confession for my priest. I have waited patiently all this time, holding my own, biting my tongue, pressing down on the black smoke churning away inside of me.

No more. The time has come to let go.

For here lies my minister: Senior Pastor Olson of the Harper Community Church and former navy chaplain. At my fingertips.

"Father," I begin, "I have a confession to make."

I clamp my eyes closed and I am instantly transported back in time:

It's the evening Jenna disappeared. My father and Aaron have been arguing for days. My father has always wanted Aaron to join the ministry, but he's leaving for the military, mind made up and no way to change it. Neither of us want him to go, most of all me. It's the first and last time my father and I will ever agree on anything. He's said some vile things to Aaron. Hurtful words that are hard to come back from and normally reserved only for me. Aaron has stormed out. My father is seeking solace in the bottom of a bottle. I catch up with my brother in the backyard, pleading with him to have a change of heart, for my sake.

"Don't leave me alone with him," I beseech. "Who'll protect me?"

Aaron's face is florid, anger tightening his jaw. "Get over yourself, Jake; it was going to happen sooner or later. I can't be here forever, wiping your snotty nose. It's time you stood up for yourself and grew a pair."

His words are hard, cutting. I know he doesn't mean them. Nevertheless, a red veil descends and I launch myself at him. We scuffle on the lawn. Not exactly landing blows, but not exactly play-fighting the way we used to, either. We roll together, limbs flailing, teeth gritted, sweat flying. Then we're on our feet, gasping for breath, staring each other down like dueling stags.

Insanely, Aaron scoops up a shovel and rushes me. He swings it like a batter hitting a home run. There's a glint of something in his wild eyes that reminds me of our father. I duck aside at the last second, landing heavily on the grass. His momentum pitches him forward and he falls headfirst through the open hatchway leading to our grandfather's defunct bomb shelter. One moment Aaron is there, raging and snarling, and the next he is gone.

The silence is deafening.

"I didn't mean for him to die," I whisper to my father, back in the hospital room. "I was going through grandfather's stuff, down in the shelter. I can't remember why. The hatch was up. Aaron's head hit the metal ladder. It snapped his neck. When I got down there he was still alive, but he couldn't feel anything from the neck down. Couldn't move, not even a finger. He begged me to end it, pleaded with me. He was all about fitness and health; he couldn't bear the thought of being paralyzed. I didn't want to do it. It was a mercy killing. I loved my brother. I worshipped him."

In my mind's eye, the image of Aaron lying dead in my arms is burning through my brain. Fingers still throttling his throat. My beloved brother. My idol. Eyes wide and staring. Warm but lifeless. Fear wells up within me. It isn't the authorities I'm scared of, it's my father. He's a man of the cloth. His whole life is based on Old Testament teachings. He will surely kill me for taking the life of his firstborn son. It must never come out. I can never let him know.

And so, irrationally, I bury my brother behind the timber wall of the old bomb shelter, near the stinking septic tank, hoping that the stench will mask his decomposition. My grandfather blew his brains out inside this underground box; his ghost stills lingers, an air of badness that is more than the odor of rust and mold. No one ever comes down here. Only me. My secret is safe, here in the darkness.

In my darkness.

Then, within weeks, I am sentenced and sent to Stillwater, to relive the last moments of my brother's life every night for years, until I am unable to separate the real memory from the nightmares.

Reality blurs, and the first thing I do when I arrive at the house on Prescott is to dig out the hatch, compelled by guilt and a need to check that I haven't been imagining Aaron's death all these years.

But the arrival of Kimberly Krauss denies me the truth.

Back in the hospital room, the black smoke inside me is breaking through the surface. With my confession, the floodgates have opened, and a suppressed memory flows to the fore—one I haven't thought about since I was seven years old. Unrestrained, the darkness bursts through, seething with prickly memories. An unstoppable geyser of repression, an uprush, spiked with the thorns of my past, exploding into my consciousness, as real as the moment they were made:

I am up at Hangman Falls, on a brilliant blue-sky day, with the late afternoon sun pulling rainbows out of the waterfall. I am inside my seven-year-old brain, in the springtime, sitting on a rocky ledge with my feet dangling over the edge. Mere yards away, the thunderous wall of water plunges into the ravine below, peppering my skin with a fine cool spray. One by one, I am dropping rocks into the pool below, feeling as stony inside as they are to the touch, wondering what it would be like to tumble over, to go with them, to let go.

"Jake, honey!"

It's my mother's voice.

At first I think it's inside my head, dimmed by the anger rolling around inside of me—an anger fracturing my reflection. Days have passed since she walked out. Days since she abandoned me to the wrath of my father. Days since my world split in half and I sought refuge in darkness. I have spent those days in turmoil, missing her, wanting her, hating her.

When her voice sounds again I realize it's outside, drowned by the crashing of the falls. I turn to see her clambering up the steep slope, clutching handfuls of roots and undergrowth to prevent her from slithering to the ravine's edge and plummeting over the drop.

"Jake, come away from there!" Tears streak her flushed cheeks, sweat dampening her shirt. Her breathing is labored from the arduous climb. She drops her purse and snatches me from the edge, pulling me out of harm's way. She stands me on my feet and shakes me, hard. "Jake, I've been looking everywhere for you! I was so worried, panicking, thinking you were hurt somewhere!" I'm unresponsive and so she shakes me some more. "You gave me the fright of my life!"

Then the tears on her cheeks flow red. She stares at me through disbelieving eyes, eyes growing big as eggs as confusion contorts her face.

"Honey?"

I pull my fist from her temple, and with it the rock in my hand. It comes away with skin and hair on it. Blood runs into her eye socket. I smash it against her head again, same place, this time harder, rage feeding adrenaline into my veins, giving me strength beyond my years.

The only thing in my mind is hate. Blood-red hatred. It veils the world in crimson and eclipses the sun.

The rock strikes her skull and something cracks. Her eyes roll back in their sockets and her fingers spring free from my waist. Even as she slumps to the ground I am over her, pounding away with the rock, venting every bit of anger, every bit of hurt she's put me through, every bit of my father hammered into me. We become covered in hot sticky blood. It sprays up onto my neck, my T-shirt, into my hair. Her hands flap uselessly against the ground, body convulsing. I pound away until my arm hurts and the rock is too heavy to hold. A blood-curdling scream gurgles in her throat, then she's quiet, still.

I sit there for long moments, panting, pulling bloodied hair from her face as the darkness inside me hardens.

Then I drag her body to Hangman's Tree. It's only a few yards away, but it takes nearly all my remaining energy to haul her dead weight to the V formed by two exposed roots, each thicker than my waist. Where they join at the base of the trunk there's a hole, leading to a hollow, scooped out by some forest creature a long time ago. First, I throw in her purse, then roll her in after it, force her in, stuff in her limbs, push with my feet and every bit of strength I have left. My heart feels fit to burst. Ears ringing. Once she's inside, I kick soil and loose rocks into the hole after her, filling it completely, stamping at it and packing it down tight.

Then I breathe.

It's like the hole never existed.

It's like she never existed.

Seconds later, I am scrabbling up the steep side of the waterfall, puffing and panting, programmed fingers hooking into cracks in the sheer rock face. I scramble over boulders, through thickets, scratched and clawed at, scraped, cut, and bruised. I rush out onto the grassy meadow sloping down to the picturesque lake. Sunshine sparkles on blue water. I don't stop running until I am at the muddy shoreline, breathing hard, with blood dripping from my hands.

Then I stand there, motionless, eyes closed, ramming the memory down into the abyss, making sure every trace of it is covered with black smoke, until it is not only invisible, it is undetectable.

It's like it never happened.

The memory completely concealed from my seven-year-old consciousness.

And I grow from child to man, through that difficult metamorphosis, oblivious to the fact I killed my own mother.

I open tearful eyes and I'm back in the dimly lit hospital room with my father, my palm sweaty against his cool fingers. More sweat streaming down my sides, stinging at my wound, and my heart beating out a death dirge behind my ribs.

I glance toward the door, fearing the doctor has returned and glimpsed the horror that lurks within my darkness, glimpsed my own demon that possessed me in the past and lay hidden, until now. But I am alone with my ghosts and the rotting husk of my father.

I killed my mother.

The realization is earthshattering, horrifying. It's as though the recollection belongs to somebody else, alien, planted in my brain to ruin my cherished memories of us together.

But half of me has always known I killed her, the half that lives within my darkness. Terrible memories repressed and smothered in smoke. Hidden when I was a boy, hidden from my own conscious mind, like my mother's dead body in its tangled grave.

I realize, with fear and anguish knotting up my insides, that there is no coming back from what I've done.

I murdered my mother.

Through pulsating eyes I gaze at the unanimated face of my father, at the plastic breathing tube wedged within the slash of his mouth. The edges of my vision are dark, ghostly. Not sure if it's in my head or if demons surround me, waiting to pounce. My shirt is damp, sticking to my ribs. I mop sweat from my brow with the cuff of my coat.

"I'm not asking for your forgiveness," I tell him as I reach for the power switch on the medical ventilator. "I just wish things could have been different. In a perverse kind of way I thought with Aaron out of the picture it would change how you felt about me, him not being there. But it didn't. It just gave you reason to hate me even more." I squeeze his limp hand one last time. "Goodbye, dad."

Then I flip the switch and walk away, trailing spots of blood all the way through the hospital and out into the snow.

Epilogue

Most people think they're in the driver's seat, in complete control of their direction, their destiny. But we're all passengers of life. Some of us lean on the gas and race down the fast lane, living for the blur. Some of us trundle along in first gear and never get to feel the rush. Most of us are glued to the center line, going along for the ride. Sooner or later it's our stop and we all get off. Life carries on down the road without us. For a while those still engaged in the journey keep our memory alive. But they, too, have their own destinations, their own points to disembark. And eventually nobody remembers.

The drive up to the lake is the longest journey of my short life. The sun is yet to rise and the nighttime canvas is still painted with stars, but the quicksilver moon has slipped behind the hills, its icy glow silhouetting saw-toothed trees.

Inside the Bronco, the blowers are on full heat, fans rattling, but it's wasted on me. I don't feel it; I am as cool as a corpse.

I pass Meeks's dead Mustang and keep going.

Surprisingly, my head isn't heavy with guilt. My thoughts are light, in keeping with my lightheadedness. Buoyant memories of happier times abound—long summer days, out here on the edge of the great outdoors, when I was a boy, free from my father's reins, exploring, conquering, imagining a life so very different than my own.

It seems closer than it is, within touching distance—as though the farther I drive, the deeper back in time I go.

After another mile I leave the highway altogether, following the switchback road as it winds its way up and over the hillside. Then I take the circuitous lake road, heading in the opposite direction from the smoldering remnants of Krauss Outfitters. This trail is out of bounds for the snowplows. No other vehicles have traveled this route all winter. The Bronco bucks and kicks through the deep snow, churning its way around the edge of the lake. Limply, I cling to the wheel, rolling with the bumps.

The public rest area sleeps under a heavy blanket of woolly snow. Equally spaced humps formed by picnic tables. Going slow, I thread the Bronco through and bring it to a stop a few yards back from the edge of the lake, so that the headlights spear out across the frozen surface.

The hole that swallowed Tolstoy's truck is invisible, either with distance or because it's already iced over. Like many of the lakes hereabouts, this one is deep, might as well be bottomless; it's unlikely anyone will ever find the vehicle or its owner.

I slide a hand into my waistband. It comes away covered in dark blood, cool to the touch, tacky. I have no idea how much of it has oozed out of the bullet holes, front and back. The leather underneath me is pooled with it. I'm not worried by the discovery. Strangely, there is no panic, no pain. Just a surreal sense of calm and acceptance.

"Jake!"

I look through the windshield to see my mother standing on the snowy shoreline, illuminated in the bright headlights. A childlike giddiness spreads through my chest. She's how I remember her: early thirties, with long mahogany hair and porcelain skin.

With adult eyes I can appreciate her timeless beauty, her soft feminine figure, her mesmerizing smile. I can see why both my fathers fell in love with her. She is angelic. Hypnotic.

She waves a hand: *"Jake, be with us!"*

Standing at her side are my brother and my father, both of them lit internally, like those life-sized Christmas characters people put out on their front lawns during the holidays. Aaron is young again, no more than ten or eleven, a big grin splitting his wide face. He looks genuinely thrilled to see me, eager, his excitement infectious. My father is my age, strong again, powerful. I have no sensation of fear at the sight of him. He is smiling, broad and wholesome. It's the first time in my life it's ever been directed at me.

He waves a hand: *"Jake, come join us!"*

Obediently, I open the door and slide out. The air is frigid, but the cold doesn't dare touch my skin. My footfalls are light, leaving no prints in the snow as I descend to the shore. No droplets of blood trailing behind. I am a moth, drawn to their light.

In my wake, a dying leviathan bellows at the night. A glance over my shoulder shows me the Bronco is spluttering, juddering, lights dimming as the tank runs dry.

Inside, a man is slumped behind the wheel. He has the appearance of a thug: an unshaven face, mashed up and slack, pale and lifeless. He looks like someone I once knew, but I can't quite place him.

"Jake!"

My gaze returns to my glowing family. Their arms are opened wide, their pull magnetic, inescapable. Happy eyes rimmed with tears of joy. My giddiness is overwhelming. I sink into their warm embrace, light banishing dark. My boyhood fracture sealing within.

Both halves rushing together, eliminating the abyss and vanquishing the black smoke forever.

It is the first time we are united as a family.

And I am a child again, wanted, loved.

Home, at last.

Acknowledgments

The year taken to write this novel was both the best year and the worst year of my life. After being engaged to Lynn for fifteen years, I finally won her hand in marriage on a sunny beach in Florida. And after almost a quarter century of joy and happiness, I lost my son, Jason, suddenly and devastatingly. Throughout the highs and the lows, my family has been my unwavering support, my life, my love, and I am truly blessed to be surrounded by such heavenly hearts.

Thank you Gemma and Sam, and Rebecca and Ruben, my lovely daughters and sons-in-law, for outshining the sun with your brilliance and your warmth. And thank you Lynn, my dearest wife, for making me the happiest man alive, even in my darkest hours, and there were many. You make me greater than the sum of my parts.

Without you, this novel would not exist.

Writing can be a solitary process, but where would any writer be without those able to see beyond the words?

With this in mind, my sincerest thanks go to: Mary Endersbe of Minnesota, who proofread the first draft, kindly ironing out my kinks and setting me straight; to my eagle-eyed editor, Charlotte Herscher, for her illuminating editorial insights; and to Emilie Marneur, Senior Editor at Thomas & Mercer, for having the vision to suggest I write this novel in the first place. You guys are awesome!

And last, but by no means least, thank you, the Reader, for reading my story.

Keith Houghton, March 2015